# Vengeance

# Simon Dinsdale

Copyright © Simon Dinsdale 2023.

The right of Simon Dinsdale to be identified as the author of this work has been asserted by him in accordance with the Copyright, Designs and Patents Act, 1988.

First published in 2023 by Sharpe Books.

To my darling wife Liz.

The author would like to thank Dea Parkin, and her staff at Fiction Feedback for their help and advice in the development of this story. My daughter Katie Dinsdale who helped as well and Richard Foreman and the wider family at Sharpe Books for their continued support and patience.

# VENGEANCE DAY

## Prologue

**Derry. November 1998.**

Liam kicked the front door of his mid terraced home and pulled the oversized fleece jacket around him. It was cold and miserable out, with a fine drizzle already settling on his shoulders. He shivered, then pressed his nose up to the parlour window and knocked. His brother Martin was in there, sitting in the warmth. 'Come on, let me in,' he shouted, rapping his knuckles on the glass. Liam jumped back as Martin yanked aside the net curtain. 'Away to the shop with you, do as you're told,' he shouted.

Liam hunched his skinny shoulders and trudged up the hill, past the long line of shabby houses. Rainwater seeped through the hole in the sole of his trainer and saturated his sock. A hundred yards in front of him, a red hatchback car turned into the street from the main road at the top of the hill. As the vehicle passed him, it threw a spray of water up and over Liam's legs. 'Ah, you...' he shouted and flicked a V sign.

The car's brake lights flared, and it slowed, then tucked into a parking place at the end of an alley. The door opened and, thinking the driver was going to shout at him, he spun on his heel and scampered up the road to Kath's corner shop.

The tinny bell rang as he pushed the door open and stepped inside to a blast of warm air. It was small and cluttered, with two banks of shelves beside a central aisle stacked with a wide choice of tins, packets of food, cleaning products and newspapers. Martin had once told Liam that Kath sold everything except condoms and booze. Liam wasn't entirely sure what a condom was, but he still thought it was funny. The till was at the far end of the shop, opposite the door. Behind that was an opening covered with a bead curtain leading to the storeroom. Liam was the only customer and there was no sign of Kath. He selected two chocolate bars and placed them on the counter. All was quiet. He leant to his right to see where Kath might be. As he did so, he picked up three bags of sweets and stuffed them inside his fleece.

## SIMON DINSDALE

Kath swept aside the curtain, making Liam jump. She was a plump, middle-aged lady. Her usual smiling face wore a stern expression as she took up her customary position behind the till.

'Hello Liam. What can I do for you?'

'Hi Kath. Just the chocolate and twenty Bensons please.'

'These two bars here, is it?' she replied, tilting her head and raising an eyebrow.

'Yes, and the fags.'

'What about the sweeties, eh?'

Liam felt his face burn, 'I don't...'

'Do you think I'm stupid? I saw you on the camera. Now, hand them back and be on your way before I tan your backside.'

'Can I have the ciggies? They're for mum,' Liam wheedled as he pulled the offending items out.

The doorbell rang, and Kath looked up over Liam's shoulder. 'You'll not get cigarettes from me. Your mammy told me she would buy her own.'

'Oh, go on, Kath...'

'No. Now, I've got real customers to be serving.' She smiled at the customer who had just walked in.

'Kids, eh.' He dropped the local newspaper and some chocolate by the till.

Liam glared at the man, who wore jeans with tatty trainers. Long fair hair hung over the collar of his windcheater.

'Who're you, anyway?'

'Away with you, Liam. And don't come back until you can keep your sticky fingers to yourself. I'll be talking to your mum about this,' Kath snapped.

Liam ran to the other side of the road. Anger and humiliation burned through him. For a moment he considered putting a brick through the silly cow's window but stopped himself. He could see the man at the counter paying Kath. Liam had lived on this housing estate since he was born. He knew everyone in the street but had never seen him before. What was he doing in a shop, well away from the city centre? Why here? This was not an area where people made casual visits. Strangers were not welcome.

Liam sprinted home and had to bang on the front door for a

frustrating minute until it was wrenched open by Martin.

'Keep the noise down. Did you get our smokes?'

'Kath wouldn't let me have any. But there's a guy up there who doesn't belong around here,' Liam blurted.

Martin led the way into the front room where three of his friends were sitting. He looked through the filthy net curtains.

'Is that him?'

'Yes, he's the one.'

'That's his car parked there,' Martin said, and pointed. 'He arrived a few minutes ago.' Liam saw it was the one that splashed him earlier.

The slim, scruffy looking man walked down the pavement and turned straight into the alley opposite their house. The boys crowded round the window and watched as he stopped halfway along it and urinated against the fence. A small cloud of steam billowing by his legs as he did so.

'He's spying on the place Hugh's told us to keep a watch on. He must be a Brit.' Martin turned to his friends.

'Go out and have a look around. Check every street around here. There must be more of them.' The boys nodded and scuttled out through the back door.

'He's coming back,' Liam said.

The man climbed into his car, opened a newspaper, and lit a cigarette. It looked like he wouldn't be moving soon.

'What was he doing in Kath's?' Martin asked Liam.

'He brought some sweets and stuff. Then he poked his nose in when I tried to get your fags. What's going on?'

'Never you mind.'

'Ah, come on Martin. Let me help, I can keep a secret.'

'I'm not to tell anyone.' Martin peered out through the window again, then glanced at Liam. 'Okay, just this once. Hugh's got some business in the place that bloke was watching. It's something really important to the cause, so he needs to be told.'

'What do you want me to do?'

'Run to Hugh's. Tell him Martin says we have a big problem at the house.'

Liam's eyes shone with excitement as he slipped through the

kitchen door and vaulted the back fence. Martin was a lookout, and responsible for organising the lads on the estate. They spent their days loitering on street corners, watching for, and reporting on, the movements of the hated British security forces. Liam desperately wanted to be involved. But his mother refused to allow it and forced Martin to promise not to use his brother for anything. Now Martin had given him this chance to show what he could do, and he was determined to not let him down.

It took him ten minutes to run through the estate. All the alleys had locked steel gates at each end. Put there by the police and army to cut off escape routes of terrorists. They didn't slow Liam down, and he barely noticed the puddles as he squeezed under them. He was soaking by the time he arrived at Hugh Murphy's house to find him busy on the phone. As Liam waited, he bent over with his hands on his knees, gasping for air.

Liam knew Hugh was a big man in the republican movement and controlled everything that happened on their estate. Martin reported directly to him. Hugh replaced the receiver and regarded Liam.

'Well now, you're looking puffed out. What's happening?'

'Martin sent me.' Hugh listened intently as Liam described his encounter with the stranger and passed on Martin's message.

'You've done well there, son. Kath didn't like the look of him either. I have put things in place to take care of the situation. Now, you get back and tell Martin that I'm pleased with him. He must keep the Brit under observation but do nothing else. Do you understand?'

'I'll tell him that,' Liam replied.

'Kath tells me she caught you stealing. Is that right?'

Liam hung his head and stared at the floor, then nodded.

'I'm disappointed in you. We don't steal from our own.'
'Sorry, Hugh. I won't do it again.'

'You will make a good volunteer one day, but we don't want thieves. We never disrespect our own. Always remember that. A little bird has told me it's your birthday?'

'Yes, I'm eleven today,' Liam replied.

'Well, happy birthday, son. Take this and buy yourself

something. Better not go to Kath's for a few days, though.' Hugh smiled and held out a five-pound note.

Liam looked at the small blue note in his hand with disbelief. No one had ever given him this much money for himself.

'Thanks Hugh,' he stammered.

Liam set off, but his legs felt like lead. Halfway back, a painful stitch in his side made it difficult to breathe, slowing him down until it wore off. He got snagged on a gate and wasted valuable seconds as he ripped his fleece to get free. He reached home, exhausted.

'Martin. Martin, where are you?' The house was empty. He peered through the front window and spotted Martin with his friends hiding by the entrance to the alley. The red hatchback was still there. Then Liam saw the Brit walking towards Martin.

'No. No, you mustn't,' Liam shouted. He moved the curtain aside and banged on the window, but none of them heard him. He opened the front door to shout a warning, but as he did so, Martin took a step and swung his hurling stick. It struck the Brit full in the face, dropping him to the floor. The other three weighed in and the four boys delivered a vicious beating. Liam clenched his fists with excitement as he listened to the dull thuds of the sticks striking the body and the cries of pain.

Two men came from the house and joined them as Martin bent down and picked something up. Liam guessed Hugh must have sent them and saw Martin hand what he had collected to one of them. The group talked together before the man handed it back to Martin. The other boys ran off as Martin turned. Liam realised he was holding a gun and was now pointing it at the man curled up at his feet.

'Shoot him,' Liam muttered. 'Go on, do it.'

Liam saw a tall figure burst out of an alley about forty yards down the street. He was carrying a pistol and sprinting hard. With a swoop of dread, Liam realised this was another Brit, he screamed out a warning, his voice shrill and catching with fear, but no one heard him. Gunshots rang out, the sharp cracks echoing off the walls and making Liam jump. Hugh's men fell and Martin ended up on his backside, clutching at his bloodied and misshapen left leg. The world went into slow motion as the Brit calmly stood over Martin and shot him in the head.

The area quickly filled with police and soldiers. They formed a barrier on each side of the entrance to the alley. An angry crowd of residents confronted the cops as they carried the injured Brit to an ambulance. Men and women in white forensic suits with masks and gloves moved through the alley. They photographed the bodies that still lay on the floor. Liam remained rooted on his doorstep, shivering from the cold and shock of what he had witnessed. He watched in a daze as two men zipped Martin into a black bag and dumped him into a van. In all the confusion, the killer disappeared.

Liam did not know how long he stood there. His tears dried up to be replaced by a dull ache of loss, then raw hatred bubbled through him. Someone gently took him by the elbow. He turned and looked up to find Hugh Murphy beside him.

'Come inside now. You've seen enough.'

'They shot Martin.'

'I know. It's a terrible thing to happen.'

'Why?'

'Because that's what they do.'

Liam shook his head as if to clear it. Nothing made sense. Then he stared into Hugh's eyes. 'I will find them. I swear I will kill them all.'

# VENGEANCE DAY

## Chapter 1

**Twenty-five years later**

Liam Rafferty's eyes blinked against the harsh fluorescent lighting. Images flash in his mind. Concrete stairs, pain, someone supporting him, choppy seas. He's lying flat on his back. The ceiling beyond the lights is white. Where am I? He glances around to find he's alone in a private room and covered with a crisp sheet. A drip is beside him, dispensing a clear fluid through the cannula in his right hand. Machines bleep as they monitor his vital signs, connected to him by leads stuck to his body. A sling secures his left arm across his chest. He wriggled the fingers on his left hand, and, to his relief, they all move.

A blond nurse appears at his side. She presses a button, and the bed lifts him into an upright position.

'Drink,' Liam croaked.

She handed him a plastic beaker and Liam swills the ice-cold water around his mouth before swallowing with relish.

He takes another sip and looks through the window. The view is enough for him to recognise Bruges. A smile creases his lips. Mary. She got him out and over here, after the shooting.

The nurse placed a plastic button on his hand.

'Press this once for pain relief. Do you understand?' Liam nods. She made some notes on his chart and left him alone.

Liam relaxed into the pillow, trying to get his thoughts in order. The events of the last few days fall into place and a sense of euphoria settles over him. He's done it. Finally fulfilled the vow he made on his eleventh birthday. To avenge the brutal murder of his brother, Martin.

Martin Rafferty had been fifteen and Liam's sole carer. Their mother admitted to hospital months before, screaming at her demons, and their father long gone. They lived in a two-bedroom terraced house, on a housing estate close to Derry city centre. The area had then been a renowned republican stronghold.

## SIMON DINSDALE

Martin led the local boys who monitored the streets, looking out for the hated British security forces.

That fateful day remained clear in Liam's mind. He spotted a stranger and told Martin. The man, who Liam had since learned was a British Army undercover soldier, was part of a team spying on a nearby house. Martin knew the property was being used as a bomb factory and dispatched Liam with a message to Hugh Murphy, the commander of the south Derry Real IRA company. Hugh sent Liam back with orders for Martin to maintain surveillance on the Brit, but to do nothing more. But Liam didn't get back in time, and Martin had already acted.

Liam shuddered at the memory. He watched from their front doorstep, excitement coursing through him, as Martin and his friends ambushed the soldier. Then a second Brit appeared from down the road, sprinting towards Martin. Liam shouted a warning, but no one heard him. The look of terror on Martin's face as he died still woke Liam, panting with fear in the depths of the night. Those nightmares would stop now he had killed the men responsible for Martin's murder.

After Martin's death, Hugh Murphy took Liam in. It was November 1998, a time of upheaval in Northern Ireland. The Real IRA was newly formed dissident republican terrorist group violently opposed to the Good Friday agreement. Liam recalled many long conversations with Hugh when his mentor imbued him with a deep sense of pride in his Irish heritage. These history lessons developed Liam's determination to join the fight for the liberation of their people. They also fuelled his pathological hatred for the British. Under Hugh's sponsorship, he joined the Derry company as a fully-fledged volunteer on his seventeenth birthday. Liam never refused an order or failed to complete a mission and remained as dedicated to a united Ireland as ever.

Liam owed his swift rise through the ranks, to become the quartermaster, to Hugh. The position allowed him to travel the world, buying weapons and equipment for the cause and making invaluable contacts along the way.

He took part in operations in Ireland and Europe. The Derry brigade had mixed results. They hit the odd police, or prison officer, but nothing bigger or more spectacular. As the failures increased, Liam realised something was very wrong in the organisation. Virtually nothing planned ever came to a successful conclusion. Volunteers found themselves under arrest and attacks disrupted. The British had completely penetrated the organisation.

During a foreign trip, Liam discovered that someone had diverted donated cash to a German bank account. He enlisted one of his many contacts to follow the money. Within a month he knew those funds had been used to purchase a hundred kilos of hard drugs, and it wasn't an isolated incident. It took him a further year to track it all back to Hugh and three other senior commanders. At first Liam refused to believe what he'd uncovered. He had looked up to these men, idolised them. To discover they had betrayed everyone's trust was a shocking revelation. To make matters worse, none of them denied it when he confronted them. Hugh made some half-hearted excuse that the money from the sale of the drugs improved their ability to fight the enemy. Liam knew it was a lie. Then they ordered him to stand down from operations, saying he had become a nuisance. Liam considered his position and decided enough was enough. He set about recruiting his own band of fighters, concentrating on young volunteers. All of them as passionate as him to win their freedom and he chose well. By the time the hierarchy got wind of what he was doing, he was ready. Liam took his group and disappeared with the munitions they had stolen. Hugh and the organisation have been hunting him ever since.

A twinge of pain in his shoulder made him wince. He pressed the switch, but nothing happens. In frustration he kept pushing it until he felt the dose of morphine flood his system. As the pain receded, he thought back to the circumstances that led to him being in this bed.

Liam always blamed himself for Martin's death. If he'd only run faster, or hadn't got snagged by that gate, he would have saved his brother's life. On the night of the murder, Liam made a vow to find and kill the men responsible, and Hugh heard him make it.

## SIMON DINSDALE

Hugh helped Liam's attempts to obtain information about the soldiers. But they were obstructed at every turn and learned very little. There had been no press coverage, and no government ministry would answer his letters. Hugh discovered that a year after Martin died an inquiry into the incident had exonerated the soldiers. A result that surprised no one in the republican community. Liam made more progress after he became a volunteer. He then gained access to the organisation's intelligence database. With Hugh's permission, he researched what they knew about Martin's death. It proved a disappointing exercise because they did not know the identity of the two men.

The soldiers had belonged to a notorious unit called 14$^{th}$ Intelligence Company. That later became a Special Forces regiment and still existed. The men he sought would have left the military years before, but he refused to give up. A friendly lawyer and a journalist from Derry submitted a Freedom of Information request to the government, demanding the disclosure of the soldier's identities. That was refused on the grounds of national security. A former member of the surveillance unit wrote a book about his experiences. Liam tracked him down to his new home in Australia and, posing as a journalist, secured an interview. The retired soldier had served in the province years after Martin's murder and professed to know nothing about the incident or who was involved. Liam had listened to the self-aggrandising fool for more than an hour and gleaned some interesting information, but not what he really wanted.

The closest Liam ever came followed his successful recruitment of a woman who worked in the personnel department at the Ministry of Defence in London. She was proud of her Irish heritage and wanted to help. But it proved impossible for her to see their personal records. Rather than expose her, Liam admitted defeat. She remained in place, willing and able to answer his call in the future.

As the years passed with no new information, Liam wondered if he would ever find them. Then, when he least expected it, he got the breakthrough. He had been in the Middle East working on his current project when the British press exposed a police officer

## VENGEANCE DAY

in Essex as Martin's killer. They only identified one of them, but that didn't matter.

Very few people knew of Liam's vow to exact revenge. The men and women he had recruited did, and they all committed to help him, even though it distracted them from their current mission. For a moment the copper's name eluded him, and he had to concentrate. Dane, Christian Dane, that was it.

Liam's anger had boiled as he watched the press conference where Dane gave his excuses and laid the blame on Martin. He re-ran the footage incessantly, to fix the police officer's image and the sound of his voice into his memory. It proved easy to find where Dane lived and within days Liam got his first sight of him. With four of his group, Mary, Michael, Eddy and Carol, Liam followed Dane, looking for that opportunity to fulfil his vow.

The officer was leading the hunt for a multiple killer and spending days on the road. But someone always accompanied him. Liam wouldn't baulk at killing another cop, but he remained cautious, not wanting to get caught and ruin his chance. An attempt to place listening devices in Dane's home failed when one of the team was confronted by Dane's girlfriend. Liam was concerned that might have alerted the authorities, so he reluctantly backed off for a few days. But the urge to kill Dane soon overcame that worry and they resumed their watch.

Three nights before, they followed Dane to a block of luxury flats in an area of East London called the Isle of Dogs. Liam and Mary sat together in their car through the night. They watched as a police cordon moved into place surrounding the building. Then heavily armed officers raided the building early the next morning. A crowd of onlookers formed through the day, watching the excitement. Liam mingled with them, and spotted Dane come out talking on his phone. They were no further apart than when Martin hit him with the stick. Liam smiled to himself. He had nearly lost control and had fought to suppress the sudden urge to draw his pistol and shoot. When Dane turned in his direction, Liam avoided eye contact and sidled behind a couple of press photographers. Dane had then gone to the boot of his car and changed his jacket before running away from the cordon alone. Liam decided his chance had come and followed.

They had soon realised that Dane was tailing someone else. Then Mary saw Dane's target and realised he must be the murder suspect. Liam's desire to kill the police officer had become overwhelming and, he now had to admit, affected his judgement. When Dane followed his quarry into a multi-story car park, Liam went after him, against Mary's entreaties.

As Liam reached the bottom of the first flight of stairs, he heard a loud cry of pain from below. He crept down to the basement level. The murmur of voices drew him towards a doorway. Liam realised Dane and the other man stood less than a yard away. What did it matter if he killed a murderer as well? Surely that would be a public service. Liam drew his pistol as he prepared to move. A voice said, *'Why did you kill the boy?'*

Liam recognised Dane's south-eastern accent. He listened to their exchange with growing astonishment and then Dane said, *'You didn't have to kill him, though.'*

The second man, who had a posh voice, replied. *'No, but he was no loss to society, just another filthy little guttersnipe. And by doing so, I saved your worthless life, and this is how you repay me?'*

Liam then realised that Dane had inadvertently led him to the second soldier. The two men who murdered Martin were only feet away. He recalled his heart pounding in his ears, and having to take a moment to control his breathing before he moved in.

Liam replayed the scene in his mind's eye and knew he'd been sloppy. Dane lay on the ground, the murderer holding him at gunpoint. His sudden appearance surprised the killer and allowed Liam to get the drop and disarm him. Then he ordered him to kneel on the floor. Things went wrong when Liam told them why they were about to die. His bragging gave the man time to roll to his side, draw another gun, and shoot him. The bullet hit him high on the left side of his chest. It felt like a heavy punch and knocked him back half a pace, but not off his feet. There had been no pain, but he lost the use of his left arm. That didn't stop him from returning fire and killing the man. Then more police appeared. He scared them off with a few shots before turning to deal with Dane.

Liam relished the memory of putting two rounds into him. The first to the chest and second to the head. He saw the blood spray up the wall as he fell and moved forward to make sure, but his pistol was empty. He had a spare magazine in the back left pocket of his jeans. But his shoulder wouldn't work, and he couldn't reach it. It didn't matter. Dane was dead, and he had to escape. Liam remembered staggering up the stairs to where Mary had waited. Everything after that was hazy.

A sharp knock on the door brought Liam back to the present. Mary came in and stood by the bed. In her late forties, slim with long chestnut coloured hair swept back in a ponytail. They had served together on several operations and were kindred spirits. Mary hadn't hesitated when he asked her to join him.

'That looks sore,' she said, nodding to the dressing.

'It does sting a bit.'

'Here, I've got a present for you.' She dropped a small misshapen bullet in his palm. 'Souvenir from the doctor. He's fixed your collarbone with a plate and screws. If you follow the instructions I have here,' she waved the envelope in her hand, 'he assures me you should make a full recovery. But you must wear the sling for at least six weeks.'

Liam protested, but Mary stopped him. 'Come on. You've been lucky. We need you fighting fit for what's coming up. So, don't get stupid.'

'Okay. I will if it'll keep you off my back. Thanks for getting me out.'

'No worries.'

'Did you have any problems?'

'Not really. You passed out as soon as I hid you in the car. We got you to the boat. Pete informed the port authorities in Ostend that there had been an accident and you needed urgent medical help. They couldn't have been more helpful, and the clinic sent an ambulance to collect you.'

Liam nodded. He'd stayed in this discrete and expensive private hospital before. The staff here treated those who could not avail themselves of their home state's health services, for whatever reason.

Mary collected him the following morning and they travelled to the safe house in the small village of Zedelgem, five miles from Bruges. Liam locked himself in his bedroom with a secure mobile phone. He emerged twenty minutes later and called his three companions together.

Liam regarded them as they settled down. The only woman there was Mary, his trusted right hand. Brave and resourceful, she had suffered most at the hands of the British. Her hatred of them was even more implacable than his. Her commitment to the cause had been unshakable until the Good Friday agreement and the capitulation of the leadership. Eddy and Ruari were both much younger and came from a similar background. They possessed the added advantage of not being known to the authorities, so-called clean skins. This anonymity helped as they set up five safe houses in England where the other dozen members of the group waited.

'Thank you for your support recently. I killed the men who murdered my brother. Without your help, I couldn't have managed it.'

Mary coughed and glanced sideways at the other two as they lowered their eyes.

'What is it?'

'I have a wee bit of bad news. Dane survived. He's badly injured but will recover.'

This bombshell stunned Liam. He turned away as raw acid burned through the pit of his stomach.

'I hit him in the chest and the head...'

They all remained silent as he gazed out of the window. He drew a deep shuddering breath, then blew it out.

'Okay. I've allowed my personal issues to distract me for long enough. We have more pressing things to attend to. Our friend has a delivery for us. But before we can get to that, we will have to make a quick visit back home. Patsy has completed the arrangements for my meeting with our old comrades in arms.

## VENGEANCE DAY

Once we've sorted that, they'll be out of our way forever and we'll move on.'

Liam returned to his room and lay down. His shoulder throbbed so he swallowed some tablets and took a hot shower. As he towelled himself down, he caught sight of his reflection in the mirror and paused. He was in his mid-thirties but looked much older. His dark hair showing flecks of grey at his temples. The wound site and dressing stark against his pale wiry frame.

His mind turned back to the events in the car park. How did I miss him from only ten feet? Liam had dreamt of killing those two. The relief he felt when he believed he had finally succeeded was now a distant memory. There could be no peace for him until he had dealt with them both. Liam's only consolation came from the knowledge that he had killed the one who fired the fatal shot into Martin. But that was only half the job. Once the upcoming operation was completed, he would give Dane his full attention.

Mary brought him a mug of tea. 'Listen. We don't have to go to this meeting.'

Liam shook his head. 'If we cancel now, they'll take Patsy as a hostage. We can't afford for that to happen. And they won't stop looking for us. That will cause more problems and interfere with what we are planning. They need to see we are serious and not to be messed with.'

'I don't trust them.'

'Nor do I.'

'You know they'll send Hugh, don't you?'

'So what? He's made his choice. There's nothing I can do about that now.'

Mary nodded. 'It just doesn't feel right. We'll be fighting our own side.'

'They are no longer our people. Hugh and the others have betrayed everything. They're no better than some filthy mafia gang. If they left us alone, there would be no trouble with me. But they won't. Will they?' The effects of the injury and surgery made Liam feel very weary, so he got an early night. He woke with a shout, bathed in sweat.

## SIMON DINSDALE

The same old nightmare. The image of his brother haunting him again. He shivered in fear, not wanting to open his eyes in case Martin was still there. Powerful arms enveloped him, and Mary's voice whispered in his ear.

'It's okay, I'm here.' She stayed until dawn.

# VENGEANCE DAY

## Chapter 2

Christian Dane had been awake for half an hour, struggling to concentrate on the events that led to him being flat on his back in the hospital. He regained consciousness, confused and in pain following brain surgery two days ago. A couple of days before that, someone shot him twice. The first bullet hit him in the chest. His body armour saved his life, but the impact left him with broken ribs and bruised organs, making it difficult to breathe. The second kissed the top of his skull. This caused a fracture that sent bone splinters close to his brain. Dane survived thanks to the skill of the doctors and nurses. Apart from the physical injuries, he had no memory of what had happened.

Dane knew he was a detective superintendent with Essex police and in charge of a major investigation team. For the past few weeks, he had been leading the hunt for the murderer of five men. Three in Essex and one each in Dorset and Cambridge. He had identified the killer, James Anderson, and had been tracking him down.

Dane lay back on the pillows and closed his eyes. He had driven to a block of flats on the Isle of Dogs in East London. Detective Constable Hayley Cross, his best officer, was by his side. They had traced Anderson to an apartment on the estate. Dane visualised his conversations with senior officers in the Met police, then briefing the armed police who raided the flat. He could even remember the disappointment when they found the place empty. Dane and Hayley spent hours searching it, and he vaguely recalled a telephone conversation with his boss, Assistant Chief Constable Perkins.

Everything beyond that point was a complete blank. The doctors warned him to expect memory loss, given his injuries. They also assured him it would return but wouldn't commit to when that might happen.

Hayley had filled in some blanks. She explained how he'd spotted Anderson outside the building and followed him. While doing that, he provided a running commentary on his mobile phone as she scrambled armed officers to support him. Then

## SIMON DINSDALE

Dane pursued Anderson into a car park and lost the signal. He knew that when the back-up officers arrived, they heard shots. As they investigated, a man fired on them before disappearing. By then Anderson was dead, and Dane was seriously injured. The identity of the man and why he had shot them remained a mystery.

Anderson had saved Dane's life when they were serving soldiers in Northern Ireland twenty-five years ago. To do so he had killed three people, two hardened dissident republican terrorists and a fifteen-year-old boy. The kid had been about to murder Dane, so it had always seemed reasonable for Anderson to have shot him. In the years since Dane became concerned that the death of the young lad might not have been necessary. Those thoughts had been playing on his mind and he had resolved to find Anderson and question him about it. This all happened before Anderson was identified as the suspect. The revelation that the man who had saved his life was the killer placed Dane in a dilemma. He desperately needed to talk to him and get answers about the death of the boy.

To ensure he could do that, Dane had not been honest with Perkins. When he briefed him, Dane neglected to tell him about his personal connection to Anderson. When Perkins found out, had been less than happy about the situation. Dane explained his reasons and apologised for the deception and promised it wouldn't happen again. Although young for a chief officer, Perkins had earned the respect of everyone for his skills as a senior manager. His acceptance of Dane's apology and his decision to move on showed his skill as a leader. But Dane felt acutely embarrassed to have let someone he liked down in such a way.

Dane knew he and Anderson must have spoken, but he had no recollection of what they said. Nothing he did would shake the memory loose, and he was losing patience.

He heard a faint rustle beside him, he glanced down at the petite figure sound asleep across two armchairs. He smiled as he watched Vicky's shoulders gently moving up and down, her face was serene. Vicky Needham was a chief superintendent and the police commander in Cambridge. They had met when Dane

## VENGEANCE DAY

travelled to the city while investigating the murders committed by Anderson. Together they had discovered Anderson's fifth victim. That all happened mere weeks before and Dane marvelled at how quickly their relationship had developed.

She was a Hong Kong Chinese. Her birth mother abandoned her close to Victoria Harbour, where a British couple found her. They adopted her and called her Victoria. Vicky was a beautiful, intelligent woman who spoke with a lovely cut glass English accent. Her dark eyes shone, her pale skin was smooth and as soft as silk. She had graduated from Cambridge University, astonished her parents by joining the police, and would soon be a chief constable. Dane had liked her immediately, and they worked well together. He had been reticent about asking her out, telling himself he didn't want to appear pushy. Although his real reasons for hanging back had been fear of her rejection.

Vicky was a highflyer with the police, and he worried she would not want to jeopardise that by having a relationship with him. He had expressed those fears to her, and Vicky put him straight with her customary forthrightness. She told him she found him very attractive and saw no reason why they shouldn't see each other. Their time together so far had been eventful. When Vicky visited Dane's home for the weekend, she confronted a burglar while he was out. When she heard he had been shot she immediately took two weeks leave to assist his mother and stay at his bedside

It had been many years since Dane had experienced a proper relationship. There had been plenty of dates with different women, but none of them developed into anything beyond a few evenings out together. The demands of Dane's job had often interfered and caused a relationship to break down. It was difficult for someone unconnected to the police to understand when they are abandoned halfway through a meal and left to make your own way home. As he watched Vicky, he knew he wanted this one to continue. They understood each other and made no demands. Dane knew she was determined to pursue her own career and he was happy to support her in that. He was touched that she had dropped everything to help him now and knew he would do the same if things were the other way round.

## SIMON DINSDALE

Was he in love with her, he wondered, then his natural reserve kicked in. One step at a time, he thought. The one thing he was certain of was that he would be devastated if he lost her.

A sudden shiver made him pull the bedclothes up over his chest. He felt clammy and nauseous, and he needed the toilet. Not wanting to disturb Vicky, he manoeuvred himself off the bed. Once his feet hit the floor, he steadied himself.

His movement woke Vicky, and she jumped up, 'What are you doing?'

'I need the loo.' He trembled, and the room spun, 'I'm not feeling that good, to be honest.'

She laid the back of her hand on his forehead, 'You're burning up.'

'Just let me go to the bloody toilet.'

'Come on, then.' She took his elbow, and he managed three steps before his legs sagged. Vicky helped him onto the bed and pressed the call button before getting a small cardboard bottle.

'Here you are. See if you can fill that up without making a mess. I'll hold it steady for you.'

'Thanks,' he replied, resigned to the humiliation of peeing into a urine bottle in front of her.

'Does this mean we're dating?' she whispered, readjusting his pyjama bottoms.

Dane managed a weak smile, 'I think it does. Sorry I snapped.'

A nurse bustled into the room, 'Good morning, how are we feeling this morning?'

'He's got a high temperature,' Vicky said, and nipped into the toilet to empty the bottle.

Mr Hurrell, the surgeon who operated on Dane, breezed in, followed by his usual retinue of junior doctors. He checked the nurse's observations then examined Dane.

'It looks like you've developed an infection. It's not unusual, but we don't want it turning into anything more severe. We'll do some blood tests and put you on a course of intravenous antibiotics. That'll knock it on the head, but you must stay in bed for another day. I'll pop back this afternoon to check on your progress.'

## VENGEANCE DAY

'Thanks,' Dane replied. The nurse plugged a bag of clear liquid into the cannula on his arm.

Vicky squeezed his hand, 'Just take it easy and let the medicine do its thing. I'm off to do some errands. I'll be back later. Make sure you do as you're told.' She gave him a peck on the cheek.

\*

Dane fell asleep and woke with a start, still feeling nauseous. He glanced at the clock and saw it was two in the afternoon. A man wearing a white coat with a stethoscope around his neck stood at the foot of the bed. Dane had never seen him before, but assumed he must be a doctor. Vicky appeared at the door and stopped when she saw the stranger.

'Who are you and why are you here?' she demanded.

Without warning, Dane vomited. Vicky rolled him onto his side, getting covered in a stream of bile as the man scuttled out. As he heaved, Dane experienced excruciating pain in his chest, and couldn't get enough oxygen into his lungs. He thought he was suffocating and started to panic as a rush of people surrounded him before he slipped into blissful darkness.

\*

Dane slept for fourteen hours and felt better when he woke. The nurse filled half a dozen blood tubes which were sent for testing and he managed to eat some breakfast. Vicky arrived, showered and fragrant, and began by puffing his pillows up.

'I could grow used to all this pampering.'

'Well, don't. It all stops when you're back on your feet,' she smiled.

'Did I throw up all over you?'

'Yes, you did.' She recounted her encounter with the strange man, 'We've established he's not a member of the hospital staff. He avoided all the security cameras around the buildings. Hurrell thought you'd damage yourself if you kept being sick, so he sedated you.'

'Thank you for being here. It means a lot to me.'

'Is it any easier to breathe?'

'My chest is still sore,' he took a deep breath, 'It's not so painful though. How're my parents doing?'

## SIMON DINSDALE

'Your dad is responding to the medication. Your mum and I have spoken regularly, so she knows what's happening here.' Dane's father had been in hospital suffering from a vicious bout of pneumonia.

Mr Hurrell bustled in and spent some time examining Dane.

'The blood tests have shown the infection is receding. I think you have recovered enough to attempt a few steps around the room. Try not to overdo it though. I've asked a colleague to pop in. He is a psychologist and can give you some information and advice about memory loss. Have you remembered anything more?'

'I can remember everything up to the point when I spoke to my boss on the telephone. But after that, nothing.'

'This is a normal consequence of the type of injury you received. It will return to you in time.'

Hurrell left them. Not long after a small Asian doctor arrived and introduced himself as Dr Khan. Dane described his symptoms and mounting frustration.

'How much can you remember of what's happened to you since you arrived here?' Khan asked.

'Yesterday afternoon I found someone in here and there was a bit of a fuss. But I only have a sketchy recall of that.'

'I'm not surprised. You were medicated and disorientated. But it's a positive sign, and shows your mental function is operating. You're suffering from post-traumatic retrograde amnesia. The violent blow from the bullet coupled with the surgeons rummaging in your skull being the cause. That level of trauma can't help but bruise your brain and will inevitably lead to a range of issues. Your symptoms are minor and what I'd expect. There's no treatment. But the important thing is that in the coming days and weeks, memories will slowly return. Very often it all comes back in one moment of recollection.'

Their conversation allayed some of Dane's fears.

Assistant Chief Constable Colin Perkins arrived. He was tall and well-groomed, with short black hair and a fashionable beard.

'You're featuring in the media again. A chap called Boyd has found out that you've lost your memory.'

# VENGEANCE DAY

Dane read the article. It covered his recent history with the police and the Anderson investigation. But most of the piece referred to the incident in Ireland. The journalist quoted his sources and revealed Dane's amnesia. He made much of the fact that he'd suffered from the same condition after the shootings in Derry.

Vicky peered over his shoulder. 'The only people who know about this are us and the doctors, and they'll not blab to the press.' She paused and glanced at his medical notes, 'He was reading them. The intruder must be the journalist. What's his name?' she studied the paper. 'Boyd. What a miserable thing to do.'

Her anger touched Dane, 'It's alright, I'm used to this. Let him write what he likes. Once I've remembered everything, I'll give my side and it'll all pass over.'

'Do you know when you might be released?' Perkins said.

'I am hoping it will be tomorrow,' Dane replied.

'I will let the occupational health people know. They will look after you and decide when you are fit to return to work.'

'I promise to do as I am told,' Dane said, glancing at Vicky.

'That will make a nice change,' Perkins said. 'The Met SIO would like to visit you, if you're up to it.'

'Who is he?'

'DCI Caldwell.'

'Sure, tell him to come in whenever he likes.' The telephone rang, and Vicky picked it up, 'Hello. Oh hi, hang on.' She smiled and handed him the receiver, 'It's your daughter.'

'Robyn?'

'Hi dad. How you doing?'

'Still battered and bruised. I'll be going home soon.'

'That's great. Do you mind if I come over and visit? Would that be okay?'

'Of course, I would love to see you. When are you thinking of coming?'

'I'll be there the day after tomorrow. I've got the ticket.'

'Seems I'm getting a visitor,' Dane said after they had hung up.

## SIMON DINSDALE

'That's terrific. I'm looking forward to meeting her. She sounds delightful,' Vicky replied.

Dane's spirits lifted at this news. When Robyn was four, her mother suddenly left him. Their marriage had never been the happiest, but it still surprised Dane to come home from work one evening and find their house empty. It took him a month to track them down. Dane discovered she had moved in with an army medic with whom she had been having a long affair and was determined to keep Robyn with her. Dane recalled the pain and misery of being on his own, not being able to see his daughter, the endless rows and court hearings. After a protracted, acrimonious and expensive battle, Dane got his divorce and, to the dismay of his ex-wife, joint custody of their daughter. On Robyn's eighth birthday, he went to collect her but found the house empty. His ex-wife's new husband had taken a posting to a military base in Canada, and they'd all gone together. It took another month before he traced them to a town called Medicine Hat in Alberta. Dane travelled over to try and see Robyn once, but it had been a disaster. She had been told he didn't want her and her angry accusations that he had abandoned her still burned in is memory. He'd written to her, but she'd received none of the letters.

Then his wife informed him that Robyn never wanted to hear from him again. As much as it pained him, Dane realised that to protect his daughter from more distress, he must leave her life. So, there'd been no contact between them for ten years. Never a day passed when Dane did not think about her and dream of a reconciliation. But knew that would never happen while she remained under the influence of her mother. That all changed when Robyn rang the hospital. She was studying oceanography at the University of British Columbia in Vancouver. He opened the pictures app on his phone and gazed at the photographs she had sent him. His little girl had blossomed into a beautiful young woman.

He turned to Vicky, 'This is all you're doing, isn't it? Oh, I forgot to ask her when she's arriving at Heathrow. I'd like to go and meet her.'

## VENGEANCE DAY

'It's all arranged, and I've done nothing. Your mum will tell you how this all happened tomorrow.'

\*

DCI Ian Caldwell called in to see Dane and they discussed his investigation. Caldwell knew he couldn't recall anything of the shootings.

'You gave Hayley Cross a little information before you passed out. Does that ring any bells?'

'No. What did I say? Hang on, let me try.' Dane relaxed, then realised he was holding his breath, as if that would force him to recall something. A fleeting image of a small, dark-haired man flashed through his mind's eye before it disappeared.

'Quite short with dark hair. Is that what I said?'

'No. You didn't give any description, so that's interesting. You only spoke one word. "Irishman." Does that help?'

Dane shook his head, 'No, I don't remember that.'

'Look, there's no need to worry about it. Leave it to us, we'll find him.'

'What else can you tell me?'

'We have finished at the scene and recovered a lot of forensic material from there. I will let you know if there is anything positive or interesting from that. My guys are following several lines of enquiry searching for witnesses and into the man who shot you. He hit Anderson five times. Then fired six rounds at the armed officers before putting a couple in you.'

'That's a full load for most automatic pistols. He couldn't have had another magazine.'

'Or he didn't have the time to reload. Remember, support was flooding into the car park and whoever this mystery man is he wanted to escape. You were lucky. Good luck with your recovery and I will keep in contact.'

\*

Dane was discharged the following morning. A car picked them up, and drove to his house in Benfleet, where he found his mother waiting.

'How's dad?' Dane asked as they hugged.

'He'll be coming home next Monday. They're pleased with his recovery,' she replied.

'Will you be able to cope with him on your own?'
'Of course. I've been looking after him for long enough.'
'What's the story with Robyn?'
'Facebook.'
'What!'
'I set my page up and searched for Robyn. I found her and we've been exchanging messages. She was desperate for news of you and keen to get in contact. We'd agreed that I'd tell you on the day you ended up in hospital. I gave her Vicky's number and they spoke before you woke up.'
'Facebook.'
'Amazing, isn't it?'
'I hate it. But it might grow on me.'

Vicky left after breakfast, returning a few hours later. Dane felt a lump in his throat as he saw his daughter for the first time in ten years. Robyn had grown tall and slim, her long blond hair hung in a ponytail. She was wearing a bright red sweat top with VRC emblazoned on the front and jeans. Her skin shone with the lustre of youth, and she oozed healthy grace. She stood still when she spotted him, tears brimming in her deep blue eyes.

'Hello Dad.' She ran into his arms. He held her tight, ignoring the pain.

# VENGEANCE DAY

## Chapter 3

The national media had been interested in Dane for weeks. They had grown used to seeing him during his investigations into the five murders. Then an ambush by a tabloid reporter during a press conference changed that to fascination. The questions revealed that he once served in the British Special Forces and the details of the incident in Derry. Dane's superiors were just as surprised at the revelations because they hadn't known about his past.

The following morning, Dane had given his account, with the support of the chief constable and MoD. But the story was out. Some reporters, Angus Boyd amongst them, did not accept the version of events put forward by the police or government. Boyd believed there must have been a coverup. Why else, he wrote, would the authorities rush to defend Dane so quickly? The revelation that Dane was a decorated former covert intelligence operative only added spice to the tale.

Within an hour of the shooting on the Isle of Dogs, the press pack arrived outside the car park. Any incident involving guns and the police always produced that level of attention.

Boyd's scoop detailing Dane's amnesia and identifying James Anderson as the man who'd saved him in Derry had the editors licking their lips in anticipation.

What started as a common or garden police involved shooting took on a whole new slant and the clamour increased. DCI Caldwell and senior officers in the Met and Essex faced questioning from excited journalists. Every allegation received a polite but firm rebuttal. All requests for interviews were declined, which only fuelled the speculation.

Boyd had several pieces published in a national newspaper and a weekend magazine that specialised in left leaning stories. In his opinion, the authorities should have replaced Dane as the SIO once the story became public knowledge. When the police complaints watchdog announced Dane had no case to answer in relation to the shootings and Anderson's death, the mainstream media lost interest. Boyd had authored another article. To his disgust, no one wanted it. He decided to bide his time and keep a close eye on his activities.

\*

Dane was soon feeling better. The headaches became less frequent, and the scar on the top of his head itched. A sure sign of healing. His chest muscles still ached when he drew a deep breath, but even that was easing.

Vicky had to return to work and his father was about to go home from the hospital. Dane's mother needed to be there to care for him. Robyn had another week before going home, so Dane booked a few days in a holiday cottage on the Suffolk coast.

The couple went for long hikes. They talked about their lives over the past ten years. The excursions got longer each day as Dane's strength increased. They ranged for miles along the beautiful costal walks. Robyn spoke with a soft Canadian accent and referred to herself as an Albertan with pride. She described growing up in the prairie town of Medicine Hat. She had vague memories of arriving there in the middle of a freezing winter. They settled in a small house, with her stepfather, Kevin.

Dane was fascinated to hear about Robyn's life at the University of British Columbia in Vancouver. She was studying oceanography. It was her first experience of a big city, and she loved it. The learning, the social scene, and the sport. She'd joined the local rowing club, competing in competitions, and winning some races.

'I chose Vancouver because of the course. But also, so I could get away from home. I had decided to find you and get in contact. I mentioned it to mum,' Robyn said.

'How did she react?'

'She screamed at me for even thinking about it. So, to keep the peace I told her I wouldn't and waited until I'd settled in at Uni. First thing I did was Google you. There are pages and pages about you on the web.'

'That's news to me.'

'Most of it covers your cases and the press releases you've done. When all that stuff about Ireland blew up, mum called and took great delight in telling me. She said it would show me what sort of person you are. They reported it in the Canadian media, and I saw all the British papers online,' Robyn paused for a moment and a tear appeared in her eye. 'I watched you on the TV and it made me so proud of you. And then you got shot.' Her voice caught, Dane hugged her.

'I rang Grandma, and she said you were out of danger and gave me Vicky's number. I was so scared you wouldn't talk to me. It took me hours to pluck up the courage to ring. Vicky answered, but you were still unconscious. We talked and talked. I called mum to tell her what had happened, but she wasn't interested. Anyway, here I am. You're stuck with me. Like it or not.'

Dane's ex-wife's behaviour shocked him. He couldn't understand why she remained so bitter and vicious.

'I promise you there will never be a time when I'm not here for you or be part of your life. These years have been a nightmare for me not knowing anything about you, or even what you looked like.'

'I don't want to lose you again either,' she replied and kissed him.

'Have you told her you're here?'

'No, I wimped out there. She would've gone ballistic. I didn't want to face any more arguments.'

'You should e-mail her and let her know where you are. In case she rings the university.'

'Alright, I will. She would never do the same for you.'

'I don't care what she thinks or does. It's the right thing, for you, to do.'

Their walks took up the whole day. If they were tired, they'd rest and enjoy the magnificent sea views or stop in a cafe and wolf down cream teas or fish and chips. The weather was glorious, and the sun tanned them, with Robyn turning a beautiful golden colour. They ate each evening in the local pub and would then sit in the bar chatting. It was always busy, and they would occasionally fall into conversation with other holidaymakers. But more often, they kept to themselves.

## SIMON DINSDALE

After their last evening meal, they discussed the future. Robyn intended to become involved in the study of marine pollution and was passionate about rectifying what humanity had done to the seas. Dane could have listened to her all night.

Later, as he lay in bed, Dane thought about the day he was shot, trying to will some memory to return. He had a clear recollection of the mystery man now and wrote his description down whenever it popped into his consciousness. Dane could just visualise the figure standing in front of him with a gun in his hand. But there was nothing else until he came round in the hospital. Frustrated, he picked up a book and read for a while before switching the light off and going to sleep.

Dane was woken by a dream, in which a harsh voice was sneering at him, *"You should get a grip of yourself."*

It sounded so familiar, and the phrase kept echoing in his mind, but he had dreamt it. Hadn't he? Dismissing it, he rolled over and closed his eyes.

Their final long walk was cold and cloudy, as if to punctuate the end of their holiday. They set off for his parents, where they arrived in time for dinner. Robyn hugged her grandmother, and followed as Dane led her into the sitting room where his father sat in his favourite chair, wrapped in a plaid blanket. He'd lost more weight since Dane last saw him and was almost skeletal.

'Dad. This is Robyn, your granddaughter. She has come all the way from Canada.'

The old man glanced up, and his face lit up with pleasure. 'Oh yes, how lovely to see you. I have so missed you,' his voice wavered, 'Please,' he patted the chair beside him. 'Sit here and tell me what you've been getting up to.' He looked up at Dane and smiled, 'My goodness, she's grown into a beautiful young woman.'

'Hasn't she just?'

Early the next morning, Dane drove Robyn to Heathrow. As they cruised round the motorway, they chatted and made plans for keeping in contact. Dane and Vicky had already promised to go and visit Robyn in Canada, but they were both subdued. Robyn didn't want to leave, and Dane was loath to let her go.

## VENGEANCE DAY

They hugged for more than a minute at the entrance to the security zone before he handed her a thick packet.

'What's this?'

'Some light reading for the flight.' Robyn looked puzzled. 'These are all the letters I've written to you. There's at least one for every month since I last saw you in Canada. I never posted them because you would never have received them.'

Robyn stared at him, tears brimming in her clear blue eyes, 'She always told me you wanted nothing to do with me.'

'Well, let's move beyond that now. We're in contact, and your mother can't stop that from happening. There are a lot of letters there so you can catch up with me on your flight.'

Robyn hugged the packet to her chest, 'Thank you and don't hang about marrying Vicky. I love her too, and I want to be a bridesmaid.'

'We've only just started seeing each other. It's a bit early for marriage,' Dane stammered.

'She loves you to bits, so why're you hanging about? You're not getting any younger. Ask her to marry you.'

'If I do, you'll be the second person to hear what my decision is.'

'Good, I'd better get going. I love you.' With a parting smile, she hurried through the barriers and out of his sight.

She'd gone. Dane was bereft, and the tears rolled down his cheeks. He blew his nose and composed himself as he returned to the car.

SIMON DINSDALE

**Chapter 4**

Liam completed a last check around the remote property. Everyone was in position and his visitors were on their way. He gazed through the window down onto the rugged coast of southwest Ireland. It was a lovely evening, with the sun descending towards the horizon, and a beautiful location. But his mood didn't reflect the vista. A pulse of pain lanced through his shoulder. Liam had taken no tablets to ensure he remained alert and avoid another slip up. He also refused to wear the sling and had hooked his thumb into the waistband of his trousers.

This meeting was inconvenient, but unavoidable. The politics and personal enmity against him were implacable. He had reluctantly agreed to meet a representative from the Army Council to discuss the terms of his surrender.

A dark saloon appeared in the distance and soon crunched over the gravel to stop outside the cottage. Liam stood inside and waited the delegation who had once been his comrades. Together, they fought a long war with a savage resolve to get the Brits out of Ireland. But they had then betrayed everything Liam held dear and turned themselves into drug dealers. It wouldn't matter what they said, he would never forgive them for that.

Footsteps approached the door.

'Is it safe to enter?' a voice called out.

'Of course. Come on in?'

Three men appeared at the door and walked in. The first was Patsy, one of Liam's group. He'd handled all the negotiations, and a much older man followed him.

'So, they sent you, Hugh. Do they expect you to persuade me to hand myself over?'

'Hello Liam. I take no pleasure in this, but it must be done. You'll remember Sean?' Hugh replied, nodding to the third visitor. Sean was heavyset, wearing jeans and a denim jacket over a dark shirt. A vertical scar ran from his right nostril through his top lip, giving him a permanent, grotesque sneer.

## VENGEANCE DAY

'Sure, we've known each other for years. We're old friends, aren't we? How're the false teeth? Do they fit your ugly gob yet?' Liam replied, and vividly recalled causing that injury with the butt of an AK47 rifle.

Sean's face clouded with anger, 'You're under arrest for the theft of guns, ammunition, and explosives. I'm going to enjoy your interrogation and then we'll execute the lot of you.'

'Straight to the point, as always. But what makes you think I am ready to come with you?'

'Let's all calm down a bit, shall we?' Hugh said, silencing his companion with a withering glare, 'There're things to talk about. I'm sure we can reach an amicable agreement, as old comrades.'

'Well, sit down and say what you have to say. But I am disappointed. They promised me only one person would be coming. Should I assume that as Sean's here, the council has seen fit to break that undertaking?'

'You're in no position to negotiate,' Hugh replied. 'We have sealed the place off, and there is a team down the hill. I persuaded them to give you the opportunity to return what you stole. Oh, and they want the money you and your little band have accumulated as well.'

'And what do we get?'

'Your life. If you cooperate, you go free. With your friends.'

'And if I decline your kind offer?'

'There'll be no amnesty for any of you. But we're merciful. The war's over, and although you've caused us a lot of trouble, you're all good patriots and veterans. Because of that, I believe you deserve some credit. That's why the court martial has extended this last chance.'

'Do you hear that? Should we accept their offer?'

'I think you should listen,' Patsy replied.

'We've convinced him of the error of his ways. He thinks you should stand down,' Hugh said.

'Let's get on with it, shall we?' Sean said, pulling a walkie-talkie from his pocket, and clicking the send button three times. 'You have a minute to make your mind up.'

Liam rubbed his face. A hint of desperation crept into his voice.

'There's so much more to do. I've made plans, something to further the cause. It'd be such a waste to abandon it.'

'You mean the mad mullahs? Do me a favour,' Sean sneered.

Hugh growled at Sean, silencing him before turning to Liam.

'The choice is yours. Come with us and give it all back or face interrogation. You know better than most that we'll find out where everything is. Then you'll all die. You can avoid that. But I must have your answer now.'

Liam looked through the open door and saw two saloons and a van driving slowly along the track.

'A full team, I see. I guess they'll have brought their Black and Decker's?'

'Oh yes.'

The cars crossed a narrow stream covered by a metal cattle grid and drove into a cutting through a hillock. One side of it suddenly erupted with a huge orange flame and an ear-splitting bang. Dirt, rocks, and a shower of deadly shrapnel tore into the vehicles, shredding them and the men inside. The van jolted to a halt and a second later, another tremendous explosion catapulted it thirty feet into the air. The thunderclap echoed across the landscape, followed by an eerie silence.

Liam watched the carnage with a mirthless grin as Hugh and Sean jumped up and stared in horror.

'Now, I don't suppose that was in the plans, eh? But that's my answer.' Liam stood and, without warning, shot Sean in the head. He turned his weapon to cover his old mentor.

'What are you doing here, Hugh?'

Hugh stared at Sean's body. 'They hoped I might talk some sense into you. I told them they were wasting their time, but they insisted.'

Liam knew those fools in Belfast sent Hugh because they didn't believe his protégé would harm him. Hugh would have known better, but he still came. The loyal volunteer to the last.

'What did that idiot mean? About the Mullahs?'

## VENGEANCE DAY

'You won't get away with it. We might have given up the armed struggle, but we know what we're doing and how to keep tabs on things. What are you doing dealing with those lunatics? They'll never play you square. You can't trust them.'

'Like I can trust you lot? I'll take my chances. So, what have you heard?'

'Enough to know that your scheme is madness. You'll never succeed.'

'You don't really believe the struggle is over. Do you?' Liam said.

'Of course, it is, you fool. The only person who doesn't see that is you.'

'You are going to betray everything you have ever taught me.'

'I'm done with it. It is time to move on and lead a life.'

'By stealing from the people and selling your filthy drugs?'

Hugh gave Liam a look of contempt and turned to gaze at the view.

'You once told me we don't steal from our own or disrespect them. I can't believe you've really changed that much. Come with us Hugh. With your help, we can make a real difference.'

'Grow up Liam, it's finished. And you and your deluded friends here will be soon.'

Liam's was stung by the vehemence in Hugh's voice and his face fell.

'I'm sorry to hear you say that. Okay. You're free to go. Get back to your friends and make your money by poisoning our kids. But tell them to stay out of my way. We haven't given up the cause. If you try anything else to disrupt my plans, you will have the mother of all fights on your hands.'

The door crashed open to admit Mary, her face flushed. 'They're all dead. Blast caught the lot. There's another vehicle down by the road with a couple of lads in it. We need to go.'

They all turned to face her and using the distraction, Hugh made his move. He grabbed a pistol tucked into the waistband of his trousers and pulled but the foresight caught on the lining, and he wasn't quick enough.

## SIMON DINSDALE

'Look out,' Patsy shouted. Liam had seen the movement and levelled his own weapon. Hugh froze, his gun down by his side.

'I don't want to hurt you. But I will if I have to,' Liam said.

'I have never doubted that' Hugh replied.

A spasm of pain coursed through Liams shoulder, and he gasped. The muzzle of his pistol wavered, then fell away as he hunched over. Hugh brought his pistol up.

Liam was quicker and fired once. The bullet drilled through Hugh's left eye. His legs gave way and he collapsed to the floor as a fountain of blood pumped from the wound. Liam looked down at the body of his old mentor and shook his head, 'Oh, Hugh. Why did you come?'

Mary grabbed his arm, 'Come on.'

Eddy joined them as the group sprinted down the path to a rocky inlet where a dinghy was waiting. Once everyone was aboard, the helmsman gunned the engine and surged away to the open sea. Mary passed Liam his sling with a look that left him in no doubt he must put it on. He slipped it over his shoulder and regarded his companions as they skimmed across the water. Their next operation would be momentous. When they succeed, Liam knew their countrymen would welcome them all home as heroes. He looked back at the building on top of the cliff and felt a moment of sadness. Despite their differences Liam really had wanted Hugh to go free.

They swept alongside the luxury yacht Water Horse. The skipper, Pete Higgins, watched from the bridge as his passengers scrambled aboard. Once the motorboat was safely secured turned her bow to the new heading and got underway.

Liam joined him a few moments later.

'I hope everything went as planned?' Pete asked.

'Pretty much as expected. How long to Portugal?'

'Weather is set fair so we will be there day after tomorrow.'

Liam nodded, 'Good. I'll head below.'

The yacht was owned by Hank O'Halloran, a New York property billionaire and the descendent of Irish immigrants. He had been a passionate supporter of a free and united Ireland all his life. To hasten that glorious day, Hank had facilitated several

# VENGEANCE DAY

large shipments of arms to his ancestral home. He was a cautious operator, so no law enforcement organisation ever suspected him of involvement in these enterprises.

The political manoeuvring in Northern Ireland and the Good Friday agreement had sickened him. In his opinion, the job was only half done and said so forcefully for years while continuing his support for the dissident movement. One evening in New York, he met an intense young woman called Mary. She introduced him to Liam Rafferty. They impressed Hank with their commitment, and he gave them his backing in furthering the struggle. His major contribution was free use of Water Horse whenever they needed it. She was a hundred and seventy feet long and capable of transatlantic voyages in luxury. There was a permanent crew of three, and quarters for six more. It was ideal for Liam to travel around Western Europe and the Middle East without being noticed.

They sailed to Lisbon, where Mary, Eddy and Ruari disembarked. The following afternoon, Hank, his wife, and four friends embarked for a week's cruising in the Azores. The harbour authorities were familiar with Water Horse, and its meandering cruise through the archipelago caused no comment.

Pete Higgins was a third generation Irish American who shared Hanks's view on a united Ireland. The two other crew members, Billy Ellis, and Neil Luckett had a similar heritage. They all guessed what Liam, and his friends were. They had heard the explosions and even the gunshots. It wasn't their business, so they didn't care. In return for their silence, they enjoyed salaries that were many times higher than they could have hoped to earn from another owner.

They'd sailed all over the world using the cover story that the boat belonged to a tycoon who liked to have it handy to where he was on business. Hank was frequently on the yacht, and no one ever questioned why it should turn up in a particular port.

While Hank and his companions enjoyed their holiday, Liam and Patsy stayed out of sight in the crew's quarters. Liam was experiencing a lot of discomfort. He rested and did his exercises. As usual, he could not resist pushing himself, which was why he was still in pain. Liam originally intended to use the time cooped up in his cabin to fine tune his plans. But whenever he tried to concentrate, the events of the Isle of Dogs intruded. He would find himself re-running what happened in his mind. Liam knew he'd spent too long gloating. He had to make sure the two men knew who was executing them and, because of his vanity, he missed. Never again would he show that sort of weakness. Next time, there'll be no hesitation, no bragging and no grandstanding. Liam would look Dane in the eye and kill him without mercy. But that would have to wait. The priority now was this operation.

After the passengers disembarked in Santa Maria. Liam joined Higgins on the bridge and after handing the skipper a sheet of paper said, 'We've to rendezvous with a ship in this position at six in the morning on that date. Can you do that?'

Higgins checked the coordinates and did a swift calculation in his head.

'Sure, no worries, we'll make that easily. And the weather looks fair. Should be a pleasant trip, enjoy the cruise.'

Three hundred nautical miles northeast of Santa Maria, Higgins saw a large vessel on the horizon. He glanced at his watch and allowed a smile to crease his face. They were bang on time. There was a four-foot swell, but otherwise it was perfect. A clear sky with a hint of cloud cover that turned it the colour of faded denim, he thought, in a whimsical moment. Atlantic dolphins gambolled through the waves in front of the bow. The pod had been with them since first light, and their antics always fascinated him. He picked up the telephone.

'I've sighted the freighter.'

Liam joined him and peered through binoculars at the approaching ship, 'Is it the right one?'

'Yep, we've made contact and exchanged the codes. I'll take station on their port side. We'll maintain a steady five knots alongside for the transhipment.'

'You won't stop?'

'No, that might cause a radar operator to think something's wrong. Look,' Higgins pointed, 'They're all ready.'

## VENGEANCE DAY

They watched as a group of tiny figures scurried along the freighter's deck and opened a hatch while the crane next to it swung over. They lowered the hook into the hold. It reappeared a few moments later hauling a cargo net containing a pallet with four silver coloured boxes strapped to it.

'We'll move up alongside and they'll lower it onto the swim platform behind the cockpit. I'll swing about as we stow the gear in the salon, then come back for the next one. This won't take long. The difficulty will be hiding everything below,' Higgins announced.

He'd been optimistic because the wind picked up, increasing the swell as they manoeuvred alongside. It took several attempts to get into position, and they almost dunked the first load into the sea. Liam prowled around the bridge, becoming frustrated and angry at the delay. He screamed over the radio at the stupidity of the crane operator. This brought a furious response from the captain, threatening to stop the work and sail away. Higgins tried to calm Liam down.

'Take it easy. We'll do this.'

The first pallet landed with a crash on the swim deck, Patsy and the others swarmed over it, releasing the hook. Higgins turned the yacht hard to starboard and swung in a wide circle as the crew hauled the cargo into the main salon and threw the rubbish overboard. They returned and took possession of the second load, colliding with the bigger ship and leaving an ugly scrape along the yacht's starboard side. As they veered away, the freighter sailed into the distance, plodding across the North Atlantic towards the next port.

With everyone looking on, Liam unclipped the fastenings and lifted the lid of a box. He stared down at its contents and couldn't help the grin of triumph. There would be no stopping him now. The crew watched in silence. Liam hadn't told them what they were picking up, and their surprise was obvious.

'With this little lot, we'll give the enemy a shock they won't recover from. You're all part of something you can be proud of. Your grandchildren will sing about this in the years to come.'

He turned to Higgins, 'Now, we need to reach Dorset in four days, where we'll unload half this gear. I'll take the rest with me in Essex. Any problems doing that?'

'None whatsoever.' Higgins plotted his course, and the distances involved. They would run close to the end of their fuel by the time they reached home. There was little margin for error, but they would make it.

As they turned Northwest for Britain, Liam returned to his cabin, where he made a call on a secure satellite phone.

'We have taken delivery.'

'Yes, I understand the exchange passed successfully. So, my friend, you have the means to fulfil your mission.'

'Thank you. We must arrange for your payment. How do you want me to do that?'

'I am instructed to inform you that your determination and the justness of your cause have impressed my superiors. They have decreed that this is a gift with their blessings and best wishes for a successful operation.'

'That is a very kind gesture. Please convey my sincere respect and thanks for their understanding and generosity.'

'I will do that. When can we expect to see the outcome of the plan?'

'You will see the result before the year is out.'

'I wish you luck, and the blessings of the Allah on your enterprise my friend,' the voice said, then broke the connection.

The Iranians' generosity was a surprise. They had demanded a substantial fee for the delivery, and Liam had been ready to pay. He considered the implications of accepting the gift. They would want something from him in return, but he decided it was worth the risk. Although Liam had stolen a lot from his former comrades, he'd been unable to acquire any hi-tech or heavy weaponry. His contact could fill that requirement, and while Liam didn't like him or his masters, he would still use them for his own ends.

The crew, assisted by Patsy and Liam, worked hard repairing the scrapes on the hull. Close up, it looked a mess, but the paintwork would pass casual observation. It would be repaired

## VENGEANCE DAY

properly in the home port. On schedule, Cornwall appeared out of the haze. Higgins contacted the Falmouth Coast Guard station and informed them of his proposed course through the channel to Harwich. They'd hidden two boxes under the beds in the staterooms and another couple in the engine room. Although they wouldn't be difficult for any border force man to find if they conducted a cursory search of the boat. The remaining kit was on the floor of the salon, waiting to be loaded in the dinghy. The plan was for Liam and Billy to sail it into Worbarrow Bay on the South coast of Dorset, where they would meet their comrades and unload the equipment.

They were an hour away from the drop and Portland Bill was appearing through the gloom. Liam stood on the bridge as Higgins spotted a ship appear from behind the headland. At first, he assumed it was a warship, but then recognised it as the British Border Force Cutter Vigilant and swore under his breath. The last time he had seen her was in Harwich and her primary mission was intercepting migrants attempting to cross from France. *Why is she here?* They were closing fast, and even though the light was fading, there would be no chance to hide the contraband or dump it if the cutter's crew boarded her. Higgins grabbed the microphone and hailed the distant vessel.

'Water Horse to Vigilant, Water Horse to Vigilant, come in over,'

'Vigilant to Water Horse. Good evening. Where are you bound over?'

'We're heading to Harwich from the Azores. I had my owner on board for a cruise, and we need a service and some minor repairs.'

The two vessels sailed past about a hundred yards apart, and Higgins could see the officer of the watch on Vigilant looking back at them through binoculars. They heard nothing for several minutes. He counted each second as it ticked by, beads of sweat prickling his forehead.

'Please don't turn,' Higgins muttered to himself. 'Oh, shit, they're gonna give us a spin.'

The radio came to life, startling them.

'Water Horse, good to see you again, bon voyage, Vigilante out.' They watched the cutter disappear into the gloom.

'That was close. I thought they were going to board.'

'Well, they didn't, so there's nothing to worry about,' Liam replied, although he also looked relieved.

They passed Portland Bill, with the lights of Weymouth twinkling a mile away. Patsy and Billy loaded the boxes and lashed them down in the dinghy before they winched it over the side. The extra weight put it low in the water as they slipped the line out and drifted astern with the engine idling.

Billy needed all his skills as he swung the bow towards land. The sea conditions were choppy, and the wind was stiffening. A wave broke over the gunnels, almost knocking Liam overboard. He just kept his balance as Billy navigated straight ahead until they were inside the protective ring of Worbarrow Bay. Liam strained to spot any landmarks, then made out Worbarrow Tout looming above him and a single pinprick of light from the beach. Billy nosed up to the shoreline where five people were waiting, ready to guide them in. They exchanged muted greetings as they started unloading. A tiny figure hefted a box, then lost her footing, dropping it. There was a chorus of muffled oaths and lots of splashing until they retrieved it. They carried the boxes along a narrow track to two 4X4s parked with their engines ticking over. Liam held a whispered conversation with his friends before they all drove off into the night. Liam rejoined Billy as he reversed into the surf. Free of the weight, Billy could open the throttle and they re-joined Water Horse an hour later.

They repeated the process near the small town of Frinton on the Essex coast, where Liam and Patsy went ashore. After loading the gear, they shook hands with Higgins.

'Good luck. I think you'll need it.'

'Not needed on this mission. It'll be a cinch,' Liam replied, then slipped over the rail.

Mary was waiting for them on the beach with more members of the group. Together, they lugged their contraband to a detached house overlooking the sea. The trip had been a

## VENGEANCE DAY

complete success, and they could proceed to the next phase of the operation.

*

Three hard looking men, all in their fifties, gathered at a dilapidated old farmhouse in County Donegal. Alex and Dermot had driven from Belfast with a small group of tough minders who secured the property.

The third, Mick McArthur, arrived with a driver from Dublin.

'Alex, Dermot, how are you both?' he shook them by the hand.

'Oh, we're just grand,' Dermot replied.

'What have you found out, Mick?' Alex demanded, getting straight down to business.

Mick looked at the ceiling for a moment, gathering his thoughts.

'It took months of negotiations before Liam agreed to the meeting. Sean was sure he had turned Patsy Moran, and he was there to escort them up to the cottage. A team was waiting nearby, and they got the signal to follow. Some lads remained to mind the entrance. Anyway, soon after they set out, there were two bloody great explosions. The boys they'd left behind saw wreckage spread all over the countryside. There was no movement, and they couldn't get a reply from Sean, so they withdrew.'

'Didn't they search for survivors?' Dermot snarled.

'No. They're experienced men. It was obvious no one survived in those vehicles. The bang could have rattled the windows in Dublin, so they got out quick. If they'd hung about, the Guards would have lifted them, so they did the right thing. They sealed the area as tight as a drum. I have some excellent sources down there, but even I couldn't get any information until yesterday. They hit the cars with military grade claymore mines and everyone in them died. A big culvert bomb under a cattle grid caught the van. Sean and Hugh Murphy were still in the house, each with a bullet in the head. Just the way we trained him.'

'Where did he lay their hands on claymores, for God's sake? They didn't come from our stores because we had none. I tried for years to lay my hands on some. So, who sold them to him?' Dermot asked.

'We now know that Liam was freelancing while still working for us. I've spoken to people who worked with him. They all say he was recruiting for at least a year before dropping off our radar three years ago. Several senior operators, including Maire ó Suilleabháin, have gone with him.'

'What! You're kidding? What's she doing with him? She knows better than that. I served with her dad when the Brit's murdered him. He'll be spinning in his grave,' Alex said.

'Liam's been very persuasive. We know about Patsy Moran, and I've confirmed Eddy Buckley and Ruari ó Caoimh have also joined him. There's at least another dozen with him, and I'm struggling to identify them all. Liam sold them the line that the movement has betrayed the people, and the fight goes on.'

'And they've all swallowed that crap, have they?'

'He chose wisely from amongst the youngest volunteers, and they're all loyal to him. You'll remember that one of his followers got arrested after a bank robbery last year?' The group all nodded, 'He was a tough nut to crack. We persuaded his mother to intervene, and he spoke to me. Even then, he only gave me the bare minimum. Liam isn't working with any of the other dissidents. He hates them almost as much as us, by the sounds of it.'

'What do the Guards think happened down there?' Dermot said.

'They're convinced it was internal feuding. We've used channels to assure them it wasn't us,' Mick replied.

'What about this other business in London?'

'That was Liam. The papers identified the police officer Dane as an ex-army intelligence man who was involved in Martin Rafferty's murder. Liam wanted revenge and went on the rampage. He shot and wounded Dane and killed a murder suspect.'

'So, Liam missed the one he was after? Will he try again?' Alex asked.

# VENGEANCE DAY

'It's not like him to give up. His vendetta won't end there. I'm positive he'll have another go.'

'It'd be nice to figure out what his plans are.'

'My sources have informed me he's had meetings with some Iranians. I have taken steps to find out what they were talking about.'

'How in God's name did he meet them?'

'Liam used a contact in Sweden who put him in touch with the Iranian. He was planning this when he was on our side.'

'The Iranians have never worked with us before. They think we're a bunch of heathens, don't they?' Dermot added.

'Yes. On principle, they only ever give aid to Islamic groups. But, once again, Liam's been resourceful. I know he's putting something together with them.'

'Can we find out what it is?'

'I'm working on it, but I need more time.'

'We've got to cull this lunatic. How did we end up in this mess? If he's allowed to keep going, it could ruin everything. I don't care what it takes, but we must stop him and carry out the sentence of the court martial,' Alex ordered.

'What about those with him?'

'If they get in the way, then they go down as well. Is that clear?'

'Are you happy for me to deal with this matter?' Mick asked.

'Yes, we are. Make sure Liam bloody Rafferty is stopped in his tracks and none of it leads back to us.'

'I've an idea, but it would mean getting the Brits to do our dirty work for us. Are you willing to support me in this?'

'You do whatever it takes, and quickly.'

# SIMON DINSDALE

## Chapter 5

In the weeks following Robyn's return to Canada, Dane concentrated on regaining his strength. He was running further, taking the opportunity of the solitude to search his memory. He still couldn't remember much apart from the tantalising snippets he'd already dragged from the furthest recesses of his mind. The fleeting image of a small dark-haired man remained a firm recollection. The mocking Irish voice frequently popped into his mind, but he still wasn't confident it was real. The scar on his head healed and his fair hair re-grew, albeit thinner.

He spent a morning with Dr Hurrell, who subjected him to a thorough examination. The doctor expressed his pleasure with his progress and agreed Dane could return to work with the caveat that he settled in slowly. The force medical officer insisted Dane must complete a course of counselling before they would allow him to return to work. The following day, Dane met his counsellor, Liz, who he had helping him for several years. She had been instrumental in Dane finally controlling the PTSD he'd suffered since his army days.

Liz welcomed him into her office and pointed to a chair.

'You're looking well, considering what you've been through.'

'I'm feeling good and can't wait to get back to the day job.'

'Is there any rush? They're not putting you under pressure, are they?'

'No, quite the opposite.'

'Why don't you tell me about what's been going on?'

Dane described everything he'd done since their last meeting. She let him talk without interrupting, making the odd note.

'You're keeping yourself busy then?'

'Yes, there's no point sitting about is there. I need to get on with my life.'

'Good. How are your parents?'

'My father is home, and my mother is doing well. Which is amazing, given what she's been through.'

'What are your feelings about what took place?'

## VENGEANCE DAY

'I've spent a lot of time thinking about it. I'm not responsible for Anderson's death. Some might say I shouldn't have gone after him without backup. But I needed answers, and I wasn't being reckless. It was my duty to bring him to justice and if I didn't follow him, he would have escaped, so I did my job. If the stranger hadn't intervened, Anderson would now be in a cell awaiting trial for five murders.'

'Did you get what you needed from Anderson?'

'I don't know. We were alone in there for several minutes before the shooting started. There was certainly enough time to ask him. But if he told me anything, I can't recall.'

'Is it a problem for you?'

'I found it all frustrating to begin with. I'd spend every waking moment trying to force a recollection. But I am more relaxed about it now. Dr Khan assures me it will all come to me one day without warning. I must be patient and wait for that to happen.'

'I'm no expert on amnesia, but it sounds right to me,' Liz wrote a note, then looked up and held his gaze, 'And you still want the answers?'

That surprised him, and he took a second to gather his thoughts.

'Of course, I do.'

'We must consider the possibility, however remote, that you are suppressing it.'

'Why would I do that? If Anderson did tell me, what do I gain from not knowing what he said?'

'Is there something related to the original incident in Ireland that causes you pain, or guilt, or shame?'

Dane frowned and considered that for a moment.

'I've grown increasing uncomfortable about what happened to the boy in Derry. The last few weeks of the investigation and the problems I experienced sleeping, with the constant nightmares, brought those feelings out. That's why I became so determined to find and confront Anderson about it. He wasn't the suspect then, and when I discovered he was, I risked my life and career to get the answers. Why would I suppress that memory, however unpleasant it is? I need to know what he said.'

## SIMON DINSDALE

'I know it seems strange but think about it. Anderson might have said something you didn't want to hear. The more you open your mind the more you can let in. Are you still suffering from the night terrors?'

'No. There have been none since I woke up in the hospital. Nor do I have the constant anxiety, as if something dreadful was about to happen. It's helped to be reconciled with Robyn and spending time with her. I wonder if Anderson gave me what I wanted, and that knowledge is sitting there in my subconscious, negating the nightmares.'

'It is a possibility.'

'So, what do you think? Am I fit to work?'

'I don't see why not. We'll meet once a week for another month to monitor your progress. I'll write to the welfare department and recommend your return. But make sure you pace yourself to begin with. You will be surprised how weak you are.'

Dane left the meeting with a spring in his step. The possibility he didn't want to remember his encounter with Anderson filled his thoughts over the weekend. His involvement in the death of three people had always concerned him, and a young boy dying made it even worse. Yes, he felt some culpability, and a certain amount of shame, but he now doubted the boy's death was necessary. That was why he went after Anderson. To find the truth. Dane needed those answers to put his mind at rest and couldn't accept that if Anderson had told him anything, he would hide it from himself.

Dane arrived at his desk the following Monday, six weeks after getting shot. Angela, his secretary, met him with her customary smile, and a welcoming hug.

The investigations into the murders committed by Anderson had continued in Dane's absence. The enquiry team had worked hard to tie up all the loose ends up, and Dane's deputy, DI Lamb, had submitted a file to the Crown Prosecution Service. Dane had to content himself with catching up on his e-mails and the other cases he was responsible for. By lunchtime a headache was pounding behind his eyes. He took two Paracetamol and attempted to work through the pile of paperwork in his in-tray but found it hard to concentrate. The warnings from the doctors and Liz were correct. He would have to pace himself.

Dane was about to leave for the day when received a call from Caldwell.

'I thought you would like a quick update on the investigation so far.'

'Yes, please. What have you found?' Dane replied.

'We recovered fresh bloodstains in the stairwell leading up the two flights above the scene. The blood is all from the same person, but there is no match on the DNA database. There are no eyewitnesses, apart from you and the armed officers. Several locals heard what they assumed were shots. We've had no luck with House to House, and there's not much CCTV in the area. What there is has been no help. But a few minutes after the shooting, a couple of our guys got to the rear of the car park and stopped a motor. It was being driven by a lone female. She told the officers she had just left the car park but hadn't heard anything. They searched it and reported the encounter, which included her description and the registration number. We've since tried to locate her but, lo-and-behold, the car number is a clone. The actual owner lives in Penzance and has never been to London, and we've confirmed that. This could be a coincidence, but I doubt it. We're happy the woman is involved and either the cops missed the shooter when they searched, or she picked him up round the corner. The vehicle is now on PNC with a stop marker, but there've been no sightings of it since then.'

'Not even on ANPR?' Dane said. Automatic Number Plate Recognition cameras capture the licence details of every vehicle passing them. There are thousands monitoring the roads all over the country.

'No sign of it after our officers spoke to her. Our thinking is they changed the plates soon after being stopped.'

'Makes sense. And tells us a lot about the people we're looking for.'

'I agree, they're not amateurs. We'll keep searching. So, we've got your partial description of the man and the quote you recalled.'

## SIMON DINSDALE

'I'm still uncertain about his voice,' Dane cautioned, 'It's difficult to describe the sensation of not having a complete recall of something. The description is accurate, but the accent. I can't be sure.'

'You're probably on the right track. The ballistic scientists compared the forensic results from the bullets with other shootings across Europe, and there is a match from Ireland. The Garda are dealing with what they believe to be internecine warfare between rival dissident republican groups. Ten people died in explosions outside a remote property in the far south. The cops found the bodies of two well-known former IRA men in the house, both shot in the head with the pistol used to shoot you. This happened five days after you were hurt.'

Dane half expected there to be a flash of light, then a memory, but nothing came.

'So, you're saying an Irish terrorist attacked us?'

'It seems likely. Once they identified you in the press, they wanted revenge for your past service and hit Anderson by mistake. I can't think of another explanation for the pistol being used on you, then over there within a week. My working hypothesis is whoever shot you also killed the victims over there or handed the gun to someone else.'

'That's extreme. To send people over here to knock me off for what I did after all these years. Have they ever done this before?'

'I'm not aware of anything like it,' Caldwell replied, 'But it's the only thing I can think of at the moment.'

'Who were the victims?'

'They wouldn't give me their names. I asked for more information through higher channels here at the Yard. The head of counter terrorism in the Met, told me in no uncertain terms that knowing the identity of the dead men was above my pay grade and would not assist my investigation.'

'Sounds familiar. They could have passed the gun on, I suppose. But is it likely? A pistol is an asset any self-respecting terrorist is going to want to keep hold of. Criminals pass their weapons around, but not terrorists. I suppose this means he has unfinished business with me.'

'Unless Anderson was the target, and you got in the way.'

'How would they know he was there?'

'Perhaps they realised you wanted him and followed you. You publicised his picture, although you hadn't named him. But you said someone might recognise him from the photo.'

'Yes, provided they knew him.' Dane conceded.

'Maybe he was punting his drugs and fell afoul of a dealer over there. It's been common knowledge for years the republican terror groups are the major source of cocaine in the North. Or they caught your man at it and wanted him out of the way.'

'But I was being watched long before I identified Anderson as the suspect.'

'That doesn't mean they didn't know who he was. They used you to locate him.'

Dane couldn't accept that line of thinking. It was much too far-fetched for his liking. If Irish republicans were after Anderson, they wouldn't need to follow him around to get to him. No, Dane was sure he'd been their objective all along. That being the case, whoever it was would be back to finish the job. He considered his family's vulnerability and doubted they would go after Robyn in Canada. But his parents were soft targets. This wasn't over, and he would have to keep a wary eye out for the foreseeable future.

'Thanks for bringing me up to date on everything. If I remember anything else, I'll be in contact,' Dane said and hung up.

SIMON DINSDALE

**Chapter 6**

Liam and Patsy found Mary waiting for them at the reception of a bleak travel lodge close to Luton airport. She led them to the conference room they had booked for their half day meeting. Without a word, Patsy swept for surveillance devices. They didn't expect to find any, but it would be foolish to drop their guard. Everyone kept quiet until he pronounced the place safe.

The hotel had provided flip charts and cheap plastic folders containing headed notepaper and complimentary pens and pencils. Flasks of tea and coffee sat alongside plates of biscuits, Danish pastries and little glass bowls filled with sweets. Liam tipped the contents of one into his pocket, and Mary raised an eyebrow.

'I like boiled sweeties,' he declared.

The others arrived in dribs and drabs over the next hour, having all travelled up that morning. This was the first time they'd all been together for several months, and they greeted each other with a lot of handshaking and joking. Mary had booked the room in the name of an IT start-up company, based in Dublin, for a strategy meeting for the area managers. Liam took his seat and observed the eleven men and women for a moment. He was not a man who had many personal relationships, but these people were the closest he ever had to friends. They were all kindred spirits and as dedicated to the cause as Liam. Mary sat on his right, and Patsy plonked a chair in front of the door to prevent any uninvited visitors. When they saw Liam was ready, the noise died down.

'It's good to see you all together again. I want to bring you up to date with some things we've been up to and let you know what's coming up. You've all been lazing about on your fat arses for a while, so now's the time you earn your corn.'

Laughter rippled around the room.

'First, I'd like an update on how you're all getting on.'

The four team leaders briefed the group on how they were all settling into their respective safe houses. None of them had experienced any issues with their neighbours who took little notice of the new people living amongst them. They all varied their movements daily to build the legend that they were working. Once they finished, Liam brought them to the principal item on the agenda.

'We've all worked hard to develop our ability to take the fight to the enemy,' he declared. They all looked at him in anticipation, 'I can now tell you we're going to decapitate the British state in a co-ordinated attack. They won't know what's hit them. Or where it's coming from.'

Mary let out a warning hiss, 'For the love of God. Keep your voice down.'

Liam grinned, 'Sorry, got carried away. This operation will show the world we haven't given up the struggle. It will force their lying politicians back to the negotiating table.'

'I've never used this type of equipment before, and I don't think anyone else here has either,' Jo said to nods of agreement around the room.

'Neither have I,' Liam acknowledged, 'So, we'll have to have some help with that. Mary, tell them what you've been up to.'

'I just got back from the States. I met some friends who support our cause and liken it to the grievances they have with their own leaders.'

'Militias?'

'Not your normal militia. Most of the so-called Patriot groups over there are red neck Protestants who hate everyone and are barking mad. The people I have been in contact with are Catholic and Irish by heritage. They've formed an association for mutual protection and support and call themselves "The Sons of Erin". They have agreed to train us to use our little toys. I have tickets, documents, and hotel reservations and, as usual, we'll all travel separately. We will meet up in New York City a week today. One member of each team is to stay behind to guard the houses. It'll be boiling hot over there, so make sure you bring sunscreen and insect repellent. If you forget, you'll regret it, and I won't lend you mine.'

Liam took over, 'Follow your instructions to the letter. Our old friends in Belfast are still looking for us. I suspect they'll have some of our names by now, so don't take any chances. If you think you've grown a tail, abort and use the fall-back procedures. Before we leave, I want you all to search for a van. Transit size or larger. Make sure it's legal, in good condition and not white. Make sure there is no signage written on it. You'll need to cut a section of the roof out to shoot through.'

There was a general murmur amongst the group as they realised what he had in mind.

'Great, so find them and crack on with the modifications. I'll see you in the Big Apple next week. Questions?'

'How long have we got to prepare them?'

'Be ready to go at the end of October. So, you have four months.'

\*

Mary travelled out to America a couple of days later, where she rented a party bus. She was waiting outside terminal eight at Kennedy airport when Liam and Patsy cleared immigration. After negotiating the maze of roads to get out of the airport, she joined the Belt Parkway towards the New York city. Mary soon turned off the freeway and onto the surface streets to avoid as many cameras as possible. They made good time as they drove through Brownsville and Crown Heights. Eddy and Ruari were waiting at a McDonalds on Flatbush Avenue, in Brooklyn. They piled in and passed round coffees and hot dogs. As they approached the East River, the traffic increased and reduced them to a crawling pace. It got worse as Mary negotiated the Brooklyn Bridge and entered lower Manhattan, where they came to a standstill. The entire area was grid locked, with stationary traffic in every direction. Liam contacted Kath and Jo, who were at the junction of Chambers Street and West Broadway. He told them where they were and to walk to them. Five minutes later, they both climbed in with their backpacks, in that time the bus hadn't moved an inch.

'I spoke to a subway inspector. There's a big diplomatic event at the United Nations building. Loads of roads in downtown

## VENGEANCE DAY

Manhattan have been closed and there are diversions all over the place,' Jo said.

'Great, just what we need,' Liam replied. His temper was already fraying at the delay, and there was still a lengthy road trip ahead of them.

'There's no way we'll reach all the pickup points in this mess. I'll ring Carol and she can gather the others and meet us outside the subway station on Columbus Circle. If we don't do something, I will grow old in this place. Move it!' he screamed at the cars in front in frustration.

Jo unfurled and studied a map, 'Go straight along Chambers Street. When we hit the West Side Highway, turn right. That's a big dual carriageway. It might not be so congested.'

Mary nodded and crawled ahead. Liam finished his call, 'They'll wait for us there. How long to Logan's?'

'It's the best part of two hundred and fifty miles, once we're clear of this madhouse. We won't be there till late,' Mary replied. She flinched as Liam bellowed abuse at another driver and punched the dashboard. The guys in the back were settling down to catch some sleep.

'Don't get too comfortable,' Liam shouted, 'Everyone will have a spell at the wheel before long.'

Mary made the turn onto the highway successfully. It was as clogged as everywhere else and controlled by traffic signals at regular intervals. It took nearly an hour to crawl north past the Intrepid aircraft carrier museum and cruise terminals to West 57$^{th}$ Street, where they turned right. By this time, Liam's temper was in danger of boiling over. Twenty minutes later, Mary crawled round Columbus Circle, stuck in the wrong lane. She spotted their friends and would have got their attention with a blast on the horn if every other driver wasn't doing the same thing. At the last moment, Carol saw them and waved, and her companions picked their bags up and trotted to the roadside. Mary swerved and bullied her way in front of other vehicles before bouncing up on the kerb, the sliding door was pulled open, and they all tumbled in. The lights changed, but they were blocking the road. The drivers behind let rip with another cacophony of angry horns, furious at missing the opportunity to get a hundred yards closer to home. A taxi driver hurled abuse, and Liam snarled back. The argument became more heated. Liam went to open the door, but Mary grabbed his arm.

'Careful,' she muttered, pointing to a motorcycle cop on the far side of the junction. As they pulled away, the officer followed and put his blue lights on, blipping his siren for her to pull over.

Mary watched in the mirror as the cop walked to the driver's window, 'Calm down, Liam. Let me do the talking.'

'Good afternoon, ma'am. Is this your vehicle?'

'No sir, it's a rental. I collected it at Kennedy this morning.'

'I noticed you stopped back there and picked some guys up. That's a traffic violation. I could give you a ticket. Where are you headed?'

'Up state to go hiking. Then on to Canada. We're over from Ireland.' She gave him a beaming smile.

'Well, be careful and watch the local laws. I'll let you off this once and only because my grandpa would kick my butt if he knew I had cited an Irish lady.' He looked across at Liam, 'It's not a great idea to have a fistfight with another driver, sir. I'd appreciate it if you kept your temper under control.'

'Thank you, officer. I will take more care, and this one will behave in future.' Mary breathed a sigh of relief. 'Okay, let's get the hell out of here.'

Mary drove north past Central Park, through Harlem, over the Macombs Dam Bridge and into the Bronx. Eddy took the wheel outside the Yankee stadium, and they soon swapped the hustle and bustle of the city for rural upstate New York.

The contrast was stark, and the traffic reduced to nearly zero the further into the outback they went. They passed through tiny hamlets comprising nothing more than a few houses and remote farmsteads.

Five hours later, they arrived at the town of Frazer and there was a request to stop for a stretch and to find some food. Mary cruised along Main Street until she spotted a gas station with a diner. A teenage waitress was serving while a man in dirty chef's whites crashed about in the steaming kitchen behind her. A row

## VENGEANCE DAY

of bar seats stretched the length of the counter, with booths opposite. Mary sat next to Liam and studied the menu.

'What do you fancy?'

'A cheeseburger and fries.'

They gave their orders to the girl, who made a laborious note and passed that to the chef. She returned with the ubiquitous coffee jug and poured, 'Where are you guys all from?'

'We've driven up from New York. We got held up in the city,' Mary replied.

'Yeah, I'm told it gets crazy down there. You're not American, are you?'

'No, we're British, on holiday.'

A tall female state trooper walked in to sit at the counter and call a greeting to the chef. Their order arrived and as Mary went to pay the bill, the rest grabbed their food and wandered out to the bus. Liam jumped into the front passenger seat and saw Mary having a brief conversation with the cop.

'What was that all about?' he asked when she climbed behind the wheel.

'That was my new friend, officer Ramirez, trying to be helpful, she even gave me her number.' Mary laughed at the look on his face, 'Just joking. She was advising us all to be careful in the mountains, that's all.'

'She's watching. Come on, let's go.'

After the last streetlight, the pitch black of the countryside enveloped them like a thick blanket. Half an hour later, they turned onto a narrow dirt track and stopped at a pair of securely locked gates. Liam had called ahead, but they still had to wait until someone arrived in an SUV to let them in.

As they drove through, Liam noticed another vehicle approaching on the main road. It cruised past, and he saw it was a police car. It didn't slow down and disappeared into the night. Mary followed the SUV along a track up and over a hill into a deep and secluded valley. A property appeared in the distance, its lights twinkling in the darkness. It took another ten minutes to reach the two-storey house with a paddock in front and a line of cabins behind. Their host owned this remote homestead and used it as a base for the militia group who would train them. They all climbed out, stretching the kinks out of their backs. Apart from the ticking of the hot engine, there was complete silence. The sky was clear, and Liam and his companions all gazed up at the billions of stars filling the heavens.

'No light pollution up here,' a voice behind them said in a low American growl, 'Hi, I'm Sean Logan and I own this place. You must be Mary?'

'I am and this is Liam.'

'Pleased to meet you. We've set the cabins aside for you all. You'll find food and drink in them.'

'Sorry we're late. The traffic was a nightmare, and we hadn't realised how far out you are. We only do short distances back home.'

'It takes getting used to. Once you've been here a while, you won't want to leave. Get settled in and come over to the house and we can talk.'

After dropping their bags in the cabin Liam and Mary joined Logan on his porch.

'We're heading out early. I know what you are keen to do, and it's all set up. To maintain your cover, we'll do some weapon training as well,' Logan said.

'That's fine by us. Are there others here?' Liam asked.

'Only some militia members for security and the instructors. I trust my people. They are all Irish by descent and sympathetic to the cause.'

'Do they know who we are?'

'No, only that you're from the old country. But they'll speculate, I'm sure. I suggest you stick to your agreed cover story. I own twelve thousand acres of land and guard my privacy. I get on well with the folks in the local town and the cops know better than to come out here. So, we'll be alone and uninterrupted.'

'That all sounds fine,' Liam replied, 'I think we could use some sleep.'

'I've arranged an early call for 0600hrs, to leave by 0700hrs. You're moving out to a remote camp. Make certain your guys

# VENGEANCE DAY

take everything they need in the way of clothes and sleeping bags.'

'How are we getting there?'

'On horseback,' Logan replied, a smile creasing his lips.

'Horses,' Liam yelped.

'Don't worry. They're all placid mounts and you won't be going any faster than a brisk walking pace. So, you shouldn't fall off.'

'I'll not say anything to the others. This should be good for a laugh.'

The alarm woke Liam with a start. He'd not slept well, suffering the same re-occurring nightmare. Sweat soaked his body and a dull ache throbbed behind his eyes. He sat up and stretched before heading to the bathroom.

Everyone assembled outside the big house and Liam admired the splendour surrounding him. The property was in a natural bowl with the hill they had driven over the previous night to the east. He could just make out the track as it snaked over the ridge. The sun was up, and the sweet scent of flowers and hay lifted his mood. In the paddock a herd of horses were munching their breakfast from nosebags. Most had riding saddles on their backs, while the rest carried equipment.

Logan joined them, looking like the Marlboro man, 'Good morning all. I hope you all got a decent night's sleep. We've a bit of a ride, so best we get moving.'

Liam laughed at his comrades' reaction when they saw their mode of transport.

'What's wrong with you? They don't bite.' He went to the biggest animal and tried to jump up into the saddle. He made it on the third attempt amidst loud encouragement. When everyone was mounted, they moved off in single file, with Logan leading. The horses all knew where they were going and followed each other nose to tail.

They walked for two hours through some of the most beautiful countryside Liam had ever seen. He felt an enormous sense of anticipation as they skirted a lake and arrived at a campsite. Six large tents were nestling in the trees and his taste buds sprang to life as he smelt coffee and bacon. They all dismounted and tied their horses to a line before congregating at the cookhouse.

'This is our primary base for the next few days. The latrines are over there,' Logan said and pointed over to two small square structures surrounded by sheets of hessian.

'Be sure to take a rifle with you whenever you go. There're bears in the woods, they just love the smell of our cooking. So, keep your eyes open.'

They all cast nervous glances towards the dense forest that came right up to the camp perimeter. After dropping their gear into the tents, Liam sorted them all into teams. Logan issued everyone with an AR 15 assault rifle, and with the instructors, they moved out to the ranges. They spent the rest of the day firing hundreds of rounds of ammunition at skilfully placed targets. As the sun disappeared behind the mountains, they collected their spent brass and returned for a campfire meal and an early night, exhausted.

There was no complaining when they rose before sunrise the following morning. They improved their marksmanship with a selection of automatic weapons. Logan had built a killing house. An extensive structure containing a dozen rooms in which they practiced armed entry and hostage rescue. The instructors taught them how to predict, and counter, the tactics used by law enforcement and military forces. Knowledge that could prove priceless in the future. The quiet determination of the militia members impressed Liam. He guessed they were all former soldiers. There was no limit to the amount of ammunition available. The group were all enthusiastic marksmen, and fiercely competitive, so there was some betting on individual scores. It was another long, tiring but productive day.

That evening, Logan joined them for their meal. As the darkness fell, Mary asked, 'Do you believe you will have to fight?'

'Yes, I do. There's too much hatred and distrust of the government. Most of the militias you see on the TV are nut cases. But some are extremely dangerous indeed. They hate anyone who isn't the same colour, sexual orientation, or religion

## VENGEANCE DAY

as they are, and by religion I mean Protestant. They believe the state is coming for them and that the politician's favour everyone else but them. To protect themselves from this perceived bias, they have amassed a considerable armoury, which is easy to do over here. I'm convinced they plan to attack selected targets soon. Our Catholic communities will be at the top of their list. We've recruited a few hundred members into The Sons of Erin. We're all prepared to face that threat.' He checked the time and stood, 'It's another early start tomorrow. We'll be moving up to another range for a day and a half, so grab some shuteye.'

'More bloody riding, then?'

'Yes, afraid so. At least you know how to handle the horse now. The journey will take about an hour.'

They left at first light and soon arrived in a clearing. It was on a plateau with tents and a corral at the edge of the campsite. A big marquee contained tables and a camp kitchen where sandwiches were being prepared.

'Unsaddle the mounts, and join me over there,' Logan said, and pointed to the edge of the clearing where a short, stocky man was waiting.

Once they were all assembled. Logan introduced the man beside him, 'This is Jake, who will be your instructor for the next couple of days.'

Jake stumped forward and turned to face them, legs apart, with arms akimbo. His face was clean shaven but craggy. He was wearing olive green military fatigues, desert combat boots and a wide-brimmed hat tilted over his eyes. Liam guessed he must be in his seventies.

'Good morning. I'm a forty-year veteran of the US Marine Corps. The finest fighting force in the world. I'm an expert in using this little baby,' he pointed to a mortar tube standing beside him.

'I've fired it in anger in several wars from Vietnam to the second Gulf war, and I never, ever, missed what I was aiming at.' His voice sounded like it had been marinading in whisky and cigarette smoke for fifty years.

## SIMON DINSDALE

'My task today is to give you folks a demonstration and some instruction on the use of this beauty, so listen up. This is the M292 81mm medium weight mortar. It is a smoothbore muzzle-loading weapon used for long range, indirect fire support for infantry and marines. The United States Government adapted it from the British equivalent and, although almost identical, I can say without fear of contradiction that this is the best.' Jake glared at them, as if to dare anyone to do just that.

'The total weight is ninety-one pounds. The barrel is just over four feet in length. It is man portable but not for far, unless you're a United States Marine of course. It fires a variety of bombs that are 81mm in diameter by the simple system of dropping them down the tube. They fall to the bottom, where they impact on a firing pin that ignites the propelling charge. This pushes the bomb up and away towards which ever gang of desperadoes you have decided to obliterate that day. This baby has an effective range of six thousand yards, and a trained crew can fire up to twenty rounds a minute. I'll put that many into an area the size of your soccer goalmouths from seven thousand yards. Anyone stupid enough to be within sixty yards of that will have the worst experience of their lives.'

Liam's eyes were shining as he listened.

'They won't have a clue what's happening,' he whispered to himself.

'This weapon is in four parts. The cannon, or barrel. Base plate, the bipod, and the sighting mechanism.' Jake tapped each component part with his metal pointer as he described it.

'You can't fire this beast unless it is complete and fitted together. The individual rounds come with an inbuilt primer charge. On its own, that is enough to throw the projectile about two hundred yards. For longer ranges, the crew calculates the distance to the target, then fits further donut charges, up to six, for the furthest distances.' Jake held a small semi-circular fabric bag that resembled a fat letter C above his head.

'The operator slips these over the tail of the bomb, which increases the range. Questions so far? None? Good, then let me give you a demonstration.

# VENGEANCE DAY

'Look at your front. At one thousand, two thousand and three thousand yards out, you will see targets marked by a flag.'

The land fell away from the campsite, covered in scrub with a few trees. They all peered through binoculars and picked out the flags fluttering through the heat haze.

Jake pointed to three bombs lying on the ground, 'Let's shoot one at each target. You observe one has got one donut charge, the second has two and the third, three. Okay. Stand by, watch and learn.'

He strolled to the mortar and checked the sight, turned with a grin, and shouted, 'Ready, fire.' Jake lifted the first round into position and dropped it, then bent his torso and twisted away. There was a load bang, causing them all to jump. It was much louder than Liam had expected and made his ears ring. Jake fed the next two rounds in and nonchalantly turned to them after the last had fired.

'Now look to your front and behold a master mortar man.'

Liam watched through his binoculars and saw the puffs of smoke as the bombs all exploded on target simultaneously. They cheered and clapped the achievement and Jake gave them a gap-toothed smile.

'Okay guys. Let's teach you how to shoot this beauty and have us some fun.'

# SIMON DINSDALE

## Chapter 7

Detective Chief Superintendent Grant poked his head out of his office.

'Angela, find Mr Dane and tell him I want to see him.'

'Yes, of course.' She swivelled her chair round until she faced through the door to her left. 'Excuse me, sir, Mr Grant would like you to go to his office.'

Dane saw him standing beyond her with a sour look on his face, 'I'll be with him straight away.'

Jonathan Grant was one of the governments new breed of senior police officer. A mature graduate recruit with a background in the retail industry. He'd never previously worked in law enforcement, arrested a suspect, or investigated a serious crime. After a year's basic training and some time with a tutor constable he was given the rank of superintendent. Eighteen months later, the chief constable promoted him to head of the crime division, and he became Dane's immediate supervisor. While Dane was away from work, Grant never contacted him to enquire after his health or make sure he had the correct support. It didn't bother Dane, but it spoke volumes about Grant's abilities as a leader and a manager.

Grant sat behind his desk as if to put a barrier between them.

'I've had a call from the coroner asking us to investigate the sudden death of a Brit who had an accident in Bahrain. The family and his employers have been badgering him since they repatriated the body. Go down there and pick up the papers. I think he wants to cover his backside.'

Dane doubted the Essex coroner would be as shallow as that but kept his own council.

'This should be a simple task. It won't be too taxing for you, will it?' Grant said.

'A nice, straightforward job to settle me back in. I'll manage without too much trouble. By the way, don't treat Angela like a skivvy. She's a good worker and deserves to be treated with respect.'

## VENGEANCE DAY

Dane walked into the town for his appointment. The sun was shining, and he felt relaxed as he strode into the refurbished County Hall. Dozens of people packed the recently completed steel and glass atrium, all scurrying about their business. Dane wondered what they all did as he found his way to the small office tucked at the rear of the building. The coroner rose to greet him with a firm handshake.

'I am so pleased to see you looking so well.'

'Thank you, sir, it is good to be back,' Dane replied as he took a seat.

Giles Burlington-Haynes was a distinguished looking man, with a full head of white hair over a kind face and dark brown eyes. His nickname was GBH, although no one called him that to his face, and he'd been the Essex Coroner for fifteen years. He had a formidable reputation, for being stern and unyielding one moment, then showing considerable compassion the next. Dane had worked with him before and liked his no-nonsense approach.

Giles got straight down to business.

'This is a sad case. The remains of a British subject were repatriated from Bahrain last week. According to the reports the man died following a fall in his hotel room three weeks ago. The local police conducted what I can only describe as a perfunctory investigation. They decided he must have fallen backwards from the shower and hit his head on the sink unit. Nothing was missing, nor were there any other suspicious circumstances, so they classified it as an accident. The deceased lived near Earls Colne with his wife and worked for a security company in London. His employers wrote to me expressing their concern about the way the investigation was handled and are requesting another inquiry. After having seen what little the authorities did, I agree with them. I'd like you to do what they should have done and report your findings to me. I have a copy of the Bahraini police file for you and the deceased's personal details. Dr Hume will do a forensic post-mortem tomorrow morning at Broomfield hospital.' Giles pushed a thin folder of papers across the table.

## SIMON DINSDALE

Dane glanced at the first page and his face dropped when he saw the name of the victim. 'George Blaine. Oh dear. What a way for someone like him to go.'

'I am so sorry. Was he a friend? Is it a problem for you?'

'No, he was one of my instructors in the Army many years ago. I met him again quite by chance recently and I know his employer. It will be easier all round if I did this.'

'I'm pleased to hear that. I have spoken to his widow, and she is expecting you.'

Dane glanced through the rest of the file, 'Are there any photographs of the scene?'

'No, not a satisfactory state of affairs.'

It didn't take Dane long to drive through the Essex countryside to the picturesque village and find the address. He rang the doorbell and admired the front garden as he waited. An immaculate lawn disappeared around the side of the house. It was lined with borders planted with a variety of English country flowers and shrubs. A slight woman in her late fifties with bright blue intelligent eyes opened the door.

'Hello, you must be Mr Dane, I'm Anne. Please come on in.' She had a faint Scottish accent and led him along a short corridor into the kitchen. As they passed the foot of the stairs, he noticed a worn and dusty military rucksack.

'My son's. He arrived about an hour ago. He'll be down in a moment,' she explained.

Anne bustled about making tea and, as she did, Dane gazed through the window at the garden. It stretched away from the house for more than a hundred feet to a wooden fence. A large shed and an even bigger greenhouse nestled alongside it.

'You have a beautiful garden, Mrs Blaine.'

'Thank you. Please call me Anne. George told me all about you, and how you met. He liked you.'

'The feeling was mutual. I'm so sorry for your loss. It is terrible for you and your family.'

'I have lived with the possibility of his death for all our married life. But I'd rather expected it to happen when he was serving with the Regiment. Not after he'd retired. That's fate, I suppose.'

## VENGEANCE DAY

A tall, lean, tanned man in his mid-thirties joined them.

'How do you do? I'm Nick Blaine,' he said with a dazzling smile, 'Please, call me Nick.'

'Detective Superintendent Christian Dane. Are you just home from somewhere hot and dusty?'

'Yes, I couldn't get a flight any sooner,' Nick replied, glancing towards his mother.

'Who're you with?'

'Para's.'

They sat at the kitchen table. 'I've come to inform you what I'll be doing in the coming days. The coroner has tasked me with investigating what happened to George.'

'John Lord raised the issue at first,' Anne said. 'And I have to say, he has a point. George never slipped in the bath in his life.'

'I'm meeting Lord tomorrow. Before that, we'll do the post-mortem. Once that's finished, I will give you a ring and tell you the outcome. How long are you here for?' he asked Nick.

'Until after the funeral, which we need to plan. When will they release my father's body?'

'Detective Constable Hayley Cross will be in contact with you this afternoon. She will make sure you have everything you need, and she will arrange for George's body to be released.'

Dane stayed for another hour. He could see that both Nick and Anne were badly affected by the death. If this wasn't an accident, then he would be investigating a crime in which George was the victim. But Nick, Anne and the wider Blaine family were also victims and would need support. This was something Dane felt very strongly about and always made a point of making sure they had it. Before he left them Anne showed him the garden.

'This was George's pride and joy and he spent hours working out here,' Anne said sadly.

'I detect a woman's touch as well.'

'We had a partnership. He did the heavy work, and I took care of the plants. The greenhouse was my territory, and his was the shed.' It surprised Dane that apart from Nick's kit, there was no other reference to the military or George's service.

## SIMON DINSDALE

'The Army was his job, but he left it all at the front door. When he came home, we liked to keep it just family. All the usual mementoes are in boxes in the loft. It seemed a natural thing for Nick to follow him. George was determined Nick would have the education he didn't have. We were so proud when he got into Sandhurst.'

Nick walked with Dane to his car, 'Do you think my father's death is suspicious?'

'I won't know for certain until after the postmortem. If it is, I promise you. I will move heaven and earth to bring whoever is responsible to justice.'

'I can't ask more than that. We spoke about you when I was last home.'

'George and I met in another life. He had a tough job to do but always did it with a smile.'

'You got him to admit something. He couldn't believe how easily you caught him out,' Nick said. Dane smiled at the memory. George had rung Dane's office to pass some information relating to the murder in Cambridge. The next day Dane had met George with his boss, John Lord, in Vicky's office.

'I recognised him straight away, although he didn't remember me. I was surprised to see him, but his voice gave him away. When we spoke on the phone, he refused to give his name and said I would recognise his voice when we next spoke. I did.'

'He admired you for that and your military record.'

'Are you with the Regiment?'

Nick hesitated for a second, 'Yes, I suppose it was inevitable I'd join the SAS. I gained my commission to the Para's and went to Hereford for my first tour as a lieutenant. I got another stint, and I now command A Squadron, dad's old lot. He was so chuffed when I achieved that,' There were tears in the tall soldiers' eyes, 'I look forward to hearing from you tomorrow, Christian.'

*

Dane arrived at the mortuary the following morning. It was tucked out of sight at the rear of the sprawling hospital complex

## VENGEANCE DAY

in Chelmsford. Scenes of crime officers set up their kit, and they got ready for the examination. Dane had lost count of how many of these he'd watched. His friends, including Vicky, often asked how the sights, sounds and smells of the forensic dissection of a human body didn't affect him. He couldn't explain why, but the experience never bothered him. It was a necessary part of the job and an exercise that frequently produced crucial evidence.

The mortician laid George on the slab, and the thick, nauseating odour of death permeated the room. They had removed him from the freezer to defrost the evening before and, as the body thawed, the decomposition process re-started. The cadaver was a deep purple colour with olive green and yellow streaks under the skin, and the belly distended. Dane just recognised his facial features, but they would soon deteriorate. Dr Hume examined the corpse, prowling around, speaking sotto voce into the tape recorder he held in his gloved hand.

'There's a severe sprain in the left ankle. He wouldn't have been able to put much weight on it after he sustained that injury,' Hume said.

'The police report says he fell heavily while out running. The hotel receptionist saw him hobbling to the lift,' Dane replied.

'He must've been a tough old bird.'

'George was very tough.'

'There's bruising around both upper arms. The marbling is masking it. You can also see the grazing to his left arm and shoulder. Probably caused by the fall in the street.'

Hume shaved all the hair off, exposing a bruise and an obvious depression in the skull.

'A substantial blow with a blunt instrument caused this,' He selected a scalpel and made a sweeping incision around the back of the head from below the right ear to the same position on the other side. Hume pared, then peeled the scalp away until he had exposed heavy bruising throughout the layers of flesh.

'There's a second injury here. Same as the first and just as fatal.'

'Not looking good for a slip in the shower then?' Dane asked.

## SIMON DINSDALE

'These injuries are too far up on the skull to have resulted from a fall backwards.' Once the examination was complete Dane joined Hume in the mortician's room.

'This victim was murdered. The assailants attacked him from behind and hit him twice. Those blows caused him to collapse and die within a minute or two. The grip marks on the upper arms show the victim was held while being manhandled.'

'Concise as always.'

'My pleasure dear boy, it's good to see you with your nose to the grindstone, no ill effects, I trust?'

'None, the doctors say I've got a thick head.'

'An attribute all police officer's need, I think. Full report will be with you within the week.'

Dane called Giles and informed him of Dr Hume's findings.

'Thanks for letting me know. I'm meeting the chief constable later today. I'll make a formal request to her to investigate. Are you likely to be doing that for me?' Giles asked.

'I've started the work, so I might as well keep it. But that decision is for my boss. I'd better tell him the good news.'

'I will contact the Foreign Office and put them on notice. It's their responsibility to get whatever information we need from Bahrain.'

Dane rang Grant, who was less than amused.

'Are you sure he didn't fall over?'

'Someone bashed his head in. Mr Burlington-Hayes is going to request our help. Do you want me to take it?'

'Yes, you'd better. Watch the expenditure and update me daily.' Grant hung up without waiting for a reply.

Dane glared at the handset. 'What a pillock,' he muttered then called Nick Blaine to tell him the outcome and what would happen next.

'How does that work? Will you be able to prosecute anyone?'

'It depends on several different factors. All the evidence I find goes to the coroner who will hold an inquest. If that returns a verdict of unlawful killing, he'll pass it to the Bahraini authorities via the Foreign Office. Murder is a criminal offence there. If I identify a suspect, that evidence would be admissible

## VENGEANCE DAY

in their courts. It is possible to extradite someone back to this country for a prosecution. But in these circumstances, I think that would be unlikely.'

'Thanks. I'm going up to Hereford tomorrow and will be back at the weekend. My Aunt is staying, and dad's boss is helping.'

'He's my next call. I'll keep in touch.'

Dane met John Lord at the headquarters of the Wilmington Corporation that afternoon. The security consultant was tall and dressed in a handmade suit and looked every bit the city entrepreneur. Lord was a veteran of the Special Air Service and set up his company after leaving the army. George followed, becoming his most valued employee. Dane had met the pair in Cambridge during his investigation into the five murders. One of Lord's clients, Sir Gordon Wilmington, had sent them there to investigate the death of Wilmington's daughter Clarrie and her boyfriend. What they uncovered led them to contact Dane anonymously and entice him to Cambridge, where he discovered the fifth victim of his killer. Lord had since proved to be a useful contact, and they had become friends.

'Good to see you and I'm pleased that something is being done. I've been banging my head against a wall for the last week. I spoke to a rude sod called Grant at your headquarters. He fobbed me off.'

'Grant never mentioned that when he gave me the job. When did you talk to him?'

'The day after we flew George's body home. I received a much better reception from the coroner. So, what can you tell me?'

'We've confirmed someone hit him on the head twice from behind. So, I am now leading a murder inquiry. Can you tell me what he was doing over there?'

Lord explained that amongst the myriad of business interests of Wilmington Holdings was the export of arms. A small subsidiary company managed a contract with the MoD to supply military equipment to half a dozen friendly countries. They purchased old surplus kit including weapons, ammunition, vehicles, uniforms and other items of use to military and police units. Everything is then reconditioned before being sold at auction on the open market. The business is carefully controlled and sanctioned by the Government. At the beginning of the year the company had sent a huge shipment to Bahrain. On arrival it had been stored in a warehouse at the port. Three months later, the Bahraini military discovered a small number of items were missing.

Lord handed Dane a thick file, 'I sent George to investigate, and this contains everything he discovered. Look at page five.'

Dane read for a few moments, then looked up.

'Four mortars and forty bombs, is that all they took?'

Lord nodded, 'George confirmed the kit had arrived in Bahrain on schedule and was stolen from a warehouse in Manama. Almost certainly with the collusion of the dock workers.'

'What had he discovered?'

'He could prove that the crates had been opened in the store at the docks. The weapons head been removed and replaced with scrap metal and the boxes placed at the bottom of the pile. He found some CCTV coverage from a camera on the dock which shows a truck pulling into the warehouse and leaving an hour later. George and Captain Abbass, the officer he was liaising with, were due to start the interviews with the staff that morning. Abbass arrived to collect George, and when he didn't appear went to his room and discovered his body. The police were determined to prove that it had been a dreadful accident. As a result, nobody did a proper investigation.'

'What happened to the inquiry into the missing munitions?'

'I know the warehouse supervisor was arrested but Abbass wouldn't give me any more information. I suspect his superiors told him to keep quiet. The hotel manager let me into George's room, and I got pictures of it. Nothing was stolen, and the authorities allowed me to bring back all his possessions.'

'Why didn't you trust the official explanation?'

'I send operators all over the world on these types of investigations. It's standard practice for them to e-mail their reports to HQ daily. George sent his findings home the evening before he died. The people who attacked him attempted to hack into his laptop at 0700hrs local. Now, when this happens, and it's not that uncommon, an alarm triggers the webcam. We have a sequence of film showing three men fiddling with George's computer for ten minutes before he returns. One of them works on the machine with a second, who is clearly in charge, peering over his shoulder. You hear him shouting at the hacker for taking too long. He looks petrified and keeps apologising, referring to the leader as "Baradar Husam." The third man is the muscle for the operation.'

'Baradar?' Dane said.

'It means "Brother" in Farsi. At 0710hrs a mobile phone rings and Husam answers it. I assume he's informed that George is on his way. They have no time to get out, so they ambush George as soon as he gets into the room. You can hear two blows and someone falling. They drag him into the bathroom then tidy the room up and leave.'

'I hope all of this is available to me?'

'We've preserved George's laptop and personal possessions for you. My techie has prepared the video with his statement explaining the process. I've also had a transcript of their conversation done.'

'What were they looking for?'

'They wanted to know what George had found out.'

'Did they get that?'

'No, the security system blocks everything. The hacker plugged an external hard drive in, hoping it would download, but they got nothing. They thought they had half an hour, so must have been watching George to establish his movements.'

'What language are they speaking?'

'Farsi. I've had three different experts listen to the soundtrack and they all agree the men are Iranians.'

'Who have you told about this?'

'No one.'

'Why not?'

'Because the Bahraini's weren't interested. There's virtually no crime in the capital and never any in that hotel. It's a favourite destination for visiting businesspeople. The authorities were determined to write the whole thing off. I didn't trust them enough to give them the material or tell them of its existence. But now you're dealing with it, I'm happy to hand it all over.'

'How about the CCTV of the hotel stairwells, exits and car parks?'

'All out of order, according to the manager. The only cameras still working in the whole place were the reception area. Spooky that, eh?'

'Who knows these weapons have gone missing?'

'We have informed the MoD and I suspect they will have passed the information to both the intelligence agencies.'

'What's your take on all this?'

'Must be to do with a terrorist plot. Whoever took the equipment had complete access to the bonded warehouse. They could have taken everything, but they didn't. It's probably all on its way to Afghanistan or Syria or southern Iraq or any other place that is experiencing difficulties with an Iranian influence,' Lord said.

Dane pondered that information. He reminded himself that he was looking for the people responsible for the murder. However, the apparent involvement of Iranians was significant and could make his job much harder. The tentacles of certain parts of that state reached into many places, and they didn't hesitate to take extreme action. Dane knew he would get no help from them if their agents were identified as suspects.

The phone on Lord's desk rang, and he picked it up, 'Yes sir, he's here now,' He replaced the receiver, 'The boss would like to have a quick word.'

They were both ushered into Sir Gordon Wilmington's enormous office with fabulous views of the London skyline. The tycoon greeted Dane who explained the findings of the postmortem and what he would be doing.

'I'm pleased you are leading this. George was a good man and didn't deserve to die this way. Can we get the swine responsible to our courts?'

'I will work through the usual process of gathering the evidence. But once that's done, I must pass it to the Bahraini government.'

'I have some powerful contacts over there, so let me know if I can help.'

'Thank you, I'll remember that.'

'My wife and I are incredibly grateful for everything you did to identify the scum responsible for my daughter's murder.'

'I hope you're both able to find some peace now.' As they walked down the stairs, Dane turned to Lord, 'Before I go, can I ask you a small favour?'

## SIMON DINSDALE

### Chapter 8

The time and money invested in the trip to the US had been worthwhile. Jake proved to be an excellent teacher and drilled Liam and his comrades in the basics. They were soon adept at assembling the mortars, laying the sights, and adjusting the fuses on the bombs.

With the means and knowledge to be able to fire the weapons effectively, Liam was even more confident his plan would work. All they had to do was place them properly and point them in the right direction.

The encounter with Hugh Murphy and Sean had raised a fear that his former comrades might be on to him. The more Liam thought about it, the less it seemed likely they could know why he met the Iranians. Even the date for the proposed attack was perfect. Liam didn't believe in superstition. But falling on such an important personal anniversary made him certain he couldn't fail. If they all stuck to his plan, they would inflict a devastating blow to the British establishment. And, with a little luck they might be able to escape with the weapons intact.

When military units set up their mortars, the soldiers put a ranging pole in the ground on a fixed point in front of the weapons. A fire mission would include the distance to the target and a compass bearing. The crew would centre the sights on the pole and move the barrel left or right onto the correct heading.

They couldn't use ranging poles in the vans, so Liam intended to use the tried and tested method the IRA employed to aim their home-made mortars. The teams would point the front of the vehicle on the compass bearing they wanted the projectiles to go. The terrorist mortar bombs rarely worked properly, because of the haphazard construction and unreliable explosives. But they usually flew in the intended direction, so the system worked.

With the military mortars, if they followed Jake's instructions, they could strike anything from five thousand yards. Liam intended to place each of them at that distance from the target, on

# VENGEANCE DAY

the four points of the compass. His priority now was to locate the best firing positions for his mortars.

With Mary's assistance he set about identifying sites that fitted the requirement. It wouldn't matter if they parked on public roads, so long as they didn't appear out of place or park illegally. No one would notice them until they fired. They spent a week tramping around the streets of North, East, South and West London armed with an A/Z map book of city. By the Friday afternoon they had eight suitable sites. Each team now had a primary firing position and a second as a fall-back. They returned to their safe house, excited and impatient for the next phase.

\*

Husam was careful to appear relaxed as he presented his papers to the uniformed guards. They scrutinised the picture and compared it to his face, then checked his name against their list. The younger of the two seemed to take pleasure in going as slowly as possible, double checking his credentials, before giving him an insolent look and allowing him through. He squeezed through the metal security turnstile and into the compound. This had once been the nest of the Great Satan and Husam's father had enthralled him with thrilling tales of the events that occurred within these walls after the return of the Ayatollah.

Husam took immense pride in his role as a covert operative with the Quds Force, the elite Special Forces unit of the Iranian Revolutionary Guards. The western powers considered them state sponsored terrorists peddling death and destruction, but to Husam, Quds had become his family. He spoke seven languages and had operated all over the world, assisting his revolutionary brothers in their fight against the Americans and Israelis. His controller had recalled him from Manama at very short notice, and he went straight to his office.

'Welcome home Baradar. It is good to see you.' The officer rose and embraced Husam. 'Yet another successful mission to add to the list. It is time for you to have a brief rest before we reassign you.'

'I am at your disposal.'

## SIMON DINSDALE

'We have an appointment with the General. He is keen to hear your report of the operation in Manama.'

Husam hadn't expected that, and a frisson of fear coursed through his guts. Had the problems in Bahrain blemished his otherwise impeccable record? The general was renowned for not accepting anything but complete success and punishing those who failed him in the most extreme way.

So, for all his bravery, Husam feared what might be coming. Sweat ran between his shoulders as they walked through the building to the suite containing the great man's office. They waited for more than an hour before a guard ushered them into the presence of the chief. He sat behind his desk, dressed in the dark green uniform of the guards. A living legend, having dedicated his life to the revolution and the destruction of Israel and western imperialism. Husam had heard the rumours that this titan had political ambitions and held the current President of the Republic in contempt. Regardless of the speculation, the man wielded immense power. The general's only remaining eye settled on the Husam, who felt the raw menace emanating from him.

'Welcome Baradar Husam, I'm glad you are safe and well.'

'Thank you Baradar General. I am happy to be home again.'

'Give me your report.'

Husam composed himself, 'Under your orders, I established the location of the arms and munitions we required and obtained them with the help of a local agent. All went well, and it was three months before the Bahrainis noticed the loss. The authorities concluded that the weapons never arrived in Bahrain. Sources then informed me that an infidel was investigating and had discovered something that might expose the operation. Police had sealed the warehouse with all members of staff awaiting interrogation by the Bahraini Military Police the following day,' Husam paused for a moment and drew breath.

'I discovered that the investigator enjoyed taking physical exercise early every morning. I took that opportunity and entered his hotel room to establish what information he had gathered. The Englishman suffered an injury and returned unexpectedly,

## VENGEANCE DAY

giving us no opportunity to leave. To maintain our security, I killed him and arranged the scene it to make it look like an accident. We escaped undetected. I later learned that the Bahrainis had classified the death as accidental. I regret to inform you that the security protocols in place on the man's computer prevented us from learning what he knew. However, I understand they recovered CCTV film of the truck we used to collect the munitions entering and leaving the warehouse. My agent panicked at this revelation and became a liability. I have dealt with him, and he is no longer a threat. The manager of the facility is in custody under interrogation and suspected of the theft. He had no contact with me and does not know of our operation, and the only link to me is deceased. No one knows who removed the weapons, or why.'

The general sat back in his chair and gazed up at the ceiling, his fingertips together in a steeple, index fingers on his pursed lips, the good eye half closed. He stayed like that for a minute after Husam finished speaking. The only sound in the room came from the scratching of a pen on paper as a secretary made notes.

'I congratulate you on a mission well-conceived and executed. We now have need of your skills elsewhere.' The general paused and looked towards Husam's commander and raised an eyebrow.

'We require his expertise in Syria to assist our brothers in their struggle against the imperialist aggressors.'

'Go with God, Husam. What you have achieved will further the revolution and bring pain and humiliation to our enemies.'

As the general turned to the papers on the desk, Husam and his commander bowed their heads and left.

Ten minutes later, another man entered and stood before the general.

'Good day to you, Zand. I understand you have delivered the weapons?'

'Yes, Baradar General. I supervised the exchange myself and everything is now in the hands of our revolutionary colleagues in Britain.'

'We have never dealt with these people before. Can we trust them?'

'I believe so. Their leader is every bit the zealot and we share the same desire to hurt the British.'

'What is the time frame for their operation?'

'We shall see the results before the end of the year. He told me the entire world will shudder at their achievement.'

'Brave words. Is he able to deliver?'

'I am sure he can succeed. He is a skilled freedom fighter, and his operational planning is faultless. With our help, they will rock the lickspittle British establishment to its foundations. There are no Iranian fingerprints anywhere. We achieve our desire for revenge on those imperialist bullies. They will never know who is responsible for this.'

'Yes, I like that. Keep me informed of developments and the outcome,' the general ordered and dismissed Zand.

That evening, the young woman who had taken the notes of the meetings left work to travel home to her elderly mother. The guards searched her bags. They knew who she worked for, so were scrupulously polite. They found nothing so waved her through. She possessed the remarkable ability to memorise the contents of even the most complex documents in seconds. So didn't need to take anything out of the compound. After settling her mother down for the night, she composed an innocuous letter to a long-standing pen pal in Jordon. The letter was posted with several others the following morning on her way to work. It arrived in Langley, Virginia four days later, where cryptanalysts decoded it.

Those in the CIA who were aware of the agent referred to her as Dove. She was the only effective human intelligence source the Americans had in Iran. When her employers had assigned her to the office of the commanding general, her handlers couldn't believe their luck. She had access to, and frequently passed, priceless, lifesaving information and her existence remained a closely guarded secret.

A select group known as the 'Four Wise Men' assessed and discussed her product before they would share it with anyone else. Only three people within the firm knew her identity, and US citizens could die before they would compromise her. When the

## VENGEANCE DAY

committee considered her latest information, they decreed that the British Secret Intelligence Service should be informed. But they placed a caveat that the information passed must be heavily bowdlerised.

\*

Special Agent Peter Franks began his day with a mug of strong coffee. He then switched his secure computer on to review the overnight intelligence reports. Franks oversaw the FBI Joint Terrorism Task Force office in New York.

Amongst his many areas of responsibility was monitoring the increasing number of so-called Militia's on the Eastern seaboard of the USA. A few weeks before, Franks requested information about a group calling itself the Sons of Erin. Amongst the dozens of new e-mails, he saw a report about them from a New York State Trooper named Ramirez. She described seeing a vehicle full of Irish citizens entering an up-state property believed to be their headquarters. Franks noticed the date she submitted the message and muttered an oath. The data sharing systems had improved immeasurably since 9/11, but five days to reach him was too long. He spotted Detective Carla Di Matteo, a NYPD officer, seconded to the JTTF and called her in. Carla was petite with a dark complexion, raven black hair and brown flashing eyes that betrayed her Italian ancestry. Born and raised in the Bronx, a pure-bred New Yorker and tough.

'Check this out, would you? It's a few days old but looks interesting,' Franks said, handing her the document.

As she read it, her left eyebrow rose in surprise.

'Yeah, I'll see what I can find out.'

Carla started by checking the licence plate of the bus mentioned by Ramirez and learned it was a hire vehicle from a big rental company. She rang them and established that the renters returned it to the JFK Airport branch the previous evening. The supervisor promised to fax over a copy of the documents and details of who'd hired it. Carla then spoke to the person who dealt with the customer who could only say that a woman with a foreign accent took the bus. When Carla asked what type of accent the clerk, who was Hispanic and spoke an interesting version of Brooklyn American herself, declared it wasn't English. This made Carla smile. Next, she checked the NYPD intelligence system and saw that a traffic officer had pulled the vehicle over on Columbus Circle. Carla contacted the cop who explained the encounter.

'I didn't give the driver a ticket because she was a tourist from Ireland, and they only stopped for a few moments to pick up some buddies. They were on their way to the mountains to do some hiking. There was a feisty guy in the front seat who'd almost gotten in a fistfight with a cab driver. I told him to calm down and let the driver off with a warning.'

'That's helpful, thanks.'

Carla then rang the State Police to track down Officer Ramirez. Two hours later, she returned her call.

'Hi, I'm interested in the report you submitted the other day. About the group you spotted going into the Logan spread,' Carla said.

'I ran into them late in the evening in the diner in Frazer. There were eleven of them in the party and the lady I spoke to was Irish. She spun the yarn about hiking. I only talked to her, but the server was positive they all had the same accent. I guessed they'd driven up from the city that afternoon.'

'Why did you follow them?'

'Something didn't add up. It was late to still be heading into the backcountry. The lady wasn't evasive, quite the opposite, and said they planned to start at Lake Chaplain. But Frazier is way past the turning for the Lake, so I grew suspicious. When I saw them going in through the gate there, I knew I'd been right. I've maintained a steady patrol in the area since then. I haven't seen them again.'

'Is there much movement in and out of the property?'

'No, there isn't. Logan lives there with his wife, but I have never met them. They do little business in the town and are unpopular because of that. The locals have observed small parties of men going out to the spread, usually over a weekend. It's an enormous property which backs onto the wilderness, and we're not welcome there. When my colleague tried to drive out to say

# VENGEANCE DAY

hello, he received a very frosty reception. Should I monitor the place?'

'Yes please, if you see anything ring me direct, I'm interested in what goes on out there.'

'Is there any specific reason?'

'We believe Logan is the leader of the Sons of Erin Militia. It could be that they use the land for training, which might explain the groups of men seen going there. A group of Irish folks visiting there is interesting. That was a good spot, so thank you.'

'My pleasure,' Ramirez replied.

Carla's e-mail pinged with a message from the car hire company. It contained the scanned rental form and a photocopy of the woman's driving licence. It was British and in the name of Kate Dunn, with an address in a town called Peterborough. The photograph on it showed a dark-haired woman. It hadn't come through photocopying and then scanning too well, so Carla rang the supervisor.

'Thanks for sending the documents. The picture isn't too good at this end. Is yours clearer?'

'I guess so.'

'Okay, put them aside, please. I'll be over to pick them up.'

It took an hour to reach to JFK and collect the paperwork. The photograph was indeed much better than the copy. Carla went to the JTTF office in the main administration building.

'Hi Greg, how you hanging?' Carla shouted.

Greg Wallace looked up from the sheets of paper he had been examining and smiled.

'Hey, look what the hounds dragged in. We don't see much of you hot shots out here in the sticks. You lost or something?'

'I could do with your help,' She showed him the driving licence, 'Can you check departures from today for her please, and while you're at it, do La Guardia and Newark.'

'Yes, Ma'am. While I'm doing that, go get coffee.'

'Donut?'

'No thanks, got to watch the waist and the damage it does to your arteries and other major organs.'

Carla returned with mugs of steaming black coffee to find her colleague looking perplexed.

'Are you sure she was traveling through here? Because this lady hasn't departed from anywhere today,' Greg announced.

'How about incoming? Say for the last two weeks?'

The computer keys clattered as he did the new search, 'Nope, can't find her. Who is she?'

'I don't know. But she's a person of interest. Do a nationwide check, in or out, and go back a month.'

This took a little longer, but the outcome was the same. No record of anyone using the name Kate Dunn entering or leaving anywhere in the Continental USA. That Greg couldn't locate her at all on the records was a cause for concern. No one should be able to enter the country legally without leaving a trace.

'Could we put her picture through facial recognition?' Carla asked.

At every border crossing, US immigration photograph every man, woman and child who enters the country. A full-face head and shoulders mug shot taken as the passport is examined by the surly agents. When an officer puts a person of interest into the database, it is searched against the millions of images already there. It's not a fool proof system and kinks are still being ironed out, but it's accurate enough to be a useful tool.

Greg studied it, 'This is a photocopy which affects the quality, but hell, let's try it. What sort of priority is this?'

'Just routine.'

'It'll be tomorrow before I have the results.'

'What would I do without you?'

As Carla drove back into Manhattan, she wondered who this woman might be. She found Franks in his office and updated him.

'This girl is interesting, and I'd like to track her down. Have we got any other coverage of the Sons of Erin? surveillance, for example?'

'No, I considered applying for a warrant to do that, but couldn't justify it. I agree with you though, we need to identify

## VENGEANCE DAY

this lady and why a bunch of Irish people visited that property,' Franks replied.

Carla took the hire form to the forensics department and asked them to treat it for fingerprints. She finished her days work by sending an e-mail to the counter-terrorism liaison officer at the British consulate requesting they do an intelligence check on Kate Dunn.

Carla was at her desk early the following morning and on her third cup of coffee when Greg called.

'Hi Carla. I have some results for you and I'm sending you some images.'

Carla logged into her secure mailbox and opened the attachments. Three pictures of the woman she was after appeared on her screen. Below each were different names and dates that spanned the past three years. Carla was shocked to see that her mystery woman had entered the USA so often and each time with a new identity.

'How come we didn't pick her up when she was using multiple IDs at the point of entry?'

'The system ain't that great yet. Unless there's a reason for the agent at the port to flag the image, it's not automatically searched. The computer rates it at seventy percent plus likelihood these images are of the same person.'

'Yep, got that. But it says here the last time she came in was a couple of months ago.'

'Have a look at this, then.'

A ping from the inbox, another attachment. The same woman. But the name this time was Carol Middleton, and this report was dated seven days before.

'I'm sure this is her, and it has the same hit ratio. She used this identity when she left JFK yesterday morning and flew American Airways to Paris,' Greg said.

Carla swore under her breath. They had missed the opportunity to identify her, 'Thanks, Greg, this is all great.

Carla stared at the image. The woman was in her forties, long thick brown hair, and dark eyes, with a clear complexion and a hint of even white teeth behind the full lips. She added the pictures to the thickening file as she glanced along the open plan office. Seeing Franks at his desk, she joined him and informed him of the latest development.

*

After leaving the remote farmhouse, Mick McArthur remained silent and thoughtful during the drive south. He stared out the window while the forefinger of his right hand picked at the quick around the thumbnail until the blood ran. He licked it dry, then pressed a finger into the open wound to stop the bleeding.

'How's your dad?' McArthur asked his driver as they approached the outskirts of Dublin.

The young man glanced sideways as if to confirm it was him his boss was speaking to. 'Och, he's fine. The diabetes has taken his leg but not his spirit. I still cart him down to the club every Sunday afternoon for his usual.'

'Give him my regards, won't you? He's a good man.'

'I'll do that. Is there anything you need?'

'No, son, but thanks for asking. You can drop me in the city centre.'

McArthur watched the car drive away, then turned and walked through the streets to his rented flat. He was an Irish patriot and, like most of his family and friends, had served the cause. His forte was the gathering and analysis of information, and his sources were legion. He instinctively saw anomalies and patterns where others didn't. All the major state intelligence organisations knew of his activities and recognised him as a formidable adversary. He would have achieved senior rank if they ever employed him. The loss of life on all sides during the long, armed conflict, disgusted him. But to bring about genuine change and justice, there had to be some sacrifice. McArthur had always known that it would need a political solution to ease Ireland's pain. There was no need for an armed struggle anymore because, within his lifetime, the country would become a united sovereign nation. Now all that could be in jeopardy because of the actions of a small gang of fools. Misguided idiots who clung to the notion that they could achieve their twisted aims by murder and destruction.

## VENGEANCE DAY

McArthur brewed tea and settled down on his settee to think. Liam Rafferty and his followers were fanatical and determined to create mayhem. But what was their plan? How many of them were there? That had to be the priority. Where were they? From the little knowledge he had gleaned, it seemed most likely they were based somewhere in Europe. North America was a possibility, but unlikely. Given the recent botched attempt to take them out they wouldn't be on the island of Ireland.

Liam's group had access to everything they needed to cause mayhem, including firearms and ammunition. One subject that must be kept quiet. The British would go ballistic if they found out where those weapons came from. They weren't short of money, and, it would appear, high-powered support. McArthur knew about Liam, Mary and the other two or three major players. But who were the foot soldiers? That was the key. Identify who is with the madman and isolate them. Difficult to achieve, but the best approach.

McArthur hadn't been keen on the attempt to suborn Patsy Moran, but Sean ignored his warning. The lad hero worshipped Liam and would never turn on him. McArthur took no pleasure when he discovered he'd been right all along. No, the answer lay with the soldiers. He wrote a concise list of likely candidates, and drove north, to visit their homes. Two answered their doors to him, so they could be crossed off. One girl's brothers chased him into the street, but within days McArthur had six names. None of their families would say where their sons or daughters were. He tracked down the parents of the youngest boy on the list, barely nineteen and with no family history in the republican movement. His mother had been frosty, although she invited him into her neat West Belfast home.

'He's not here,' she announced.

'Where is he?'

'He's gone to find work and better himself. I know what you represent. We kept out of the madness and want no part of it now, so stay away from him.'

McArthur found the father that evening. A workshy and feckless drunk who was full of the woes of his life. Over a few drinks, they talked about his youngest son who was clearly the favourite child.

'There's a clever lad. Always top of his class, a great wee footballer, but not quite good enough for the big time,' he said sadly.

'Where is he now?' McArthur asked.

'He's taken off to the mainland and landed a decent job, according to the wife. But he rings her every week to make sure she's fine and dandy, so he does.'

'Does he ever ring you?'

'No, I don't have a telephone. How about another then?' he hopefully pushed his empty glass towards McArthur.

'Why not? We're amongst friends here.'

McArthur enlisted the assistance of one of his many contacts in the telecoms industry. It took three days to identify the number of a public telephone box in a small town on the coast of Essex. That was confirmed seven days later, when a second call was made to the mother from the same place. With his list complete, McArthur left his flat and took a roundabout route to Connolly railway station to ensure no one was following him. In the least smelly telephone kiosk on the concourse, he dialled a number from memory.

'This is Peter. I need to meet with Ray,' Mick said when someone answered. 'Shall we say four at eight this evening?'

'Four at eight confirmed.'

# VENGEANCE DAY

## Chapter 9

Dane felt invigorated to be back in the thick of an investigation. The awful circumstances of George Blaine's death added an extra urgency to his work. He formed a small team of his most experienced detectives. Hayley Cross was dispatched to take Anne's statement and support her. Two other officers spent three days with Lord and his boffin's getting statements and documentation. In the incident office, an indexer and analyst read and filed all the material into the HOLMES computer as it came in.

The laptop went to the forensic science laboratory, where the experts found mixed DNA profiles on the keyboard. They eliminated George's and isolated fragmentary DNA belonging to two other people. A routine search of the national database didn't find a match. More advanced techniques identified the owners of these samples as natives of Iran. A result that surprised the scientists, but not Dane.

The technicians downloaded the video and interpreters double checked and confirmed the translations already completed by Lord's team. Dane viewed the film while reading the transcript of the men's conversation. The leader was obvious. A young man with black hair and a neatly trimmed full beard. He was tense, but in control of what was going on in the room. The second, the hacker, was smaller and bespectacled, sweating profusely. At one point, he almost tore the tie from his neck in frustration as he struggled to access the hard drive. The third said nothing and looked like a thug.

Dane winced as they committed the murder but forced himself to watch the video through to the end.

The Iranian agents had gained entry undetected. If it weren't for the security in the computer, no one would ever have known they'd been there. To have come with the hacker and, Dane presumed, a bit of muscle as backup showed advance planning. They must have been watching George since his arrival in the country and noticed his exercise routine. The speed of the leader's decision to kill George was chilling, there was no emotion or consideration of disabling him. Dane was sure they wouldn't have harmed George if he hadn't returned when he did. It took ten days to collect the evidence and put it together.

Dane met Giles and they spent a morning with the special crime and counter-terrorism unit at the Crown Prosecution Service in London. The senior lawyer listened to their briefing, then read the file. She agreed there was a prima facia case against the men in the video.

'Would there be any chance of prosecuting them here?' Dane asked.

'That's unlikely, I'm afraid. The murder occurred in Bahrain, and they would have first dibs at them. Even if they didn't. I very much doubt we would sanction an application for extradition to this country.'

'Then we will have to ensure they make every effort to catch them. I have received permission from the Foreign Office for Mr Dane to travel to Bahrain,' Giles stated, and Dane did a double take. This was the first he had heard of it.

'I'm sorry not to have mentioned this earlier,' Giles continued, 'But I think it would be helpful if you delivered this excellent work to the competent authority there. You will then be able to impress on them our desire to see a proper investigation conducted. The family deserves answers and, we hope, closure. I hope this doesn't ruin any of your plans?'

'No, I am happy to go. I might have a useful contact who will put me in touch with the right people over there.'

'Then please use him' Giles said.

'Mr Grant's reaction will be interesting though.'

'Don't worry about him. I have already cleared this with the chief constable.'

They left the lawyer's office and once outside, Dane turned to Giles.

'I have an idea about how we might be able to identify the suspects and would like your permission to try it.' He explained what he had in mind.

'You have my sanction for that. I'm under no illusion here. I appreciate it's unlikely we'll ever bring these men to justice, but I won't give up trying. Let me know how you get on.'

## VENGEANCE DAY

They parted company. Dane had enough time to walk to his next appointment and used it to decide how he was going to pitch his request. He strolled across Westminster Bridge and along Albert Embankment to the large beige and green building at Vauxhall Cross. This was the headquarters of the Secret Intelligence service, or MI6, as the world knows it. At the main reception, Dane handed over his mobile phone and squeezed through the airlock security barrier. A young woman was waiting for him inside.

'Hello, I'm Bonny. Come this way.'

Dane followed her through a set of double doors, across a medium-sized sports hall and up four flights of stairs.

'Is this the tradesmen's entrance?'

Bonny shrugged of her shoulders but said nothing. She turned along a corridor before opening the door to a tiny, windowless room containing a table and four chairs.

'Take a seat. They'll be in shortly.'

A few moments later a well-built man in his late forties, with a mop of unruly black hair, walked in and held his hand out.

'Hello, sorry to keep you waiting. I'm David Fawn, in charge of the mid-east desk, and this is Laura.' She was in her early thirties and carrying a coffee mug with the CIA emblem on it.

'Right,' Fawn said, collapsing into the chair. 'What can we do for you?'

'Thanks for seeing me. I hope you might be able to help with an enquiry I'm conducting on behalf of the Essex coroner.' Dane described the circumstances of George's death and the footage from his laptop.

'I've got pictures of the men, and a recording of their conversation together with a written transcript. They are Iranian and trained operatives. I would guess government agents, probably Quds Force. Would it be possible for you to search through whatever intelligence you may have on Iranians to see if you can identify them?'

Fawn glanced at the pictures and flicked through the other papers before handing them to Laura.

'What would you do with that information?'

## SIMON DINSDALE

'Pass it to Bahrain. It would assist their investigation and prosecution. If they won't prosecute, then our courts could extradite the suspects. But for that to happen, I must know who they are. I realise I am asking a lot, and we couldn't use the information as evidence but is this something you could do?'

'I doubt it,' Fawn replied, 'Not, I hasten to add, because we don't want to. But I don't think we possess that level of personal information about individual operators. Laura will check our records to see if there is anything there that could assist.'

She appeared surprised at that comment but remained silent.

'Thank you. All these documents are copies, so you can keep them. The contents may be of use to you.'

'Do you think you'll get a satisfactory result?'

Dane shrugged, 'I'll do my best, but I must be realistic. The theft embarrassed the Bahraini's. George Blaine's death being proved to be a murder is more unwelcome news they can do without. Our government wants to keep the whole thing as quiet as possible to maintain normal relations with Bahrain. George's family doesn't want publicity either, but they deserve a decent attempt to nail the men responsible. If the Bahrainis don't prosecute, I'll apply to the courts for an international arrest warrant for them. We might be lucky and pick them up outside Iran and put them before our court.'

'Is that likely?' Laura said.

'Not really, but that doesn't mean I shouldn't try. George Blaine and his family should get justice.'

'I take your point. If we can help, Laura will be in touch.'

With that, they parted company, and Bonny led him back to the front entrance. Dane paused on the street and looked up at the building. Fawn appeared interested and willing to assist, but he wouldn't hold his breath waiting for them to contact him.

\*

A mile away on the other side of the river, Karen Teller was in her office in Thames House, the headquarters of MI5. She oversaw the desk responsible for monitoring the activities of dissident Irish terrorist groups and was catching up on her e-mails when one caught her attention. The resident MI5 officer at the British embassy in Dublin had received intelligence that a

## VENGEANCE DAY

previously unknown group was planning an attack on the mainland. The source couldn't identify the potential target or when the operation was to be conducted. The best information they had was sometime this year. It was possible that a known terrorist called Maire o'Suilleabhain was involved. In addition, someone connected to the group regularly used a telephone box in Essex to contact a Northern Ireland phone number. Karen read that twice. How did the source know that? This sounded like senior levels of the republican movement were aware of an impending atrocity which could embarrass them and damage the peace process. It was not unusual for them to alert the old enemy with this type of vague message. But when that happened only the bare minimum of intelligence was passed so the leadership could truthfully say they had alerted the authorities. Karen knew they would never reveal everything, which was frustrating but still better than nothing.

The dissident republicans in Ireland are dangerous and had been trying to commit just such an atrocity on the mainland for years. Karen's organisation had penetrated most of the well-known groups, which was why they'd been so unsuccessful. But they still posed a serious threat. Karen frequently saw similar warnings, and although nearly all of them turned out to be nothing more than hot air, this felt different. This scenario was what she, and everyone in her profession, always dreaded. An unknown group full of people she knew nothing about intent on causing mayhem.

She instructed an analyst to research the named woman and got a reply within five minutes, which made her sit up straight.

Maire o'Suilleabhain, also known as Mary Sullivan, Mary O'Sullivan, Maggie Smith, Maureen Reilly, and Maureen O'Reilly. Who, they believed, had taken part in terrorist operations in Ireland, Europe and England, although there was no firm evidence to support this. She was in her forties, born and raised in Belfast to a staunch republican family. Father deceased, killed by the army, as was one of her elder brothers, and a loyalist killer murdered another brother in the Maze prison. There was a single blurred black and white surveillance photograph of an attractive young woman in her late teens with short brown hair, snapped at her father's funeral. Her violent opposition to the peace settlement was on record. Despite all the reporting about her, the police had never arrested or charged her with any offences. She had dropped out of sight three years before and her present location was unknown.

Okay, Karen thought, what're you up to? She passed the file to a desk officer with instructions to track her down. Then composed messages to all MI5 stations and departments to be alert to any similar reporting. As soon as Karen pressed send, a request for information from the American Joint Terrorist Task Force landed in her in box.

The message stated that a woman attended a property suspected of being a militia training camp in upstate New York. She had been in company with ten other people, seven males and three females, all believed to be Irish nationals. The JTTF requested all recipients to check their records to identify her. They confirmed she had left the country bound for Paris two days before. An attachment contained the names she had used when entering the USA in the past and four pictures of the same person. Karen's eyes flared with shock. It was Maire o'Suilleabhain. She was much older in these photographs, but it was definitely her. All the pictures were head and shoulder passport shots, implying that she had many different sets of identification documents. No wonder we haven't been able to track her movements for so long, Karen thought. She called her team together and briefed them on what had just been received.

'This is now a live operation. I want everything we have about this lady by close of play today.' As they scurried to their desks, Karen checked her watch and, calculating the time difference, rang New York.

# VENGEANCE DAY

## Chapter 10

Liam and Mary spent the week visiting the teams at their safe houses to check how the preparations were going. He had taken a lot of care recruiting the young men and women for this mission. The intelligence services knew nothing of their involvement in republicanism. None of them had a criminal record, so they were the epitome of clean skins. The police in Northumbria had caught one of the original recruits during a bank robbery a couple of years before. That young volunteer was now serving a long prison sentence but had resolutely kept his mouth shut.

Mary had rented five detached houses with integral double garages and large enclosed gardens. Two were in the West Country, one on the outskirts of Wareham in Dorset, and another in Yeovil in Somerset. Closer to London, the third team were ensconced in a beautiful old house in the countryside outside Ware in Hertfordshire. The fourth in Frinton-on-Sea in Essex. Liam, Mary and Patsy shared a place near Peterborough.

Each group comprised three people. They had infiltrated the quiet neighbourhoods and kept themselves to themselves. Their cover story was the same used to hire the hotel room and everyone was settled into a routine that fitted with that. Their neighbours were mainly professional people who were all out at work every day. With the usual southern reticence to talk to strangers no one bothered them or tried to make friends.

Kathy, Jo, and Martin met them in Wareham. Jo was the team leader and proudly showed them the Citroen Relay van parked in the garage. It looked in excellent condition and Liam liked everything except for the colour.

'It's white. I told you, anything but that.'

'You can't get them in any other colour,' Jo replied. 'We checked out a blue one, but it was a wreck. We've dry mounted the gear in the van, and it fits perfectly. Once you give us the word, we'll weld it in place. I've measured the part of the roof that we need to remove and had an idea for securing it back over the hole until it must come off.'

'That's good. Share that with the others. You will need to align the mortar with a set point in the dashboard. In the meantime, I want you all to start to practice parking,' Liam said.

They all looked at him in surprise, 'You must be able to get the van in position with the nose on a certain compass heading. The driver must be able to do it in one go. We don't want lots of shunting backwards and forwards because that will draw attention. Remember what Jake warned us about? If you are out by only half a degree, you will miss the target by hundreds of yards. So, accuracy is bloody vital.'

'Okay, what compass heading?'

'You chose. Do one a day or as many as you like, but make sure you're all proficient at it. I won't be telling you your firing position or the direction until the last minute.'

'We'll start doing that tomorrow. How much longer before we go?'

'Not too long. Just be patient. Everything else alright?'

'Sure, we're well set up here. We've got everything we need.'

They left Wareham the following morning and visited the others. They were all still looking for a suitable vehicle, but time was on their side. Liam gave them all the same briefing and instructions.

At the end of the week, they re-joined Patsy at their house, pleased with what they had seen. While Mary cooked dinner, Liam took a bath. He gasped and held his breath as the deep, near scalding water enveloped him. Once his body had adjusted to the heat, he relaxed and soon dropped off to sleep. The vivid image was there, crystal clear and in high-definition colour. Liam was back in the street, looking at his brother's last moments. Over and over again, the scene rolled like a continuous loop of a film. Martin, screaming in agony and clutching his shattered knee. The solider casually standing over him. The gunshot. Blood on the floor. Liam woke with a start and a gasp. He thought he was falling, his limbs stiffened, then flailed as if to grab hold of something splashing water everywhere. The door was shaking on its hinges as Patsy banged on it.

## VENGEANCE DAY

'Come on, wake up, dinner's ready. Mary says to come down while it's hot.'

Liam lay there with sweat rolling down his brow. It was always the same. Every time he closed his eyes, the images seared into his memory and the dream never spared him of the slightest detail of his brother's murder. Would he never be free of it? Patsy was back ten minutes later with the message that it would be in the dog if he didn't come down.

Mary watched Liam as he pushed the food around the plate. She was not much of a cook, but he usually made more of an effort to eat what she had prepared.

'What's up?' she said.

Liam looked up and into her eyes, 'There's something I need you to do for me.' She left early the following morning before the men were up for their breakfast.

\*

The British Airways airbus levelled out to start its final approach into Bahrain's international airport. The Foreign Office had provided all the required paperwork for him to travel. As predicted, Grant was furious when he learned where Dane was going, accusing him of taking advantage, and engineering a jolly for himself. Giles took care of that. Dane had not been party to the conversation between them, but his boss was subdued when he told him the trip was on. Wilmington had come good on his promise to help and made a call. Dane was due to meet a senior government official early the following morning.

It was mid-evening by the time the plane taxied around to the arrivals gate, and everyone stood to shuffle towards the doors. He was amongst the first off, and with only a cabin bag, could avoid the horrors of baggage reclaim. There was a long queue at the immigration control as everyone waited to dawdle past the glass booths containing the grim-faced police. When it was his turn, Dane smiled and handed over his passport. The officer examined it, then looked over his shoulder and beckoned a western man over.

'Please go with him,' he said in passable English.

'Shokran,' Dane replied.

'Al'afw,' the immigration officer replied automatically, already waving the next passenger towards him.

A timid looking man in his early thirties approached Dane and held his hand out. 'Good evening, I'm Peter Lines, assistant attaché.'

'Christian Dane.' They shook hands.

'I have a car outside, and instructions to take you to the Embassy. The Third Secretary would like a word about your visit.'

'Okey let's go.'

Dane followed the diplomat out of the terminal and into the heat of the evening. He had hoped for a breath of fresh air after spending so long cooped up in the aircraft. What he got was a lung full of hot dusty desert air and sweat bursting from his forehead. Dane dropped his bag in the boot and jumped in the back seat, almost pleased to be back in an air-conditioned atmosphere.

'Is this your first time here?' Lines asked as the driver set off.

'Yes, it is. I won't be here long, though.'

'Oh, I see,' Lines replied, and turned to stare out of the window.

Dane watched him for a second then realised the man had nothing else to say so he settled back to enjoy the ride. They were soon out of the airport and joined Airport Avenue for the three-mile trip into Manama. Dane was surprised to see they were driving on the right-hand side of the road and wondered how that had come about. The road was a modern dual carriageway and busy, they passed between the big city of Muharraq on the left and the smaller town of Busaiteen. Both sides of the road were lined with two storey sandstone-coloured homes and business premises, many with high walls surrounding them. The younger pedestrians wore jeans and T-shirts while the older generations were in the more traditional Gulf dress of Thawb and headdress. A few minutes into the drive they crossed the Shaikh Isa causeway with its famous white columns lit up and looking magnificent against the dark sky.

## VENGEANCE DAY

It didn't take long to reach the impressive embassy estate in the diplomatic area. Security was tight and after getting through the gate they drove to the side of the building and parked.

'You can leave your bag,' Lines said 'The driver will drop you off at your hotel when you've finished. This way, please.'

Dane followed to a tiny anteroom, 'Hang on here. He'll be with you in a minute.' With that, Lines left him alone. Fifteen minutes later, a door opposite him opened and an overweight middle-aged man looked out and beckoned him in.

'I'm Peter Williams, Third Secretary. Sorry to keep you waiting, but no one informed us you were coming until this morning. All a bit of a rush. Please take a seat.'

The office was no bigger than the anteroom and sparsely furnished. An old-fashioned fan revolved above their heads. It squeaked on every turn and wasn't moving any air about.

'Just need to lay down a few ground rules regarding your visit,' Williams said as he referred to a sheet of paper on his desk, 'As I understand things, you're from the plod to deliver some papers to the Bahraini police. Is that right?' He continued without waiting for Dane to reply, 'Thing is that our relationship with the government here is vital to our national interests. We don't want someone to come in and put a spanner in the works if you see what I mean. The locals can be a prickly bunch and are sticklers for protocol. So, we must make sure you cause no offence. Now I think it is best if I take care of the handover and Mr Lines will look after you. Do you know who you are seeing tomorrow?'

'Yes, I do.'

Williams waited, but Dane said nothing more.

'Well, who is it?'

'Let's get a few things straight, shall we?' Dane said, startling Williams, 'I am a detective superintendent and a police officer. Not plod, and not an errand boy. I am representing His Majesty's Coroner of Essex. He has ordered me to deliver, by hand, a file regarding the murder of a British citizen in Manama to the interior ministry.'

The diplomat put his hands up, as if in mock surrender, and tried a weak smile.

## SIMON DINSDALE

'I shouldn't have used the word plod. I apologise. We are aware of the incident you are referring to. The police investigated and ruled it was an accident. So, you can't go making this sort of accusation and upsetting everyone.'

'There seems to be another breakdown in communications with your head office. George Blaine was murdered. I'm meeting with General Suleiman bin Abdullah Al Khalifa first thing tomorrow morning. I will be briefing him on my investigation and passing him the evidence my team gathered.'

'But he's the Interior Minister and a member of the ruling family. There must be a mistake.'

'No, there isn't,' Dane glanced at his watch, 'If we're finished here, I'd like to go to my hotel and get my head down. I am expected at six, and I do not intend to be late.'

'We must send a representative from the embassy with you.'

'That's a matter for you. Good night.'

Dane was waiting in the impressive marble clad hotel reception the following morning when a car arrived. A young man in uniform jumped out and came through the revolving doors. He looked around and spotting Dane joined him.

'As-Salāmu `alayka.'

'Wa `alaykumu s-salāmu wa rahmata l-lāhi wa barakātuh,' Dane replied.

The officer blinked in surprise, then smiled, 'You speak our tongue very well, sir.'

'Thank you, although I confess, that's all I know.'

'It does not matter. I speak excellent English. My name is Abbass. I am a captain in the Military Police, and it is my job to drive you to the minister.'

They shook hands and Abbass led the way to his car. 'Are you aware of my business here?' Dane asked.

Abbas nodded, 'I was the investigating officer when the mortars and ammunition were found to be missing. And I assisted Mr George while he was here. I am deeply sorry to say that he died while I was waiting in reception.'

'I'm sure you couldn't have prevented it.'

'It is an embarrassment that it happened in my country.'

## VENGEANCE DAY

The streets were already busy, even at that early hour of the morning. Abbass drove past the diplomatic quarter where all the buildings were surrounded with concrete barriers and heavy security. High rise towers of glass and steel surrounded by six lane highways gave way to single story commercial premises and houses in tight teeming streets. Abbass drove up to a pair of steel gates guarded by heavily armed soldiers. Their credentials were closely examined before being admitted into a large modern white building.

At the reception desk they found a dishevelled and sweaty Peter Williams waiting for them.

'Can I help you sir? Abbass asked.

'I am here to attend the meeting with the general.'

'I'm afraid that is not possible. You are not on the list. I only have instructions regarding Mr Dane.' Abbass replied and steered Dane to an elevator, leaving Williams standing with his mouth open.

The lift doors opened straight into a palatial office with stunning views over the gulf. A tall slim man, with hawk like features and a close-cropped black beard was waiting. He was dressed in a spotless white Thawb, with a red and white checkered Ghutra, held in place by a black agal.

'Good morning, Superintendent. I am General Al Khalifa.' His handshake was firm.

'How do you do, sir. It is kind of you to see me at such short notice,' Dane replied.

'Not at all. Sir Gordon Wilmington is an old friend. He has impressed on me the urgent nature of this matter. I understand you possess a file relating to your excellent investigation regarding the sad and brutal death of Mr Blaine.'

Dane opened his bag and took out three folders containing the papers and placed them on the desk.

'These contain the original forensic reports, witness statements and everything we have learned about the suspects. So far, I've not been able to positively identify them.'

'But you have your suspicions?'

'They are Iranian.'

## SIMON DINSDALE

'I see. There is no doubt?'

'The experts who translated the men's conversation are certain.'

'I assume you are aware of the sensitive nature of the relationship between my country and Iran?'

'Yes sir. The coroner has asked me to assure you it is not his intention to embarrass your people or the government. I can also say that George Blaine's family has no wish for this to be publicised either. Their only desire is for a full explanation of his death, and, if possible, to see those responsible prosecuted.'

'I am told that he was a distinguished former member of a famous military unit in your military.'

'That's correct sir, he was.'

'He came here to help, and thug's murder him in a cowardly way. It brings shame on us all. I cannot allow that to pass. What would you like from us?'

'Within the file is information that should assist you in identifying the perpetrators of this crime. The Blaine's only ask that you use every effort to bring them to justice.'

'Captain Abbass will complete this task. He reports to me and has access to all the resources he needs. When we catch these criminals, I shall, of course, inform your coroner. I would be pleased if you would convey my sincerest condolences to the Blaine family. Please assure them of our determination to find these cowards and put them before our courts.'

'I will gladly do that, sir.'

'Since this appalling business happened, Captain Abbass has been extremely busy. He has established beyond doubt the weapons left this country within a few hours of being stolen. The thieves loaded them onto a dhow here in Manama and they were last seen on the quayside in Bandar Abbas.'

'Isn't that the base for the Iranian Navy?'

'It is, and also their terrorist organisation, the so-called Quds Force.' The general was silent for a moment, then smiled, 'It was good to meet you. I wish you a safe journey.'

Williams was waiting anxiously in reception and marched over as soon as Dane left the lift.

## VENGEANCE DAY

'This is most irregular. What happened in there?'

'I handed over the case papers to the general and passed on the coroner's request. I assure you I have not caused a diplomatic incident. Captain Abbass is leading the investigation and will keep you abreast of any developments. Now if you will excuse me, I have a plane to catch.'

Dane enjoyed lunch with Abbass before flying home that afternoon. The following day he drove out to inform Nick and Anne Blaine about what he'd been doing.

'They'll never catch them, will they?' Anne Blaine said.

'I must be honest and say it's unlikely. But never give up hope. The one thing I have learnt since I started investigating murders is to always expect the unexpected. Those men might slip up in a friendly country and find themselves in a cell within my reach. If they do I promise to do everything within our power to get our hands on them.'

Dane took Nick aside and showed him the pictures of the three men responsible for his father's murder. The soldier studied them all, fixing their features indelibly into his brain.

'God help them if I ever run into them,' Nick whispered, 'Thank you for everything you've done, Christian. The funeral is next week. We would both like you to be there.'

'Of course, I'll come. George was a fine man, and I won't give up.'

As Dane drove away, his phone rang.

'You and I are to attend the Met's Special Operations Centre, tomorrow at 0900hrs. There is a café round the corner, so let's meet there at 0800hrs,' Perkins said.

'Okay boss, see you there.'

\*

Perkins arrived first and ordered for them both.

'What's this all about, then?' Dane asked, sipping his tea.

'The powers that be have appointed me to an Executive Liaison Group. You're going to be the Senior Investigation Officer for a counter terrorist investigation.'

Dane's eyebrows arched with surprise. The Metropolitan police had taken the national lead in counter terrorism since the nineteenth century. The force fought a long, hard war against the IRA and were regarded as the world's leading experts in combating terrorism. But the attacks in London in July 2005 and the general rise of extremism in Britain had shown that the Met could no longer deal with it all. In 2006, the Government formed the Counter Terrorism Command as a national police response. Senior Met leaders were still in overall charge, and the organisation was administered from London. They were supported by Regional Counter Terrorist Units (CTU) based strategically across the country. Local officers from the constituent police forces in those regions staffed those teams. MI5 dispatched their agents to the sticks to fulfil their role in the fight.

The Met CTU in London covered the City of London and the Eastern counties, including Essex. As the number of counter terrorism investigations rose the government realised there wasn't enough senior investigators, so they trained officers from the provincial forces. Dane was one of those and the only terrorist SIO in Essex. If a case was based outside London, a regional Counter Terrorist SIO should lead it. But in practice that never happened. The old prejudices against using anyone not from the Met still held sway, and Dane had never been deployed before.

'The meeting starts at nine and I'm involved in the first bit. Then they will brief you,' Perkins said.

When a covert terrorist operation requires overt police action, an Executive Liaison Group (ELG) is formed. The National Coordinator for Terrorist Investigations, Deputy Assistant Commissioner Caroline Shaw, is always in the chair. Perkins was there because the case involved Essex and there would be a senior officer from MI5, who would be the deputy chairperson. The role of an ELG is to be the strategic management team, and its members would direct Dane's investigation.

They strolled round to the drab, nondescript building in central London that housed the Met Counter Terrorist Command. It took them ten minutes to get past the security and up to an anteroom on the first floor. Perkins went straight into a meeting room while

## VENGEANCE DAY

Dane waited outside. At the far end of the corridor was another door, and Dane could hear raised voices coming from behind it. One caught his attention. It was the loudest, with a strong Glaswegian accent, and whoever owned it was not happy.

'Why was I not told they've started? Who is in charge around here?'

Feet pounded along the corridor as the Scottish voice rose to a higher pitch in anger.

'Who said they could give a country boy a job?'

The door burst open, and a heavy-set man barged through it. Two others followed, almost running to keep up with him. The Scot tried to get into the meeting room, but the door was locked. His face was puce when he caught sight of Dane.

'Who the hell are you laddie. What are you doing in my building?'

Dane knew who this was, although they'd never met. Detective Chief Superintendent Alex Brown was the head of the Counter Terrorism Command in the Met, and a renowned bully.

'I guess I must be the country boy. Who're you?'

Brown hadn't expected that and appeared to swell with indignation as the other two cast nervous glances at their boss and each other.

'I'll tell you who I am…' The door behind him opened to reveal a dark-haired woman wearing a uniform with the insignia of a Deputy Assistant Commissioner on her shoulders.

'Would you both come in. Hello,' she faced Dane with a welcoming smile. 'I'm Caroline Shaw. Pleased to meet you.'

'Likewise, Ma'am.' They shook hands, and Dane found a seat at the conference table.

'I see you've met Mr Brown.'

'He was kind enough to make himself known to me.' Dane noticed Perkins had a grin playing on his lips. Apart from Shaw, Brown and Perkins, there were four others in the room.

'Let me introduce you to the other members of the group,' Shaw said. 'Alan Steele, who is my deputy chair and from the Security Service. Then Detective Superintendent Bob Thatcher, in charge of the Counter Terrorist Intelligence Unit in Stevenage.

Beyond him is Karen Teller also Security Service, she'll be our intelligence manager. And last, but not least, the lady at the back of the room is Amy, and she's our note taker. Shall we get under way by welcoming Detective Superintendent Christian Dane to the ELG. This is a matter of national security and attracts the highest security classification. Can you confirm you are a trained and certificated SIO?'

'Yes ma'am, on both counts,' Dane replied.

'And you have clearance to see Top Secret material?'

'I do.'

'Good,' she addressed the others. 'I propose we invite him to accept the post of Senior Investigating Officer for this operation.'

'Seconded,' Steele responded.

'Those in favour?' all but one person put their hands up, 'Against?' Shaw said, and Brown put his hand up.

'I object Ma'am. Dane might have done all the courses, but he has no experience. My unit will provide a suitable SIO for this task.'

Shaw paused for a moment, 'I thought we'd deployed all your people?'

'Yes, but…'

'Then who did you have in mind?'

'One of my guys could double up on this.'

'I think not. That would not do. I've listened to your objection, but Mr Dane is now the SIO.' She turned to Dane, 'I assume you're happy to accept the job?'

'I would be delighted.'

'That's settled then. In front of you is a briefing pack. The code name for this investigation is "Golden Mantle".'

Shaw summarised how Karen received the two strands of intelligence warning of an imminent terrorist attack and connected them both.

'We're certain this is a credible threat. The problem is identifying who or what the target might be. Karen's team has identified the telephone number in Frinton, which gives us a good starting point. Your job is to gather the evidence to identify

# VENGEANCE DAY

and apprehend the people involved in this conspiracy. Do you have any questions so far?'

Dane gathered his thoughts and considered what he'd learnt.

'A couple if I may. Is there likely to be any more intelligence coming from the source? And can we task them in the future?'

'You don't need to know that laddie,' Brown growled.

Shaw shot Brown an irritated look.

'You'll receive any further information in the normal way. Karen will handle that and any potential tasking.'

'What resources do I have?'

'Mr Thatcher's surveillance team, based in Stevenage, and Karen's people at the intelligence unit there will support your investigation officers.'

'The incident room must be here,' Brown interjected.

'Why?' Shaw replied.

'Because that's where the secure facilities needed for this sort of operation are.'

'Essex is not a backwater. We can provide the proper accommodation and sufficient staff to conduct the work. And it makes no sense for everyone to clatter up here every day at vast expense. A small, handpicked team of suitably trained officers will conduct the investigation, under Mr Dane's command.' Perkins said.

'I'll send two of my guys to assist,' Brown stated.

'If you insist, that would be helpful and gratefully received.'

'I have just one more question,' Dane said. 'What else is going on that might affect this operation?'

Brown was about to say something when Shaw stopped him with an impatient wave of her hand.

'What do you mean?'

'Well, you only bring outsiders like me in when you've run out of regular staff. That suggests to me there's a wider issue here. It's important for me to be aware of what else is running that could influence what I'm doing. We might turn something up that applies to another investigation. Or if I want to use a particular resource. If I know it isn't available to me, I can plan an alternative strategy.'

Shaw turned to Steele, 'I think he should be in the loop.'

'I agree.'

'Hang on a minute. Dane doesn't need to know anything other than his own investigation. I'd like to address you all and he should step outside,' Brown snapped.

'No, make your point to the entire group,' Shaw replied.

Brown was clearly struggling to control his temper.

'Dane is a minor cog in a larger wheel and should keep to his own area of responsibility. The more people we inform about the main part of this, the greater the chance of a leak. I say this only as a caution. I'm not suggesting he's a security risk at all.'

'Good because I am completely confident we can trust him, and I don't agree with you.' Shaw turned to Dane, 'There is a nationwide threat of a spectacular attack on the mainland before the year is out. We do not know what, or who the target might be. The best intelligence we have suggest its likely to involve Islamic terrorists. Exactly who they are, or where they are based remains a mystery, and is the primary objective of the overall operation. Every Counter Terrorist Unit in the country is engaged in trying to identify them. Now, this doesn't mean we are treating the Irish information as less serious. But as you guessed, we are short of staff, so you get the gig. Does that answer your question?'

'It does and I appreciate you being so candid with me.'

'This scenario has been on the cards for years. The Irish republican dissidents are keen to raise their profile on the mainland, and this could be their opportunity. We'll reconvene here once a week when you will brief us on the progress of the investigation.'

'What are my channels of communication between the meetings?'

'Any requests for intelligence through Karen and resources through me,' Perkins replied.

The meeting broke up and Dane and Karen agreed to meet at Thames House later. Then Shaw pulled him aside.

'Don't take any notice of Alex Brown. He believes they created the Met on the eighth day, and we can do without help

## VENGEANCE DAY

from outsiders. But he is a very experienced counter-terrorist officer, with an excellent record.'

'I got the impression he would rather I wasn't around.'

Shaw smiled, 'Well, you are, and I look forward to working with you.'

'Thank you, ma'am. See you next week.'

Dane locked the briefing pack in his briefcase and was about to leave when someone tapped him on the shoulder. He looked round to find the officer who had been with Brown earlier.

'The chief wants a word.'

Dane followed him into an office overlooking a storage yard full of dumpsters. Brown was working on papers at his desk and didn't look up. Dane gazed out of the window for a minute.

'Nice view. I understand you wanted to see me?'

Brown held up his hand to silence him and continued reading the document. Dane gave him another fifteen seconds, then shrugged and turned to leave. Brown's assistant moved nervously to block his way.

'Just wait there, laddie. I'll be with you in a moment.'

'I'm busy and not interested in your games. What do you want?'

Brown threw his pen onto his desk and glared at him.

'I'm the man around here, and don't you forget it. I didn't ask for you, nor do I want you anywhere near my CTU. But I'm stuck with you, so we'll do things my way. You are to report to this office daily. DCI Johnson there will give you the number to ring. He'll take your brief and pass it on to me. Do I make myself clear?'

'You do, and it's not going to happen. I don't work for you and the only person I'll be talking to every day is Mr Perkins. You'll get my investigative update at the weekly meeting, and not before. Got it?'

'Don't cross me laddie I am a force to be reckoned with.'

'I'll bear that in mind.' Dane turned to leave but found Johnson blocking the door.

'Move,' he growled, and the startled man stepped sideways.

Dane walked back to the café to join Perkins.

## SIMON DINSDALE

'Are you happy with what we've just lumbered you with?'

'Sounds like an interesting job. I'm off to see Karen Teller and get things moving. I ought to tell you she and I are old friends. We were on the same team in Ireland.'

'Did she know Anderson?'

'Yes, we were all there at the same time and still meet socially.'

'Thanks for telling me. I don't think anyone needs to know about the connection, do you?'

'It's not a secret, but I agree. Let's not mention it unless someone else brings it up.'

Perkins nodded his agreement, then hesitated for a second.

'One word of warning, though. Watch out for Alex Brown. He's furious that Shaw brought you in. I wouldn't put it past him to make life difficult for you.'

'Why would he do that?'

'Because he's typical of far too many of these old Met officers. They think that anyone outside their mighty organisation couldn't possibly catch anything worse than a cold. You saw how he behaved in the meeting. Just watch him, that's all.'

'I'm sure we'll enjoy an excellent working relationship.'

Karen met Dane at the main entrance of Thames House and took him to her office. As soon as the door was closed, she gave him a hug, then stood back to look him up and down.

'How are you?'

'Fully recovered and eager to get going. I wasn't expecting you to be sitting there, but at least I now know what your actual job is.' The last time they had met was at a regimental reunion a couple of months before. They had even talked about their mutual colleague, James Anderson, that evening.

'I couldn't believe it when I heard what happened. Tell me about it.'

Dane ran through the events of that day in the car park and his recovery.

'And you can't remember anything?'

## VENGEANCE DAY

'No, I wanted to ask Anderson about his shooting the boy, and if it had been necessary. We must have spoken, but I've no memory of it. It's frustrating to be honest.'

'You're alive. That's the main thing. Listen, I've told no one about our history. Do you think we should?'

Dane smiled, 'I've already told Perkins. I didn't tell him about my connection to Anderson when I identified him as the suspect. He wasn't incredibly happy with me, and I promised I wouldn't do it again. He's fine about it.'

'Great. So, let me get you up to speed with what we've learned.' She ran through the sequence of events leading to today.

'I know coincidences happen, but this was spooky. My guys tried to track Mary down, but we can't find her. Her real name is Maire o'Suilleabhain,'

'I'm impressed you can pronounce that properly. Shall we stick with Mary?'

'Good idea. Anyway, there's no reporting about her for the last three years. It's as if she disappeared from the face of the earth.'

'How good is the source?'

'Top class, and someone we always listen to carefully. The only strange thing for me is the telephone business. Why would they know that, and not who's involved?'

'Perhaps they've only passed on what they want to tell us.'

'That's a possibility.'

'Have you requested more from them?'

'I've already sent a questionnaire out and I'm waiting for a reply.'

'How about the Americans? Is there anything else from them?'

'No, they're still trying to learn more about the property the Irish group visited. It is owned by a man called Logan, who's filthy rich. He made his money in a variety of legitimate businesses and describes himself as a patriot and a supporter of a united Ireland.

'What's their assessment of why they were there?'

'I take it you've heard of the militias all over the US?'

111

'I've read a few articles about them. They all sound crazy to me.'

'That's what most people think. A group calling itself the Sons of Erin is believed to be associated with Logan's place. The Americans know little about them. The membership is understood to be exclusively Catholic, Irish American, and their aim is self-preservation. The FBI thinks Logan allows his land to be used to provide weapons training for them. Maire o'Suilleabhain, Mary, is now on an international watch list. If she pops up, they'll arrest her.'

'That's a start. Now, what's this about a phone in Essex?'

'According to the source, someone regularly calls a Belfast number from the public telephone kiosk outside Frinton-on-Sea railway station. We've checked for the last month and identified a call at seven in the evening every Thursday. A subscriber check has provided the name and address of a family in Belfast. They've lived at that house for years and have no known republican connections. But my guys are researching them as we speak.'

'Well, it's Monday afternoon. The next move is to identify who's making the call and where they're living.'

'I agree,' Karen replied.

# VENGEANCE DAY

## Chapter 11

They took over the special operations suite at Essex police headquarters, which was equipped with computerised smart boards and state-of-the-art communications. Dane had a tiny, windowless office next to it. The handpicked team of detectives included his deputy DI Paul Lamb, DS Dave Stone, Hayley Cross, and six others. The officers from the Met CTU arrived that morning and reported to Dane.

'I'm DS Samson boss, and this is DC White. She's an experienced counter terrorist officer. Mr Brown has sent us to give you country boys a dig out.

'Pleased to meet you both. I'm sure you'll soon settle in. See DI Lamb, he'll brief you up on the job and put you to work.'

They were like chalk and cheese, Samson tall, slim, and well dressed in a dark business suit and tie. White, with blond hair and a petite figure. While Samson was brash, White said nothing during the exchange. There was something about Samson's demeanour which Dane didn't care about. Six hours after their arrival, Dane received an angry phone call from Brown.

'What are you playing at? Those officers are top investigators. They're not there to do the rubbish jobs your people don't want to do.'

'DS Samson is the disclosure officer. Are you seriously suggesting that's a menial post? And DC White is dealing with CCTV recovery, which is just as important.'

'They should be leading the outside investigation teams. You're taking the micky here.'

'I'm not and they're working for me, not you. You stick to your job and keep your nose out of mine,' Dane snapped, and, without waiting for a reply, replaced the receiver. He called Lamb in, 'How are the Met couple settling in?'

'Samson is already strutting about as if he owns the place, and he questioned me about their roles. We had a deep and meaningful conversation, but I'll sort him out.'

Dane told him about the call, 'He'll be expecting a reaction and something to change because of his bleat to Brown, but we won't accommodate him.'

The following morning, Samson walked into Dane's office without knocking.

'We're not happy with the jobs me and Carol are doing. This isn't why the chief sent us here.'

'What makes you think I'm interested in what you like? You'll both do what's asked of you while you're here. Now go away and get on with your work.'

Dane informed Lamb of the conversation and then drove over to Stevenage to meet Karen. The offices of the Eastern Counter Terrorist Intelligence Unit (CTIU) are based with the MI5 regional team in an unassuming building in the small Hertfordshire town. No signs advertise who the residents were, but Dane thought the tight security and tall fence were a bit of a giveaway. Karen was waiting for him on the top floor with Bob Thatcher, who introduced Detective Inspector Ali Frampton, the surveillance team leader.

Karen had information from Belfast.

'We have established that the telephone number belongs to an address owned by Alison and Patrick Shanahan. They have four children, two of each. The girls are both married and live near their mum, and the eldest boy is attending Queens University. As of last night, they are all still there. The youngest, Michael, works somewhere in England. He did well at school, then spent a year at collage before dropping out. He's nineteen and there's no record of him being employed over here, and he isn't paying tax or national insurance. None of them has any known connection to the republican movement.'

'Do we have a picture of him?'

'No, not yet. My guys are researching his passport and driving licence applications, so we should find one on them,' Karen turned to Frampton, 'Tell us how you intend to cover the job on Thursday.'

'We've found an observation point with clear sight of the telephone box and the routes to and from it. Anyone going to it

## VENGEANCE DAY

will be under our control and when our target leaves, we'll follow them home.'

'The telecom companies are onside. If there's a call to the Belfast number, they'll tell me,' Karen added.

'Good,' Dane replied. 'Let's recover the fingerprints and DNA of the person who makes it. How busy is it then?'

Karen pulled a sheaf of computer printouts from her file and leafed through them.

'Most of the calls made from there are to the local taxi company, and much later in the evening.'

'The Belfast call is at seven?'

'Yes.'

'Ali, could your operators clean and sterilise the handset before the target arrives? And swab it after they finish?'

'That's no problem. I've got a couple of guys who're trained to do that,' Frampton replied.

\*

On Thursday afternoon, the surveillance team moved into their positions and manned the observation point, referred to by the team as the OP. Dane and Karen were sitting at the back of the operations room watching a screen streaming live pictures from the OP. That was situated in a house fifty yards from the telephone box, outside the ticket office. There were occasional bursts of conversation on the radio, but no extraneous chatter. Whatever was said referred to the operation. Dane knew these people were all experienced operators and if anyone could follow the target, it would be this crew. Frinton-on-sea railway station had one platform and served as a single-track branch line from Colchester, twenty miles away. A slip road gave access to the front of the building, and there was parking for only a dozen vehicles. To say it was tight would be an understatement. The surrounding area was all private housing. It was a leafy and relatively prosperous area.

Dane looked at the picture of Mary someone had pinned to the wall. She was a dangerous and talented terrorist. People like her didn't go all the way to the USA for a holiday in the outback. Every move they made had a purpose. If Mary had taken a group there, then they were up to no good. Dane was sure of that.

## SIMON DINSDALE

There was a click from the radio.

'OP to all units. The handset is now sterile.'

Dane glanced at the clock. Five minutes to go. A small knot of nerves bunched in his stomach. It always felt like this at the start of an operation. He ran through the plan for the umpteenth time. Were there sufficient troops on the ground? Had he considered all eventualities and were the contingency plans sound enough to cover them? Dane smiled to himself and gave up the pointless second guessing. There was nothing he could do now, even if he had forgotten something. Karen was across the room, and he realised she was probably feeling the same way.

The radio sprang to life.

'Stand by, stand by. A white male jogging towards the station. Six-foot, short fair hair. He's wearing black shorts and a blue vest.'

'OP has him in sight. He's gone straight in and is dialling.'

They all watched the video feed as an athletic-looking young man appeared and picked up the phone. Karen had her mobile glued to her ear. Seconds later, she looked up, grinned in triumph, and put her thumb up.

Dane interjected.

'All units, I can confirm this is the target. I say again, he is our target and designated Subject one.'

There was a heavy silence in the room as they watched the man conduct his conversation. He occasionally turned to look around but didn't seem particularly interested in his surroundings. After five minutes he replaced the receiver and left the telephone box.

The officer in the observation point came over the radio.

'Stand by. Subject one is off. He's jogging towards the level crossing.'

Frampton had sixteen men and women deployed in a variety of vehicles on foot and a couple on push bikes all surrounding the station. Each unit had their own numbered callsign which they used to identify themselves with. They had been expecting someone to arrive in a car. While the target was speaking on the phone, Frampton tried to reposition his team. But they weren't quite ready when the call ended.

## VENGEANCE DAY

A voice came over the radio. 'This is 4. Subject one has cleared the crossing. The barriers have come down and we are baulked by them. Subject one is heading north on Elm Tree Avenue. We cannot follow.'

Several minutes of hectic, breathless chaos ensued. The railway line effectively split the small town in two. Most of Frampton's surveillance operators were trapped to the south and had to wait for the train to rumble out of the station and the barriers to rise. There had been two vehicles and a bike to the north. It took another three tense minutes before one of them caught sight of their target.

'7 has Subject one. Still running on Elm Tree. Is anyone with me?'

'9, is at the junction with the B1034,'

'7, roger. I will back off.'

A couple of minutes later, callsign 9 reported that Subject one had turned right onto the B1034.

'He's running at an impressive pace towards Walton on the Naze. I need back-up.'

'7 is in your mirror.'

'9, received, we've hit some roadworks. Subject one is through them. The lights have stopped us. He's still making for Walton, and we have now lost him.'

Frampton reported the barriers had lifted and the rest of the team were heading through the blockage to catch up. Dane held his breath and listened to the officers asking each other if anyone had control of the target.

More frustrating time passed, and Dane was now concerned they had lost their quarry. Then a calm voice came over the air.

'This is 2. Contact, contact. Subject one is still on the B1034 making for the pier.'

Dane looked over at Karen and raised his eyebrows. She gave him a nervous smile.

More vehicles joined the hunt as the young man ran down through the small seaside town of Walton on the Naze to the seafront.

'This is 5. Subject one has gone onto the beach path. Heading back towards Frinton.'

## SIMON DINSDALE

Now, finally, they had him under control, and the atmosphere on the radio calmed down. Their target passed the lines of huts to his right and the wide sandy beach on his left. Frampton manoeuvred his officers to static points along the route from where they could observe Subject one as he passed them. After two miles, he turned and crossed the wide greensward to a large, detached house. A surveillance officer on a bike timed his arrival perfectly to note the number and ride on. Not wanting to expose the team, Dane instructed everyone to stand down and to return to Chelmsford for a debriefing.

As they all gathered in the office, Frampton joined them looking disgruntled.

'Sorry about the mess boss. My fault, I should have considered a bloody jogger.'

'None of us thought of that. But your guys didn't lose him, and we now know where he's living. So, I say that was a successful operation.'

The forensic team had lifted fingerprints and DNA swabs from the handset in the telephone box at the station. They would go straight to the lab. The surveillance officers had taken dozens of photographs of Subject one. Karen took them back to her office in London to start the process of identifying him. Dane dispatched Hayley to research the address Subject one had gone into. Frampton's officers had found a promising location for an observation point to watch the house from. Dane was keen to get that in place as soon as possible so Frampton left to sort that out.

Dane was left alone in the incident room, and he reflected on the last few hours. Yes, the operation had achieved its aim, but it had nearly been a disaster. Subject one's arrival on foot shook Dane because he hadn't considered that scenario. The success, or failure of this operation fell squarely on his shoulders, and depended on him making sure every possible angle was covered. The surveillance team had retrieved the situation, but he couldn't continue to rely on luck. He knew he had to pull his finger out.

Dane walked out of the building for a breath of fresh air and called Vicky.

'Hi, how's your day been?'

## VENGEANCE DAY

'Cambridge City Council has been giving me a tough time today. They're unhappy about our response to the deaths of those two students and the drugs scene in the city. They have a point of course but none of them were interested before. But that's petty politicians for you. How about you?'

'We've had an interesting but successful day. I'll have to work through the weekend, I'm afraid. Sorry.'

'Will you make it to your parents on Sunday?'

'I should be there for lunch.'

'I will go over there on Saturday as we arranged. Your Mum has asked me to give her a hand sorting the housework out and help her with the cooking.'

'Thanks for doing that. I had an e-mail from Robyn this morning. She's on a field trip to Vancouver Island but will be here for mum's eightieth.' His mother's birthday was a cause for celebration, and he couldn't wait to see his daughter again.

'That's great. Your dad is always talking about her.'

'Yes, so mum tells me. It'll be nice to have a proper talk with him. We've not had a chance since he left the hospital.'

'See you on Sunday.'

*

The office was a hive of activity, and even Samson and White had their noses glued to their computers when Dane arrived the next morning.

Frampton contacted him.

'We have the use of a detached garage with a flat over it to watch from. It's the best part of six hundred yards away, but that's not a problem with our optics. I've just watched two blokes leave the house in a car and neither of them was our young man from last night.'

'Is it all ready to start?'

'The techies have got to finish plugging everything in. But we have eyes on the place.'

'Excellent. We'll be manning it twenty-four-seven. Can you manage that level of surveillance cover?'

'No problem. I'll have most of them on during daylight hours and a skeleton staff overnight. We do this all the time.'

## SIMON DINSDALE

Hayley returned after lunch with news that the house in Frinton was rented. The letting agent had met a woman claiming to represent an Irish IT company. She had leased the property for a year and paid cash in advance.

'I showed him the picture of Mary, and he had no hesitation in identifying her,' Hayley said.

Dane's eyebrows shot up, 'Now that is interesting. Well done. What does he know about the people living there?'

'Three men moved in about four months ago. One is about twenty and the other two are a few years older. He gave me the names they are using, and I will check them out.'

As Hayley left Dane received a call from Karen. She explained that the surveillance commissioners had authorised the surveillance operation, but she would now have a problem staffing it.

'There has been a request for the surveillance team to assist the operation in London. And my boss has just told me to send three of my people back to Thames House. So, I'm struggling as well.'

Dane could guess who was trying to take everyone.

'I'll use my police officers in there. It's daft using the surveillance team when they'll be needed to follow when the suspects go out.'

'I hoped you'd say that,' Karen replied.

The investigation team all volunteered to work in the observation point. Lamb and Dane drew up a rota.

'How about we put those two from the Met together on the day shift?' Dane suggested.

'It would make life in the incident room easier,' Lamb replied.

'Why? What's the matter?'

'He keeps banging on about how the Met is better at everything. I had to stop someone from punching him the other day.'

'Is he doing his job?'

'Yes, but there's not that much for him to do at the moment, to be honest.'

'What about White?'

## VENGEANCE DAY

'She's efficient enough, but nowhere near as experienced as they led us to believe. They travel out together. I suspect they're an item.'

'Is it wise to put them in there, then?'

'I doubt it, but it would cause a lot of inconvenience if we separated them. They can't do much damage in there, can they? I say pair them up and keep them out of our hair and he'll stop whinging.'

'Okay, do it.'

Dane found Perkins in his office and brought him up to date with the investigation.

'This is going to be quite resource intensive, so I need some more officers.'

'I'll inform the Executive Liaison Group tonight and then talk to the chief about your extra people,' Perkins replied.

'I understand there's been some pressure on Frampton and Karen to provide staff into London.'

'Yes, there has. Shaw has already told me you are to keep your resources.'

'Thanks for the support.'

The technicians finished installing the high-tech video equipment, and officers moved in. They had an excellent view of the detached four-bedroom house, with its integral garage and semi-circular, tarmacked drive. By Saturday evening, they had observed and photographed the other men living there. They became Subjects two and three. Karen set about identifying them.

\*

Liam peeled the plastic lid off his cup, spilling hot coffee as it came free.

'Why does it always do that?' he snarled, sucking the scalding liquid off his fingers.

Mary shook her head, 'What am I going to do with you? You're worse than a big kid.'

It was Saturday morning, and they were sitting in her car at the end of a street in Cambridge. As he took a tentative sip, a small, dark-haired figure sprinted past them. She was wearing running clothes and opened the door to a house.

Liam smiled as he recognised her.

'Ah, the delightful Vicky.'

'Yep.'

'How did you find this place?'

'Followed her here from the police station. It wasn't hard. I could have taken her out whenever I felt like it.'

He looked round. It was a quiet housing estate of both terraced and semi-detached houses with street parking.

'It's tight for what we want.'

'I agree. I thought it would be worth spending a day with her to see where she goes.'

'I've got nothing better to do,' he replied and settled back to drink his coffee. An hour later, Vicky reappeared and drove off.

Liam soon realised Mary had been right. The woman was taking no precautions. When Vicky turned into an out-of-town supermarket Liam jumped out and followed her around the superstore as she loaded a shopping trolley with groceries. He returned to their car when Vicky went to the till.

'Did you get it on?'

'Of course,' Mary replied, showing him the screen of her mobile phone. On it was a map of the car park and a pulsing symbol.

With the tiny tracking device fixed to the underside of Vicky's car, they could stay out of sight as she drove through the countryside to a village in Essex. When she stopped, Mary pulled up by a quaint pub.

'She's parked about a mile away,' Liam said.

They waited for five minutes before following. Liam couldn't suppress the smile of triumph as they spotted Vicky's car outside a secluded, detached cottage.

'This would be perfect,' he muttered.

'I'll find out who lives there,' Mary replied.

\*\*\*

Dane made it to his parents by midday on Sunday. Vicky and his mother were busy in the kitchen, and he hugged them both.

'How's dad?'

## VENGEANCE DAY

'He's as weak as a kitten, which he hates, and still won't eat properly. It's his mental state that worries me. It has got worse this last week.'

Dane's father had been a parish vicar for over fifty years. For most of his adult life, he'd suffered bouts of depression. He understood what was happening to him and accepted help, but the condition often overpowered him, making him irascible. The illness was the source of many of the difficulties Dane had experienced with him since his childhood. Dane's twin sister, Christine, died following an accident when she was thirteen. This tragedy caused Dane to lose his faith and rebel. The old man blamed his son for what happened, which led to deeper resentment. When Dane joined the Army, against his father's express wish, the schism was complete. They barely spoke for years, but in the months before this recent bout, their relationship had improved. Dane hoped that would continue.

'I took them both to church this morning,' Vicky said, 'He shouldn't have gone because it was freezing in there.'

'He wouldn't let the weather keep him from his devotions on a Sunday.'

'Why don't you take him a hot drink?' his mother replied, passing him a steaming mug.

Dane set the tea down beside his sleeping father. He seemed to have shrunk in the couple of weeks and he looked skeletal.

'Dad, dad, wake up.'

He stirred and peered round, then his gaze settled on his son.

'Oh, it's you. I noticed you missed church again. What's your excuse?' his voice was querulous.

'I've been busy at work. I hear Vicky took you both.'

'Yes, she did. She is a lovely girl, but I don't understand why she's here.'

'She is with me. We are in a relationship.'

'I see.' His lips tightened with displeasure, 'More sin on top of a lifetime of sin.'

'That's not fair. She is someone I am hoping I can spend my life with.'

## SIMON DINSDALE

'I would expect nothing less from you. What comes next? Children I suppose, and what does the future hold for them in a Godless house with no chance of salvation?'

Dane forced himself to remain calm. He knew his father was ill but hadn't expected this. The old man's face darkened with anger as he glared at his son, then he changed tack.

'Honour thy father, do you remember that? The fifth commandment, that's how I brought you up. Honour thy father and mother and you will have a good life.'

'I do, but I have made my own decisions about how I live.'

'I had such plans for you.'

'Yes, and they were yours, not mine. Honouring my parents doesn't mean doing what you decide or leading my life in the way you think I should. I have done my best to serve my country and the public. As you did. Isn't that worthy of recognition from you?'

'You turned away from God. Then you join the Army to learn how to kill, against my express wishes. An ill-judged marriage and divorce, and now you wallow in sin. All of this you did to punish me because you blamed me for Christine. And you have allowed them to turn Robyn, from the church. I pray for her salvation every day. That she will see the light and return to the fold before it is too late.'

The tirade petered out, and he coughed, a wet hacking bark spewing thick, dark green and yellow phlegm. Dane grabbed tissues and mopped up the mess, then held him upright until he could get his breathing under control.

'Robyn's coming over for mum's birthday.'

'She is a delightful child. I suppose we will have to put up with your presence as well?'

'Yes, we'll both be here and I'm sorry for bringing you pain. That was never my intention. All I ask from you is to forgive me for my supposed sins and move on.'

'You just want to salve your conscience. You know you have sinned. It will take more than your hollow apologies to convince me you have changed.'

He turned away, faced the wall, and refused to be drawn into any further conversation.

## VENGEANCE DAY

Dane gave up and returned to the kitchen. His mother and Vicky had heard the exchange.

'We were making such good progress before he became ill,' Dane said.

'Give him time. He is so weak he can't do anything for himself and that is feeding the depression. At least he's taking his medication. That should help settle him and stop these violent mood swings. Once he's shaken this bout, he'll be better,' his mother replied.

Vicky looked shocked by what she'd heard.

'He told me he was looking forward to seeing you today. That was only just before you arrived.'

'That's how his illness works, I'm afraid,' Mrs Dane replied.

Dane could see how much this was affecting his mother and felt powerless to help. They ate lunch without his father, who announced he was going for a nap. The mood lightened a little later when he re-joined them for a while, but he was still morose. Dane didn't sleep well that night, unable to get the angry voice out of his head and worried about both his parents' health.

\*

The observation point saw no movement on the Sunday. Each morning thereafter, two of the occupants would go out together. The watchers soon established that whatever they were doing it had nothing to do with any IT business. They had the use of two cars, a Citroen C5 estate, and a Ford Focus. Both were rentals, one from a local hire company and the other from a different firm in Colchester, which they parked in the double garage. The surveillance team followed them to auctions and used car companies all over the country. Discrete enquiries revealed the men were searching for a long wheelbase van. At no time did all three leave the house at the same time. A six-foot-high wooden fence with a locked back gate enclosed the property with a row of conifer trees inside that. It was impossible to overlook the rear garden. A public footpath and the golf course ran alongside and behind it. Every evening, Subject one went for his run, and he always took the same route.

Dane thought back to the first time they followed him. Could Subject one have deliberately timed his call to finish as a train was due, so he could run past the railway barriers as they fell. Was he leading the surveillance team through a series of counter surveillance points where his friends were watching. It was a possibility, so Dane positioned an officer to watch the rear of the house when Subject one was due to start his run. No one came out that way, so it seemed to have been a coincidence.

Seven days into the operation, Subject one made his regular phone call. The next day, Subject's two and three left the house, each driving a car. They handed the Ford Focus back to the rental company before travelling together to a second-hand dealership in Northampton. From there, they collected a Fiat Ducato van and then returned to Frinton. That evening, Dane, Frampton, Karen, and Perkins reviewed the information they had discovered that week.

'The vehicle situation is interesting,' Karen said, 'IRA active service units never had the funds to swap hire cars about like this. It's expensive and having two is almost profligate. But it ensures they have a regular turnover of clean vehicles, which suggests they are flush with money.'

'I've tasked Hayley to get copies of the rental forms. We knew they were in the market for a van, but why? I think they're moving into the next phase of their operation. It'll be interesting to see what they do in the coming days.' Dane said.

'I received a copy of Shanahan's passport photograph this afternoon and I'm certain he's our Subject one. We still need to identify the other two. We might get lucky there when we see the driving licence they used to hire the cars.'

# VENGEANCE DAY

## Chapter 12

Detective Carla Di Matteo was at her desk before dawn. She liked to have the office to herself to catch up on the paperwork and review the previous day in peace. It was a habit she developed as a rookie cop in Brooklyn. Carla was a dogged investigator and the Sons of Erin case had got under her skin. The real identity of the woman calling herself Kate Dunn, and her background, shocked Carla. That information added to the pressure on her to discover more about Logan and his group. Those enquiries weren't going well.

Logan didn't fit the profile of someone involved in this type of organisation. The other better-known militias were keen to publicise their activities. They used amateurish web sites and endless social media posts to get their message out. The Sons of Erin did none of this and were shadowy in the extreme. Despite all Carla's hard work, she hadn't been able to find how many members they had or what their aims and objectives were. She circulated a request for intelligence about them to all FBI field stations. So far, none had replied, which was another frustration.

Karen Teller at MI5 wanted more information, but she couldn't give them what they needed. More embarrassment. Carla was due to meet Peter Franks later and was not looking forward to telling him she'd made no progress since their last conversation. Then her phone rang.

'Hi, is that Detective Di Matteo?' the voice at the other end said in a soothing southern drawl.

'Sure is. What can I do for you?'

'You circulated a bulletin about an Irish militia group based in upstate New York?'

'Yes, I did,' Carla replied and sat up. 'Who are you?'

'Special Agent Josh Spain. FBI field office in Columbia, South Carolina. I'm a Marine Corps brat and vet. Last week, I was at a funeral and got talking to an old guy I've known all my life. He served with my father and is a legend in the Corps. He told me he makes some extra cash teaching rich folks to shoot. These people like to play at being military and fire a few toys you can't usually get your hands on.'

'Where does he do this?'

'That's the thing, and the reason I called,' Spain said. 'It's at a large private estate near Frazier, New York. They use him a couple times a year, and he's been up there recently.'

'What's his name?'

'Edward Kavanagh.'

'Is he friendly? Would he speak to me?'

'I'm sure he would. This guy is a dyed-in-the-wool patriot. I could set up a meeting.'

'Thank you. But I would rather he didn't know we were coming.'

'I understand. My special agent in charge has said I am to assist you. I'll make the introductions to Gunny.'

'If my boss gives me the go ahead, I will be down first thing tomorrow. Is that convenient for you?'

'That's fine by me. I'll come pick you up.'

She strode into see Franks, feeling a lot better.

\*

Carla read Kavanagh's service record on the flight down to Columbia Metropolitan airport the following morning. The thick tome filled her briefcase.

Edward James Kavanagh was born in December 1950 in Nashville, Tennessee. He spent his childhood in state orphanages and joined the US Marine Corps on his eighteenth birthday in 1968. He received an honourable discharge in 2010, on his sixtieth. The record listed the many wars Kavanagh had served in, and his impressive string of medals. It also recorded his discipline offences, virtually all of which related to the old marine's excessive drinking. The Corps had frequently promoted Kavanagh during his time in the service but demoted him almost as often. At the time of his retirement, he was a Gunnery Sergeant. A mid-level, non-commissioned rank. Not very impressive after such a long service.

She walked through the terminal doors and stood by Airport Boulevard squinting into the sunshine of the October morning.

## VENGEANCE DAY

'Hi, you Carla?' a voice behind her said. She turned to find a man who looked straight out of central casting. Six feet tall, thick black gelled hair, a crisp white shirt with red tie under a smart dark business suit cut to hide the pistol on his hip.

'Yes, I am. I guess you're Josh.'

Josh nodded and they shook hands.

'The car's just up here. How was the trip?'

'Fine. I caught the first flight out of Kennedy.'

'That's good. We've got a hundred-and forty-mile drive. Shouldn't take more than a couple of hours. Gunny lives in back of a well-known bar in Beaufort. It's owned by a lady called Aggie, she's the widow of a marine he was close to. She takes care of Gunny.'

'Why do you call him Gunny?'

'That sobriquet always refers to a Gunnery Sergeant in the Marine Corps. It's a tradition and sticks with the holder.'

'Would he be alright with me calling him that?'

'Sure. He would love it.'

Josh drove out of the airport and a few minutes later they joined the I26 highway, heading south.

'What can you tell me about Kavanagh?' Carla asked.

'I have known him almost my whole life. My father retired as a Brigadier General and served with Gunny in Nam, Beirut, Granada, Somalia and the first Gulf War. I often saw him when he was invited to our house for the occasional function.'

'Was he a good soldier?'

'Marine. If you want him to talk. Do not call him a soldier.'

'Okay. Got it.'

'In answer to your question. Yes, he was. In the early days, Gunny was a superb marine. But the Beirut bombing changed his life.'

'That was the terrorist attack on the barracks, right?'

'Yeah. I'm told Gunny excelled himself that day and saved the lives of several of his friends by digging them out of the rubble with his bare hands. When his outfit returned from that tour, he was promoted to Master Gunnery Sergeant. Many people, my Pa included, had him slated to be a future Sergeant Major of the Marine Corps.'

'So, what went wrong?'

'Booze. Many of his closest friends, including Aggie's husband, died in Beirut. The loss overwhelmed him, and he hit the bottle. The hierarchy tried to help and protect him. He threw himself into alcoholics anonymous and re-discovered his Catholic faith. That helped, but he always relapsed.'

'If that's the case. How did he stay in for so long?'

'The military is a strange institution. But it tries to look after its own and he tried hard to control his problem. That earned him some credit. There were plenty of senior officers who remembered him in his prime, so they looked after him.'

'Sounds sad.'

'There are many good men brought down by the demon drink. My last post in the Corps was recruit training on Parris Island here in South Carolina. Gunny worked in the clothing stores. I saved what was left of his career then.'

'What happened?'

'I found him falling down drunk one night when he was the guard commander. By then, the official patience and acceptance of his behaviour had worn thin. There were people there who wanted to get rid of him. So, if he'd been caught, it would have been a dishonourable discharge, and the loss of what little pension he gets now. I hid him for two days until he recovered.'

'What did he tell you about the spread in Frazier?'

'Gunny was full of beer and cornered me for an hour. He was moaning about the miserable state of the country and how poor he is. Then he talked about working as a small arms instructor there. He was very enthusiastic about it. And they pay him good money.'

'Is he qualified to do that?'

Josh smiled, 'He sure is. Gunny is an expert on the use of all infantry weapons. His skill with a mortar was legendary.'

'Did he talk about the people running the place?'

'No. When I asked, he clammed up and changed the subject. I suspect he realised he'd said too much and shouldn't have been

# VENGEANCE DAY

talking about it in the first place. But I heard enough to make the connection.'

'I'm glad you did. This could be very important.'

Carla sat back and reflected on what she had heard as the miles rolled past. The highway was constructed of huge slabs of concrete, so there was a constant irritating rumbling from the tyres. Tall trees and heavy undergrowth lined both sides of the road, cutting out any view. The occasional building or gas station broke the monotony, but not much else. The lines of advertising billboards fascinated her, perched on hundred-foot-tall poles peeking above the branches of the tallest trees. They extolled the virtues of wreck recovery companies, golf courses and car dealerships. Carla was used to crowds of people, nose to tail traffic, noise, and high-rise buildings. She needed a view that went further than a hundred yards in every direction. So wasn't comfortable in this rural backwater.

'Is there anything beyond those trees?'

Josh smiled, 'Sure, there is. This is a beautiful state.'

'It would be nice to see some of it.'

'We'll be joining the I95 before long. The scenery should change then.'

It didn't. Josh negotiated the big clover leaf junction where Carla got a quick view of flat scrubland before trees enveloped them again.

Two hours after setting out, they cruised past a huge military base.

'That's the Marine Corps Air Station, Beaufort. There are thousands of personal based there,' Josh said.

'Do they keep you busy?'

'They sure do. Parris Island is only a few miles away, so you can see the influence the Corps has on this area.'

The scenery improved when they approached the town. Carla gazed over the many Sea Islands, all linked by wide salt marshes. Beaufort was pretty. Low-rise buildings dominated, and she was struck by how clean the streets were. Much different from the Bronx.

'They don't do skyscrapers around these parts, then?' Carla joked.

'Everything around here is built on marshy ground. If you go higher than two stories, it will sink. Here we are,' Josh replied. He parked and pointed to the other side of the street.

Carla saw a building with a redbrick façade. A sign proclaiming Aggie's Bar hung over the door. She could see through the windows that it was busy with lunchtime diners.

'It's a nice place. Themed on the Marine Corps and popular with the tourists. Aggie does decent food. Most of the regulars are locals and retired marines.' Josh led the way.

A line of chrome plated stools stood next to the bar with regimental precision. Twenty booths with seating for six ran along the walls. Josh introduced Carla to Aggie, who was a tall woman in her late sixties.

'How do you do, young lady,' she smiled as they shook hands.

'Is Gunny about?' Josh said.

'I've not seen him today. He'll be in the apartment. Go on up.'

'Thanks Aggie.' Josh walked past the bar and through a door marked private. At the top of a flight of stairs they came to another door which Josh knocked on. It took three more hard knocks before the was jerked open, and Carla got her first sight of the grizzled old veteran.

Gunny Kavanagh was about five feet eight tall, dressed in sweatpants and a grey Marine Corps vest. His lined face was sporting several days of stubble. He glared at his visitors through heavily bloodshot eyes.

'Morning Gunny. How are you today?' Josh said.

'Surprised to see you. What do you want?'

'Just a talk. This is Carla Di Matteo. She's a colleague of mine.'

'How do you do, ma'am.'

'I'm pleased to meet you, Gunny. May we come in?'

'I guess so.' He stood back and waved them into the small apartment.

Carla looked round the sitting room. Memorabilia recording his life in the Marines lined the walls. A settee and an armchair

## VENGEANCE DAY

placed around a small portable television. An ornate wooden crucifix stood on the side table beside a silver plate and a string of rosary beads. A breakfast bar led to the kitchenette with a picture window giving a view over a waterway. She could smell the faint tang of whiskey in the air. The place was spotlessly clean and tidy.

'I had a late night out with some buddies. I'm a little slow getting going and I didn't expect visitors. Take a seat. Can I fix you some coffee?' Gunny said.

They both accepted and as he clattered about making the drinks, Carla caught him casting surreptitious glances in her direction. She could tell he wasn't happy with the intrusion.

Gunny placed the mugs down and sat opposite them.

'How can I help you guys? I know what he does,' he nodded to Josh, 'I assume you're a Fed as well, ma'am?'

'No, I'm with the NYPD, and please call me Carla. Josh tells me you've been doing some weapons training in upstate New York. I have a professional interest in a property in that region. I wondered if it might be the same place.'

Gunny's face dropped and he glared at Josh.

'Really? I talk to you in private and you tell the world my business?'

'Hardly that Gunny. I'm a Federal Officer. I am duty bound to report what I hear if it could affect a current investigation.'

'I thought I could trust you.' He faced Carla, 'I've done nothing wrong.'

'Are you sure we are talking about the same property?'

'Okay. There's no secret. The son of an old marine friend made contact and introduced me to a pal of his. He offered me the chance of occasional work as an instructor at a spread near Frazer, New York. It's a dude ranch for rich kids who want to shoot military weapons and other cool stuff.'

'How often have you been up there?'

'Is it the place you are interested in?'

'Yes. It sounds like it.'

'Then I'm saying nothing more without good reason. Those folks have been good to me. And I don't see why the Federal Government needs to poke its nose in. Unless…'

Carla opened her arms out, 'Unless what?'

'Is this to do with me not paying tax on my earnings? Are you doing the IRSs' dirty work?'

'No…'

'Because I only have a tiny pension to live on. If it wasn't for Aggie, I would be on the streets…'

'Gunny.' Carla barked, 'I am not from the IRS. My investigation has nothing to do with your tax arrangements. I don't care if you are earning a little on the side.'

'Then I don't understand why an NYPD detective would be interested in this place. That's out of your jurisdiction, isn't it?'

'I'm attached to the Joint Terrorist Task Force. My job is to investigate the so-called militia, or patriot groups on the East coast. There is a suggestion that such an organisation operates from the property in Frazier.'

Gunny shook his head and looked at Carla, then Josh.

'Means nothing to me. And it's about time you people dealt with those crazies. They are a menace.'

'You're not impressed with them?'

'They're a bunch of nuts and I certainly don't care for their agendas. But if they leave me alone, I'm happy. If they perpetrated an attack. That would be a different story. I hate terrorists of any race, colour, or creed. I spent my entire adult life fighting scum like that and watched too many of my friends murdered by them.'

'Have you heard of the Sons of Erin Militia?' Carla said.

From his reaction, she knew she had hit a nerve. Gunny's face turned puce as he glared at her.

'You guys are something else, you know that? The Federal Government has sat back for forty years and allowed those maniacs to form and organise. You stood by as they spewed their hate. Their Nazi ideology and conspiracy theories and you have done nothing. How many of them have you closed down? Not one. Yet the minute a group of concerned Catholics get together,

## VENGEANCE DAY

the full weight of the FBI, and you, Detective, rolls into action. How do you sleep at night, lady? With a name like yours, you must be Catholic, or did your grand pappy fight for Mussolini?'

Josh started to intervene, but Carla stopped him.

'If my information is wrong, then put me right. You will save me a lot of time. Time I could use to look at the people you are concerned about. And I am a Catholic. My Great Grandpa was a paratrooper and dropped into Normandy on D-Day. He lost his legs in Bastogne.'

Gunny held his hand up.

'I'm sorry, ma'am. That was uncalled for.'

'Apology accepted. Now where have I gone wrong?'

'The Sons of Erin are no militia.'

'Then what are they?'

'It is an association of friends. Representing Catholic communities across the country. People who fear what those patriot groups and the government are planning for them.'

'What are they all afraid of?' Josh asked.

'You must have read the militia's twisted ideology. Protestant, anti-Catholic, anti-gay, anti-Jew, anti-government. They are powerful, well-armed and intend to attack Catholics.'

'And you are training people to resist and fight back on the land in Frazier.'

'No. You have got that all wrong.'

'When are you expecting the militias to attack?'

Gunny shrugged, 'If you don't prepare. You'll never be able to defend yourself.'

'Sound philosophy. But is this war imminent?'

'I have nothing else to say.'

Carla shook her head, 'It doesn't work like that, Gunny. Something is going on there and it directly affects our national security. If you think you can just clam up. You are seriously mistaken.'

'I know my rights. You can't force me to say anything.' He turned to Josh, 'Do I need a lawyer?'

'You should listen to Carla and talk to her.'

'They are doing nothing wrong up in Frazier.'

'Then explain what you do up there, and who goes there,' Carla said.

'No. I ain't snitching on anyone.'

'Are you aware it is a serious crime just to lie to the FBI?'

'Yes.'

'Then understand that life gets even more difficult for citizens who obstruct the work of my organisation. If I say the word you could disappear into a federal holding cell. No lawyer can help you out. There is no torture or mistreatment, but you will tell us what we want to know. And when we do spit you out, your reputation as a decorated veteran will be in tatters. And you can kiss your pension goodbye. How's that for the level of trouble you could be in here?'

Gunny stood and collected a half full fifth of Bourbon from a kitchen cabinet and poured a generous slug into his coffee. He offered the bottle to them, but they both declined. After taking a drink, he looked up at Carla.

'I don't appreciate being threatened in my home.'

'It is not a threat. That is what will happen if you are not straight with me.'

'Aw come on. There is nothing that could affect national security going on in Frazier.'

'Okay. Let's take the heat out of this. How about we talk in general terms? What type of people do you train?

Gunny pursed his lips and paused for a moment. His eyes flicking between Carla and Josh.

'I only see ordinary folks there. Mostly younger age groups and professional. They come out for anything up to a week and shoot on a variety of ranges.'

'Is it expensive?'

'I don't know. They pay me a thousand bucks for a few days' work. And it's not just me. So, it won't be cheap. I get food and benefits included so I'd do more if I could.'

'Where do the customers come from?'

'All over the country. Most are men, but ladies attend as well. There are some neat ranges in the wilderness. They also have two purpose-built buildings where they practise the tactics used by

## VENGEANCE DAY

law enforcement SWAT teams. Hostage rescue, invading a house, that sort of thing. It's damn popular. One big company in Silicon Valley brings their workers for an adventure holiday every year and they're not alone.'

'Do they advertise?'

'I'm not sure you'll find an ad in "Guns and Ammo". More likely on the internet.'

'What kind of weapons have they got?'

'They have a well-stocked armoury with examples of most of the military assault rifles of the world. They have several belt fed pieces, a Nazi MG 42, a US M60 and a British GPMG, and a 1919 Browning. There's a mortar, a bazooka, hand grenades and enough ammunition to fight off the Soviets. The clients buy a package to fire on the various ranges and have a go with the different weapons systems. Most folks bring their own weapons. The groups are never bigger than a dozen, and it's popular and busy. I do the Gunny act. Shouting and screaming at them as if they're recruits and they all love it. They call me Jake.'

'How many times have you been there?'

'Oh, about a dozen times over the last three years.'

'I understand a man called Logan runs the operation. Is that right?'

'He owns the spread. There are some kids who do the housework. And a few old guys like me to instruct the clients and take care of range safety.'

'What's the setup?'

'Logan lives with his wife in a big house. Out back are cabins where the guests sleep for the first night and stables for about thirty horses. We move everyone into the wilderness where the ranges are, and they live under canvas.'

'How far out are they?'

'Couple of hours on horseback to reach the campsites. You can run a jeep up to the camps, though we don't tell the clients about that. We arrive a day early and set everything up. It's all very professional and organised. There's never been an accident since I've worked with them. Worse injury is mosquito bites which are a hazard in the summer.'

## SIMON DINSDALE

'Are the Sons of Erin charged for their training?'

Gunny paused and took another slurp of his coffee.

'If a Catholic community wants to prepare to defend themselves, they can send people to Frazier. The deal is the training is free. They pay for their upkeep. That's all.'

'Is Logan the leader of the group?'

'No. There is no central structure, or leadership.'

'What do you teach the clients?'

'Basic weapons handling and marksmanship. How to protect a community in the event of an attack. But they are the minority of people who go there. Logan is running a business and making a fortune. Hell, he has another spread in Arizona, where you can drive tanks.'

Carla hid her surprise, 'When were you last there?'

'A couple of weeks ago. There was a crowd of guys from Ireland. It excited Logan they were coming because it might lead to more Europeans using his place.'

'Why is he interested in Europe?'

'Because they will pay big money. The dumb gun laws over there are about the strictest in the world and places like his can't operate. He sees it all as a great business opportunity.'

'What's your opinion of the Irish group?'

'They were all friendly people. We split them into teams, and they spent most of their time in the killing houses. One side being the SWAT team and the other the hostage takers. Then they would swap over. They got real competitive and were excellent marksmen. I took them for a stint on the mortar. Showed them how to set the weapon up and fire it. That part of the package is always at the end of their week and used as a bit of fun and to let them unwind. They all enjoyed themselves.'

'How many were there?'

'Eight men and three women. That's the usual size of a group. It's a business, pure and simple. Sure, they train a few Catholics. But only to protect themselves. Not to overthrow the government. Nearly all the folks who go there are rich kids who want to try something different.'

'Did Logan tell you anything about the people from Ireland?'

## VENGEANCE DAY

'Only that they were journalists and office staff from a magazine in Dublin. He was friendly with them and told me they were writing a big article about their trip. Good advertising. You see, Carla. There is nothing bad going on there. You are wasting your time.'

'Thank you, Gunny. That is all very helpful and explains a lot. Would you look at a picture, please? Tell me if you recognise the person in it.'

'Sure.'

She took the photo from her bag and handed it face down to him. 'You must not discuss this with anyone, do you understand?'

'Yes ma'am. You have my word on that.'

He turned it over and Carla could see immediately that he recognised her.

'Okay,' he drawled, 'What have I gotten myself into here?'

'What can you tell me about her?'

'We called her Mary. She was one of the Irish people and a crack shot. In fact, she was so good I thought she must have some military experience. Who is she?'

Before Carla answered, she took out three more pictures. Karen Teller had sent them over the previous evening.

Gunny peered at them and pointed to two, 'These guys were there. But the other one wasn't.'

'Thank you. That's been extremely useful.'

'Am I in trouble because of this?'

'No. You're doing a job of work and as far as I can see you have broken no Federal or State laws. But the Irish people are part of a terrorist group. They pose a genuine threat in the US and Britain. If you ever see any of them there again, I would like to hear from you. Will you help me?'

'Sure. I trusted Logan. If he got me training terrorists, I ain't happy. Next time they call me, maybe I can do something else for you.'

Carla travelled back to New York that evening, pleased with what she'd discovered. Karen Teller was another smiling woman when she received an e-mail telling her the outcome of the visit.

## SIMON DINSDALE

***

Liam prowled around the house. Mary was away, and Patsy was out to get some shopping. His mood had darkened as the days of inactivity passed. He had little to do now except brood about how he missed the cop and try to avoid sleep. Scared of the inevitable nightmare that would follow.

He heard a car pull up outside and Mary came in.

'I didn't expect to see you.'

'I've got news about the house Dane's girlfriend went to. It belongs to his dear old mum and dad.'

Liam smiled for the first time in days, 'Brilliant.'

'I watched your man arrive there last Sunday. It's the best place to bring him when we are ready to finish that piece of business.'

'You're a marvel. I knew I could rely on you.'

# VENGEANCE DAY

## Chapter 13

The early November evening was cold and dismal, with an incessant drizzle soaking the shoulders of his coat. Dane hated this time of the year. The heavy rain-laden clouds made it seem darker than usual, almost black. The rain smeared the windscreen, refracting the insipid light of the streetlamps and the harsh headlights of oncoming cars. He mulled over the events of the past week. Things had gone well. The Dublin intelligence had proved accurate, and he was certain they would soon confirm that Subject one was Shanahan. The surveillance was working smoothly and the purchase of the van, although expected, was significant. Dane was sure it would prove to be the key to whatever the men were planning.

His father's condition was a source of worry. The doctor was now a regular visitor to monitor him while his temperature remained stubbornly high. When Dane rang his mother that morning, she mentioned that the previous evening he'd queried if life was worth living. This was so out of character; he changed his plans and was on his way to spend the weekend with them to give his mother some respite. Vicky was coming from Cambridge, but he wasn't looking forward to the next couple of days. The pressure of the week had left him feeling drained and more exhausted than usual. Three intense headaches during that time hadn't helped. A legacy of the head wound and the surgery. Either that, or I'm getting too old for all this, he thought.

The roads became narrower the further into the countryside he got. The rain was now heavy and hammering the windscreen. His headlights illuminated the running water and leaves in the road, and it took him more than an hour to reach the village. Dane passed the cottages on the single road that meandered through its heart. The pub's lights were blazing while the beautiful Norman church was in darkness. Dane swung the car into his parents' drive and parked, leaving enough space for Vicky. After letting himself in, he called out a greeting. No one replied, so he walked through the kitchen to the sitting room. His mother was sound asleep in her favourite chair.

Dane watched her for a moment, keeping quiet so as not to disturb her. A strong draft hit the back of his neck and made him shiver. He checked and found the outside door in the conservatory was swinging in the wind. A sudden swoop of fear coursed through the pit of his stomach, and he darted up the stairs. It took seconds to confirm his father wasn't in the house. Dane shook his mother gently on the shoulder. 'Mum, wake up.'

Her eyes fluttered open, and she smiled when she recognised him.

'Oh, hello dear. I didn't hear you come in. What time is it?'

'Where's dad?'

She looked straight at the empty chair, 'He'll be upstairs.'

'No, he isn't. He's not here.'

'I only sat down for a second. I've been so tired. Where is he?' she said, her voice faltering.

'Let's not panic. When did you last see him? Can you remember?'

'The six o'clock news had started. I asked him what he wanted for his tea. But he wasn't hungry. I must have dropped off. Are you sure he isn't upstairs?'

'He's not here, mum,' he glanced up as headlights swept across the front window, 'That'll be Vicky. Don't worry, he can't be far away. Did you leave the conservatory door open?'

'No, it was raining,' she stopped, and panic flared in her eyes, 'Oh no, he must be out there. He'll catch his death.' She tried to get up, but Dane gently restrained her.

'I'll do that. You stay here.'

Vicky walked into the kitchen and dropped her bag on the floor. Rainwater dripped from her hair.

'It is pouring down out…' She stopped when she saw the look on Dane's face, 'What's happened?'

'Dad has gone walkabout. Could you ring the control room and ask for a patrol to check the village. I'm going to find him. Take care of mum.'

## VENGEANCE DAY

'Yes, of course I will,' she replied and squeezed his hand, 'There was no sign of him on the road.'

'I think he slipped out the back. I won't be long.'

Dane found his father's flashlight in the garage. He then stood in the conservatory door and shone the powerful beam around the garden. A single set of footprints was clear in the wet grass. He followed them to the gate in the fence, which was swinging open. Beyond that, a huge, cultivated field stretched into the darkness. Dane played the light over the flat ground, but there was nothing there. A footpath ran along the headland to his right, so he followed it. The rain was torrential, and it soon soaked him to the skin. His shoes slithered across the mud, making it difficult to hurry.

After a hundred yards, the path turned ninety degrees left, alongside a ditch that was rapidly filling with water. A bundle appeared in the light and his heart skipped, but it was a pile of old sacking and fertiliser bags. The road was not much further away. Dane doubted the old man had the strength to make it that far, so he continued. Within seconds, he spotted him, half submerged in the ditch. Dane plunged down beside the inert form, gasping as the icy water chilled him. His father's face was deathly pale, and his lips looked black in the torchlight. He hauled the old man over his shoulder in a firefighter's lift. The steep bank was almost seven feet of smooth, slippery dirt, and Dane struggled to gain any purchase. He kicked into the mud to create a foothold, difficult with smart leather shoes. Twice he slid back into the freezing water before finally reaching the top and rolling his father onto the path. As he let go, he lost his footing and slithered back to the bottom. It took several more attempts before he clawed himself out. Dane lay there for a moment, his chest heaving. He pulled his phone out and breathed a sigh of relief when he saw it was still working, and he had a signal. With a mud encrusted finger, he pressed the speed dial for Vicky's mobile.

'I've found him. Call an ambulance. I'm on my way.'

He wrapped his sopping suit jacket around the inert body, then gathered the old man up in his arms and started running. Three times, his feet skidded from under him, sending them both crashing to the ground. As they fell, Dane twisted to make sure he landed first. The last fall drove the air from his lungs, and it took him several minutes to recover. Vicky appeared through the rain and helped him manhandle his father through the garden and into the house. Dane collapsed on the conservatory floor, caked in mud, and drenched. His mother screamed at the sight of them. Then Vicky took over.

'The ambulance is on the way. We must warm him up. Scissors, I need scissors,' she said, and he found a pair in the kitchen. Vicky cut the soaking clothes off, then wrapped him up with blankets and towels.

Dane comforted his mother. 'I'm a weak old fool. If only I hadn't fallen asleep,' she wailed as tears fell down her cheeks.

'It's not your fault. You can't do all this on your own. This is getting too much for you,' Dane said.

'He is he going to be alright, isn't he?'

'Of course, he is. He's a tough old bird, and not ready to go yet.' Flashing blue lights appeared on the road outside and Dane let the paramedics in.

They worked on his father for fifteen minutes before lifting him onto a stretcher. Vicky and his mother travelled in the ambulance while Dane cleaned himself up. At the hospital, he found them in the waiting room outside the intensive care unit.

A doctor spoke to them a few minutes later.

'We have settled your father down. His body temperature is dangerously low. How long was he immersed in the ditch?'

'It might have been as long as half an hour,' Dane replied.

'We are treating him for hypothermia. He has also got pneumonia. We will do our best to get him through this.'

'Thank you. Can we sit with him?'

'Yes, but only one person at a time, please.'

They agreed to take turns at the bedside. Dane persuaded his mother to let him take the first shift, and Vicky took her home. Once dressed in protective clothing and a facemask, a nurse led him into the unit. The sight that confronted him brought tears to his eyes. His father lay on his back, his upper body propped at a forty-degree angle and supported by pillows. A hospital gown and blanket covered his bony frame. Machines surrounded the bed. A ventilator was delivering oxygen through an endotracheal tube to assist breathing. Monitors bleeped and hissed as they checked cardiac and other bodily functions or pumped drugs into him. A bewildering mass of leads was attached to his chest and arms. Drips supplied saline and a urinary catheter led to a receptacle that only had a dribble of yellow fluid in it. Not a good sign.

The nurse pointed to a chair.

'You can sit there. Please try not to touch any of the equipment. I know this all looks horrible, but it is all to help your father.'

'Thank you,' Dane replied and settled down, taking hold of the bony hand that felt ice cold. He stayed through the night whispering to his father. He recalled the fun they had shared in the years before their split. Dane talked about their long walks together. How his father instructed him in the art of photography. The hours they spent processing the films and developing the pictures in the cellar darkroom. Every few minutes, a nurse would appear at the bedside and check the machines.

As the night wore on, Dane could feel the warmth returning to his father's hand and the urine bag slowly filled. The more of their past he recollected, the more Dane came to realise how stupid he had been. How could he have allowed their rift to last for so long? And now his father was close to death without them resolving the problem.

'We must sort this out, dad. Please God, don't take him just yet,' he murmured.

Dane dozed off in the early hours and woke with a start as the nurse moved around the bed, checking the monitors, and replacing an empty drip. He had a painful crick in his neck and stood to stretch and walk to the toilet. When he returned, his mother and Vicky were at the door to the ward.

'You're early,' he said.

'I couldn't keep her away,' Vicky replied.

'How is he doing?' Mrs Dane asked.

'I think the correct terminology is that he spent a comfortable night.'

'Thank heavens. You must be exhausted. Get home. I will be fine here.'

'Okay, mum. We'll be back later.'

As they walked to the car, Vicky took his hand.

'She was up at half-past six. I almost had to tie her down to make her eat something.'

'She can be pretty determined when she gets going. Did you sleep alright?'

'Yes, I did. Now you need to get your head down before you collapse.'

Dane was back at the bedside on Saturday night. As the sun rose the following morning, he was reminiscing about a family trip when he felt his father squeeze his hand. Dane sat bolt upright. A nurse was on the other side of the bed.

'Was I asleep?'

'No. You were talking to your father.'

'I am sure he just responded.'

'That's not a surprise. He can hear you, so keep talking to him.' Dane's eyes misted with tears of relief. He was now confident it would be alright.

Late Sunday afternoon, the doctor examined his father, then spoke to Dane and his mother.

'His condition has stabilised. We are through the worst of it. But he is still gravely ill. I'm afraid he will be with us for some time.'

'Thank you for everything you have done,' Dane replied, 'My mother is insistent on staying with him. Can you accommodate her?'

'Yes, of course. Might I suggest you go home for a couple of hours and get some rest? I'll organise a bed and let you know when we are ready.'

All they could do now was wait. Dane's mother still blamed herself for allowing her husband to slip out.

## VENGEANCE DAY

'We'll get you help. I know you don't want him to go into a home. Nor do I, but you can't look after him on your own,' Dane said.

'Perhaps that is the best solution,' she replied.

'I'll start making enquiries about it tomorrow. Now, before I go, are there any jobs you need doing around here?'

'Could you check the trapdoor to the cellar, please? It's been creaking and I'm scared I'll fall through it.'

The cellar had once been the darkroom. A couple of months before, and without explanation, his father had packed all the equipment away, and it reverted to a storeroom. The door was in the ceiling and opened into the double garage above. Dane checked it and found it was sound.

'Try not to park the car on top of it. It's not designed to take much weight.'

'I'll keep to the side of the carpet we put down on the floor to stop draughts. I can walk on that, can't I?'

'Yes, but nothing heavier.'

Dane and Vicky left her later that evening. His mother insisted she could manage on her own and would spend most of her time at the hospital.

'You've both got important jobs to do. I'll be alright. They'll take good care of us.'

Dane hugged Vicky by her car.

'Thanks for everything. I couldn't have managed without you.'

'Your dad is a lovely man. Let's hope he's on his feet soon.'

'Crap weekend, eh?'

'There will be plenty more to enjoy. Don't work too hard. I love you,' she whispered.

Dane was taken aback. It was the first time Vicky had said this to him. It felt the most natural thing in the world to reply, 'I love you too.'

\*

Dane reached his desk at seven on Monday morning. He was fighting a pounding headache, which was resisting pain killers. He found it difficult to concentrate as Paul Lamb informed him that only Subject One, going for his customary runs, had left the house over the weekend. The observation point was operating efficiently, and everything was in place for the week ahead.

Hayley Cross came in next, armed with bacon sandwiches and tea. As they ate, she reported that both the cars had been hired both for a month. A man calling himself Michael Hanrahan, who provided a fake British driving licence as identification, paid for the Frinton car.

'Hanrahan is Subject One. I searched the car and found a pen down by the driver's seat. It's one of those freebees you get in hotels,' Hayley said.

'Do we know where it came from?'

'Yes, a hotel close to Luton airport. I'm about to go over there.'

'I've got a meeting at Stevenage this afternoon. I'll come with you. What's the score with the other cars?'

'Subject Three hired the second one. He used a British licence in the name of Smith. They're well supplied with fake identities this lot.'

'Did they provide a contact phone number?'

Hayley nodded, 'They both gave the same mobile. An unregistered pay as you go purchased from a supermarket five months ago. No calls in or out and a historical cell site analysis confirms it's always at the house.'

'Thanks for doing that. Good job.'

Dane then spoke to Ali Frampton, who told him that two of the subjects had just left in the van and they were following.

Dane and Hayley arrived at the hotel an hour later and found James, the manager. Hayley showed him a photograph of the pen with his company logo and number. He turned to the reception desk and picked up an identical one from a holder containing about a hundred of them.

'We give them away by the handful. They're in all the bedrooms and the stationery packs we provide to the conference rooms.'

'Do you recall a group of Irish people either as guests or booking a meeting room?' Dane asked.

# VENGEANCE DAY

James shook his head.

'No, we're busy here every day. Let's talk to Paula, my deputy. She looks after that side of the business. She's got a memory like a bleeding elephant.'

Paula was more forthcoming, 'That rings a bell. Let me check through the records.' She pulled a large ring binder from a filing cabinet and leafed through it.

'Here we are. Late August. An IT company according to this.' She passed over the form.

Mary Reilly made the booking. Representing Collins IT services with an address and telephone number in Dublin.

'Who filled this out?' Hayley asked.

'I did. She dictated the details for me to fill the various boxes,' Paula replied.

'But she signed it?'

'Yes.'

'How many people attended?'

'No idea, I'm afraid. I was on holiday then. They booked refreshments for a dozen. The organisers of these events are usually on a budget. They tend not to overbook the food. And this lady paid in cash.'

'Is that unusual?'

'Most use a company credit card. But it's not that out of the ordinary.'

'Who showed them to their room?'

'I was on duty that day. So, I probably did that,' James replied, 'But I don't recall them.'

'Which one were they in?'

'The smallest. We put groups of between a dozen to twenty people in there.'

'Do you have CCTV here?'

'Yes, but we only keep the images stored for a calendar month. There's won't be anything from those days, sorry.'

Hayley pulled a photo from her bag. Paula stared at it for a few seconds, then nodded, 'That's her. What's she done?'

'Nothing. But we're interested in her movements. Can you recall anything else about her? Was she alone when she visited you?'

'She was on her own. There might have been someone waiting outside, I suppose.'

'Thanks for your help. We'll need to take the original booking form please.'

'Sure, that's not a problem. We've made a copy. Are they dangerous?'

'Not to you.'

As they walked through the car park, Dane looked around.

'We'd better check with the local police to find out if there are any fixed ANPR cameras in the area. We can run the numbers of the cars we know about. What do you make of this?'

'Looks to me like a bunch of people who're spread out meeting at a central point to catch up with each other.'

'I agree. They came here a week before being spotted in the States. And it's the right number. That's a large gang for a terrorist cell, though. The classic IRA Active Service Unit would be only half a dozen operators, maximum. They might have a few backup personnel. But twelve is on the big side.'

'Two teams?' Hayley suggested.

'It is a possibility. We're expecting a spectacular, and this crew isn't your normal ASU. Let's run over to Stevenage. I've got to meet with the spooks, and I'll mention what we've found here.'

Hayley took a coffee to the smoking area as Dane joined Karen Teller. She had news of her own.

'I've just heard from the surveillance team. They've been following the men from the house who are driving around housing estates and parking. Sometimes alongside the kerbside. Or they shunt back and forward, half on the pavement or over the kerb. The team has seen nothing like this before. But they are sure it's not an anti-surveillance manoeuvre. Once they stop, they look down at something in the cab. Then check where they are pointing. Does that sound familiar to you?'

'Never heard of that.'

## VENGEANCE DAY

'They've been at it all morning. They do a couple of stops, then drive off to another part of town. There's no rhyme or reason to where they go or stop. They seem oblivious to what's behind them.'

'Weird!' Dane said, then told Karen what he'd learnt.

*

The surveillance team watched the men from the house practice their strange parking manoeuvres in the days that followed. Two of them would go out in the morning, then return for lunch. Later in the afternoon, they would change round and do the same again. No one had any idea what they were up too.

Dane travelled up to London on the Thursday and met Perkins in the café for a quick chat before the meeting.

'You look awful, are you alright?' Perkins said.

'Tired, that's all,' Dane replied and recounted what had happened at the weekend.

'Bloody hell. Do you need some time off?'

'No thanks. He's on the mend, but still extremely ill. Perhaps when he gets out of the hospital, I'll take some leave. But right now, I must concentrate on this job.'

'Remember. You put your family first. If I can help, make sure you ask, okay?'

'I appreciate that. So, what about this meeting? Do I need to know anything before we start?'

'There's been more pressure to cut back on your surveillance,' Perkins said, 'A certain party thinks you're overdoing it. He wants the resources for his operation. I've resisted and Shaw has backed me up but expect another blast today.'

They walked round to the special operations building and joined Karen in the waiting area.

'I have heard from the Yanks. My contact has given me some very interesting information. Sorry I didn't let you know earlier but I've only just got off the phone with her.' They were speaking as they filed in to start the meeting.

Shaw greeted everyone and gave the floor to Dane to brief them.

'The most significant update is the link to Maire o'Suilleabhain. I'll refer to her as Mary. Everywhere we go, we cross her tracks. She rented the place in Essex and the conference room in Luton. It's likely that at least a dozen people were there. To date, we've only seen the three occupants of the house. So, we are missing another nine. The surveillance must continue in case they meet up with their friends. We also need to establish what they are up to with the van.'

'This is all very tenuous,' Brown drawled, 'And is wasting a lot of resources for little in return. If this gang of Irish are being suspicious go and turn them over. They are a distraction and you're making a meal of it.'

Dane turned and regarded him.

'I assume the resources we release are to go to your investigation?'

'Yes, and not before time. My guys are being run ragged. It's becoming more difficult by the day to maintain the coverage. We know what the threat is, and it is not from this lot.'

'If we pop those three. What about the other nine?'

'If they exist,' Brown sneered.

Karen caught Shaw's eye.

'I just spoke to my contact in New York who has given me some interesting information. They have identified and interviewed a source who works inside the property we are interested in. Eleven Irish citizens visited for a week and spent their time in a killing house practicing how to counter hostage rescue tactics. The owner, Logan, operates the place as a dude ranch where you can shoot a variety of military hardware. The entire operation is a lucrative business venture for him.'

'So rich gun nuts go to the States and fire a few bullets. That doesn't mean that they are going to come here and perpetrate an attack,' Brown said.

'These were not any old Irish tourists. We have positively identified Mary as being there. As were Subjects Two and Three from Frinton. We stick to our original assessment,' Karen concluded.

Shaw nodded decisively.

# VENGEANCE DAY

'I'm satisfied this operation is viable and should continue with the current level of resources. Your aim, Mr Dane, remains to identify those involved in this conspiracy. That is now to include the nine other suspected members of the group. Are we all in agreement?' She glanced around the table and stared at Brown, who glowered at Dane but said nothing, 'Good, we will meet here again next Thursday.'

# SIMON DINSDALE

## Chapter 14

The bizarre driving and parking antics continued throughout the week as the three men alternated between them, never leaving the property unattended. The surveillance teams tried everything to get close enough to discover what they were doing in the cab, but to no avail. Dane knew the trip to the United States had been to prepare for whatever they had planned. The revelation that they practiced counter hostage rescue tactics caught the attention of the Executive Liaison Group. But what did it signify? Would it be a bomb, or the kidnap of a celebrity, or a Mumbai type attack? The people responsible for protecting senior royals, government ministers and retired politicians who once held sensitive posts checked their charges for upcoming movements and engagements. They were all attractive targets. In the light of the heightened threat, plans were reviewed, and even more stringent security precautions put in place. The same applied to the most obvious public buildings.

Dane and Karen spent hours together discussing the problem trying to work out who or what might be the potential target. They both agreed there was plenty for the terrorists to choose from. Dane doubted it would be a suicide attack. That had never been the Irish way. They preferred to escape once they had completed their mission, and the thought of dying was anathema to their Catholic upbringing. A Mumbai style outrage in the capital had to be the worst possible scenario. Specially trained armed counter terrorist patrols had augmented the largely unarmed British police in recent years and were on permanent standby. But even they could not respond in time to prevent the high casualty numbers such a tactic always caused.

No one knew when and where it would happen, or how the terrorists might do it? The classic dilemma for the authorities.

'Can't we go back to the original source and ask if they have anything else? There must be more than they have given us. We should task them to find out?' Dane said.

'I've already done that, but we must be patient. This one is extremely sensitive and well placed. But they're difficult to tie

# VENGEANCE DAY

down for a meeting. My masters are aware of how important this is,' Karen replied.

Dane understood the difficulties of running such an informant. At least MI5 had someone on the inside to ask. But the time it was taking to receive a reply frustrated him.

They had still not heard anything by the Wednesday when Lamb walked into his office.

'Have you got a minute? There's something you ought to see.'

Dane followed the Inspector to a small windowless room being used to view the video from the observation point. Every morning, an officer reviewed the previous day's footage and compared it to the surveillance log. It was Hayley's turn today.

'Have a look at this.'

Hayley pressed the play button and the street leading to the target house in the distance came on. Samson was walking nonchalantly along the footpath towards the golf club. As he reached the side fence, he stood on tiptoe and peered over into the rear garden before moving out of sight. Hayley pushed the fast forward, and the images whirled across on the screen until she started the film again. Twenty minutes had elapsed when Samson reappeared. As he got halfway back, she paused, freezing him in mid-stride.

'Look there.' She pointed to the top right window and magnified the image. A figure was behind the window watching Samson through a pair of binoculars.

'Where is he?' Dane said.

'He's with White in Frinton on the day shift. Do you want me to bring them out?' Lamb replied.

After a moment's consideration, Dane shook his head.

'No, we'll go up there.' He tapped Hayley on the shoulder, 'Brilliant job, well done.'

A muscle ticked in Dane's jaw as he struggled to control his anger. What on earth had Samson been doing. And why? Thirty minutes into their journey, he turned to Lamb. 'Paul, can they see the gate to the property the observation point is in?'

'No, it's around the bend.'

'That's one small mercy, I suppose. What was the fool thinking?'

'Sorry boss. I shouldn't have put them there.'

'It's not your fault. We had to use them.'

They drove into Frinton, and Dane phoned Ali to inform him where they were going.

'Everything's quiet here. They haven't gone out today. Shall we let them know you're coming?'

'No, there's no need to do that.'

They parked outside the flat. Lamb was about to knock when Dane stopped him.

'Hang on, let's surprise them.'

He took a leather pouch from his pocket and selected two slim implements. Seconds later, they walked up the stairs to the unmistakable sound of two people enjoying noisy sex. They looked at each other in disbelief, then crept along the passageway to the sitting room and found it empty. The cameras were operating, but no one had eyes on the target. Lamb nodded to the bedroom, where the grunts of ecstasy continued.

Dane took three strides and kicked the door, sending it crashing back on its hinges. He waited a moment, giving Carol White time to wriggle off the bed, dragging the sheets over her. Samson rolled onto his back with a confused expression. The colour drained from his face when he saw who was standing there. Dane regarded them both. White's eyes, wide with shock, peered back at him over the mattress.

'Get dressed,' he snapped, then spun on his heel.

'This is a first,' Lamb said.

'Change the disk. Then review the last hour's footage, please.'

Lamb set to work as Dane watched the house. Ten minutes later, and after a tense whispered conversation, the two officers emerged from the bedroom.

'I ...' Samson said.

'Don't bother to even try,' Dane interrupted. He didn't raise his voice, but his tone was unmistakable.

'I get this looks bad. But we've done no harm. The cameras are operating. Everything is recording.'

'Oh yes. It's all on record. Just like your stroll yesterday. What was that all about?'

'I don't know what you mean?'

## VENGEANCE DAY

'Do not take me for an idiot. Why did you walk to the house and look over the fence?'

'I wanted to get a feel for the place.'

'Well, you alerted them. They watched you all the way back.'

Samson recoiled as if he'd been slapped.

'They couldn't have seen me turn in here.'

'You had better hope so. But your actions have compromised this operation. Who told you to do it?'

'No one,' Samson replied, with a hint of defiance.

'Boss, see what they've missed,' Lamb said, pointing to the monitor, his face pale with anger.

Lamb pressed play and Dane watched a dark saloon arrive and swing into the driveway. Subject Two appeared at the door as Mary got out of the car. She gazed down the road while stretching the kinks out of her back. Behind her, a figure hopped out of the passenger's side and ducked straight inside. Another man rolled out of the rear seat and followed the others.

The screen clock showed this all happened two hours before. Dane glared at Samson, whose jaw had gone slack at what he had just seen. White was beside him and watched in horror. Lamb fast forwarded the film and stopped it fifteen minutes before their arrival when the same three returned to the car and drove away. There was an unobstructed view of the woman and the second male, but they obscured the man who got into the front seat. Because of the angle, they couldn't see the registration number as it left nor when they arrived.

'Paul, bring another team up to take over here.'

Dane gestured to the two Met officers, 'Gather your kit and go home. You're sacked from this investigation. Now get out of my sight.'

Samson appeared to be about to say something but changed his mind and stalked off down the stairs. White whispered, 'I'm so sorry, sir. I have no excuse.'

Dane took a moment to gather his thoughts and stared out of the window. He puffed his cheeks out.

'Right, let's try to retrieve this. Send the disk to the lab and hope they can decipher the index number. At least we've now got a confirmed connection with Mary and this place. How long before the relief crew arrives?'

'I've scrambled a couple out of the office. They'll fill in until the night shift gets here.'

An hour later they watched the garage doors open, and the van drove away. Lamb notified Frampton, who reported they had it under control. As Dane drove back to Chelmsford he rang Karen about the pictures.

'It's Mary all right. But I've no idea who the third person is and there's no clear image of the man from the front seat. We'll check our records and try to identify them. I wouldn't hold your breath, though. This is a turn up. What's so special about today that she should visit, I wonder,' Karen said.

'I don't know, but something is moving. The surveillance team have followed the van to a self-storage depot in Chelmsford. It's taken them two hours to get there. They performed three anti surveillance manoeuvres on the way. They've never behaved like this before. Have you heard any more news from the States or Ireland?'

'No, nothing yet.'

'Karen. What exactly did they do there? The information just refers to lots of shooting and the exercises in the killing house. What do they mean by that?'

'Hang on, I'll check the message again.' Dane listened as she tapped a computer keyboard, 'All it mentions is weapons training.'

'Call your mate over there and find out exactly what they fired or had a go with. We know they have extensive experience with small arms, and you can never have enough practice. But what else did they do? I think that's where the answer is.'

'Okay, I take your point. I'll ring New York.'

Dane put the phone down. He was still seething with anger at the behaviour of the Met officers. An ELG was scheduled for the following morning where they would discuss the matter.

He got back to his office and had nearly finished his notes when Vicky called.

'Hello darling. I'm heading home soon. Are you at the airport?'

'What… Oh God, I'm still in the bloody office.'

## VENGEANCE DAY

'You didn't forget, did you?'

'No of course not. Well, yes, it slipped my mind. I've had a seriously rough day. I'll tell you about it at the weekend. When did she land?'

'Not for another hour. Her flight's delayed.'

'No worries, I will make it in time.'

'How do you catch all those killers if you can't even remember when your own daughter is coming home?'

'Okay, don't rub it in. I'll ring you when we get home. Robyn will want to talk with you.'

Dane grabbed his coat and ran to his car. I should just make it, he thought, and offered a prayer to whichever deity controlled the traffic on the M25 to give him a clear drive to Heathrow. As he reached the airport, he received a call from Frampton.

'They're home. No stopping or practice parking. It's as if they've gone into operational mode.'

'That could well be what's happened. They receive a visit, then react like this. Were you able to see what they collected?'

'No. They reversed up to the loading area of the storage unit. One went in and the other stayed in the van. At no time did they leave it unattended, and the driver had eyes all over the place. The second bloke returned with a trolley carrying a box about five feet long and another half the size. Our guy described them as two heavy aluminium containers. They put a couple of large holdalls in as well. I decided not to enquire with the management there.'

'You did the right thing. We can always go back there later. Are you happy they didn't spot you?'

'We're too good for the likes of them.'

Dane made it in time and was waiting in arrivals as Robyn came through the sliding doors and gave him a tight hug. He forgot his troubles as they drove home.

SIMON DINSDALE

**Chapter 15**

Time was dragging. They were close to the end, but every hour felt like an eternity to Liam, who was becoming more irritable by the minute. He was only dozing for a few hours at night. As soon as his eyes closed the flashing vivid images taunted him, and he would wake drenched in sweat. He craved sleep but feared it more and wasn't sure how much longer he could bear the sight of Martin dying in front of him.

Everything was in place. The vans were prepared and ready to go. The chosen drivers could point the nose of the vehicle on a compass bearing with no fuss. Their security was watertight. They had visited the teams and informed them what their target was to be. Everyone was astonished, then energised by the sheer audaciousness of the plan. Liam allowed himself to daydream about success and his plans for the immediate aftermath. Only then would he purge himself of the guilt of not being able to save his brother.

The television was on, and he flicked through the channels but couldn't settle on any one program. His head was fuzzy from lack of sleep, and it was increasingly difficult to concentrate. The throbbing behind his eyes increased. He pushed his thumb and forefinger into the junction of his nose and the corner of each eye and squeezed hard. It didn't help, so went to find some pain relief, but couldn't find what he was looking for.

Liam tore at the cans of soup and cereal boxes in the kitchen cupboard, spilling them across the worktop and onto the floor. He spotted the small foil sheet on the windowsill, lying where he'd left it an hour before.

Patsy came in and glanced at the mess. 'Are you alright?'

'Sure, I am. Got a wee bit of headache. Where've you been?' Liam replied, swallowing three tablets.

'Took a walk to check about the area. It's all quiet. I've brought you the papers and some nice fish for our tea. Why don't you get some sleep? You look like crap.'

'I'll try later. Has Mary rung?'

'Yeah, she'll be here soon.'

## VENGEANCE DAY

Mary arrived and surveyed the kitchen. Without a word, she tidied up.

'Are we all set?' Liam asked.

'Yes. We can hit them in the evening after we finish the mission. It'll be quick and easy. We'll be away hours before anyone finds them.'

'You're a good comrade, Mary.'

'I only want what's best for the cause,' she replied. 'Once we've finished this. You must be ready to focus on how we win the war.'

'I'll never forget what you've done for me.'

Liam slept better that night, only having to suffer the nightmare once. Perhaps it was the imminent action that relaxed him. Or his brain had had enough of the images. Whatever the reason, his mood lightened the next morning.

*

Karen was at her desk long after her colleagues had left for the day. As the evening progressed, a sense of frustration enveloped her. Her team had been unable to identify the two men seen with Mary. She'd not received anything from the source handlers, or Carla. She didn't have the answers they needed and was feeling drained and useless. The Executive Liaison Group meeting was scheduled for the following morning and unless things changed soon, she wouldn't have much to tell them. To make matters worse, she was losing four of her staff for the weekend.

Her boss had tried to mollify her by explaining that the other threats are the more credible, and she would get everyone back on Monday. Karen knew he was right, but it irritated her. There was never enough staff to go round. It didn't matter how much extra work their masters dumped on them, they still had to deliver the same results.

Carla rang just before midnight.

'Hi, sorry it's so late. I needed to check a couple of things to make sure I've got them straight.' Ten minutes later, Karen left for home with a smile on her face.

*

The atmosphere was tense as they assembled on Thursday morning. Alex Brown was already in his place when Dane and

Perkins arrived. He didn't acknowledge either of them. Karen bustled in with apologies for her late arrival as the meeting got underway.

'The first item is the return to the Met of Detective Sergeant Samson and Constable White,' Shaw said.

Brown leant forward, his face pale, a muscle ticked in his jaw.

'I want to know who Dane thinks he is. I send him two experienced officers, at serious cost to my own investigation. They are put to work doing menial tasks. Then I'm informed Samson and White have been summarily sacked. All this without a by your leave or permission from me. Well. It's time for an explanation, laddie. And it had better be a bloody good one.'

'Before I explain my reasons. What did they tell you?' Dane replied.

'Only that you victimised and bullied them both. White has gone sick and requested a transfer to uniform. She won't answer my calls.'

'I assume you've only spoken to Samson?'

'Yes, he's an outstanding officer and I don't like what I've heard.'

'I see. Two days ago, Samson compromised the observation point by walking past the target house and peering over the fence. The occupants spotted him. They watched through binoculars as he returned to the observation point. Samson told me he did it because he wanted to get a feel for the place.'

'As I understand it, the entrance is not within a direct line of sight from the target premises,' Brown retorted.

'No, it isn't. Which is the only saving grace from this entire episode. But he was lying. He didn't do that of his own accord. Did he?' Dane replied, looking pointedly at Brown.

'He was checking the rear of that residence on my instructions.'

'I've no knowledge of a request for information from you. You're out-of-order getting Samson to do something like that. You compromised my investigation.'

'I'm in charge round here, laddie. I don't need to ask your permission for anything.'

## VENGEANCE DAY

'I think you'll find that I am running this operation,' Shaw interjected, her voice icy, 'And I hope you've got an explanation for this incredible behaviour. But first, explain why you didn't pass your request through, Mr Dane?'

'I needed the information in a hurry and Samson was there.'

'That's not acceptable. On many levels.'

'Okay. I should have gone through Dane. But he has no right to send them both back.'

'I sacked them because when I arrived in Frinton yesterday, I found Samson and White in bed having sex. While they were amusing themselves, they missed the arrival and departure of a car containing Mary and two unknown males. They were in the house for more than two hours. That's how long your experienced officers were at it.'

Brown's jaw dropped. This was obviously not what he'd heard from Samson.

'We will deal with this matter later, but I'm not happy,' Shaw said, then glanced at Dane.

'Is there anything new on the investigation?'

'Two of the occupants of the house drove to Chelmsford soon after their visitors left. They collected several large and heavy items from a self-storage facility. Ali Frampton informed me they were performing anti-surveillance manoeuvres throughout the journey and were very jumpy. My assessment is they received their instructions and are now preparing to execute their plan. Flashes of intense light have been observed coming from the garage overnight. They appear to be welding something, probably in the van.'

'I have some additional information from my contact in New York,' Karen interjected, 'Apart from the small arms training the whole group spent a day and a half learning how to use a mortar. That included how to prepare the ammunition, set up, aim, and fire the weapon.'

Dane looked around the room, his mind working. Then it all became clear.

'They're going to mortar the Remembrance Parade. Hundreds of Northern Ireland veterans are due to be marching. There's nothing else planned this weekend that could be a more tempting target for them.'

'That's a bit of a leap, isn't it?' Brown replied, 'Just because they were playing with them doesn't mean they've got one. Their record of success with mortar attacks in the past is dismal. And the security in central London will prevent them from getting within miles of Whitehall. Their home-made rubbish is no good over that distance.'

'Unless they possess some military grade pieces,' Dane replied.

'Where would they pick up that sort of kit from, for God's sake?' Brown retorted, now recovered from the shock of the Samson revelation.

'Four surplus British Army mortars, with ammunition, were stolen from a bonded warehouse in Bahrain last summer.'

There was a stunned silence before Shaw asked,

'Where did you get that information?'

'I investigated the murder of the man sent over there to look into the theft.'

'The Iranians stole them. And they passed it all to Hezbollah in Lebanon,' Brown said.

'The men responsible were Iranians. The Interior Minister of the Bahraini government informed me personally how they smuggled the weapons out of his country. You'll find an intelligence report somewhere with my name on it stating that. But who says Hezbollah got them?'

'You don't need to...'

'Oh, will you give the old "need to know" tosh a rest, and answer this,' Dane snapped, 'Why would Iranian agents go to the trouble of obtaining access to a munitions store in a foreign country and only steal four mortars? They openly supply them to terrorist organisations and boast about it. They took those weapons for a specific purpose. An attack we couldn't trace to them. Or so they thought.'

'The Iranians wouldn't pass this type of kit to the Irish. They always refused to deal with the IRA, so they won't help a dissident group. And how did they bring them into this country? It's all too fantastic,' Brown stated, then addressed Shaw.

## VENGEANCE DAY

'Ma'am, what we face is not some half-baked plan. We must put all our available resources into protecting Whitehall on Sunday. I can't do this without more staff.'

'We are all well aware of that,' Shaw replied, then turned to Dane, 'Our operation has identified ten young men who we've watched prepare for this weekend. They are intent on a co-ordinated suicide attack by detonating their bomb vests as near to the Cenotaph as they can get. I hardly need to tell you who will be there. And no one on that long list of dignitaries has any intention of not attended the parade.'

Dane knew better than to doubt what Shaw had just said. But he was certain the crew in Frinton were preparing their own attack. It couldn't be a coincidence. First, they were trained to operate a mortar in the States. Then they practise parking in odd positions. The reason for that became clear.

'They are going to use the van as the firing platform.' He turned to Karen, 'There's been no mention of mortars from any of your sources, has there?'

'No, none,' she replied, 'But it makes sense, though. Why would they bother being instructed on how to use them? They must have a good reason for doing that.'

Dane looked at the senior officers around the table.

'We're certain they number at least a dozen. There are three in Frinton and another three who turned up yesterday. Mary ordered meals for twelve at the hotel. And there were eleven of them were in the US. That adds up to a crew of three per mortar.'

'We'd know if they'd obtained stuff like that,' Brown insisted, 'There is a corroborated threat of an Islamic attack on Sunday. All you've got are the three in Frinton and a hypothesis. I'm sorry, but that's how it is.'

It pained Dane, but he had to admit Brown was right.

'May I suggest then that we arrest the men in Frinton as soon as possible? That might disrupt the others and give us more time. We can manage this and the interviews from within Essex.'

Shaw looked at Perkins, who nodded.

'We'll do that easily.'

'Does everyone concur?' Shaw said. They all raised their hands.

## SIMON DINSDALE

The meeting broke up. Dane and Perkins travelled back to Chelmsford, where they had a tense session with the chief constable. Dane outlined the tactics he would like to employ to enter the house to make the arrests.

'We've got to secure them quickly,' Dane said, 'If we follow our usual approach and breach the door to call them out, we'll have a siege. These people won't surrender willingly. They know our tactics, including how our teams enter a building, and they practiced that in America. If we give them the time to prepare for an assault, people will lose their lives. They'll also be able to warn their mates and destroy information that might lead us to the others. We don't have a choice, ma'am. We must do it this way.'

VENGEANCE DAY

## Chapter 16

Dane stifled a yawn and glanced at the clock on the wall. It was a few minutes before three in the morning. A low hum of muted conversations surrounded him as the sports hall in Clacton police station filled with people. Paul Lamb was with the team of detectives who would make the arrests and transport the suspects into custody at the back of the hall. Closer stood a group of black clad officers from the force Operational Support Group. They all carried bulky rucksacks which they dropped next to their chairs then nonchalantly placed their firearms on top. The light-hearted banter between them all reminded Dane of missions in Ireland that reached the point when things were about to go noisy, to use the military parlance. When Dane, the covert operator, handed over to the Blades from the Special Forces. It had been their job to conduct the surgical strike and arrest the bad guys.

The only difference now was police officers were going instead of soldiers. There were thirty-seven of the elite firearms team. Men, and women, who had all passed the rigorous selection and training process to handle the most dangerous of assignments. Most were in their late twenties or early thirties, with a couple of grizzled veterans. They were all fit and alert, their quiet confidence bolstered with the arrogance of knowing they were the best. A tall burly man with a shaven head in his forties arrived. Known to all as Knocker, he was the raid team leader. He strolled to his seat, then nodded a greeting to Dane. Knocker would be the first in the door with another five, including two women, right behind him. The sight of female officers decked out in the black garb and armed to the teeth was now so commonplace it no longer drew comment. Dane had spent time with Knocker earlier. Hayley had acquired the floor plans of the house and some photographs of the interior from the letting agent. The raid team took these, together with high altitude pictures of the estate in Frinton and laid out a scale model. They then talked through and rehearsed how they would assault the building. Dane admired their professionalism.

## SIMON DINSDALE

Assistant Chief Constable Perkins and Chief Inspector Alison Myers, the head of the Firearms Support Group and the operational commander for the evening, sat next to him at the table. Alison had an excellent reputation and had commanded many such high-risk operations. As she prepared her papers, Dane noticed her hands shook slightly and were red and blotchy with eczema. Which proved she was human and as nervous as everyone else.

The room fell silent as Alison delivered her meticulous briefing, which lasted an hour. The officers listened intently, taking notes, and asking pertinent questions. By the time she finished, everyone knew their positions and when they should in them.

Dane still felt nervous about suggesting this tactic. It carried a much higher risk of something going wrong.

Perkins stood to offer words of encouragement.

'We believe that the men living in this house are in the final stages of planning for their attack. It's vital you secure them all before they can react. The last thing we need is a protracted siege situation. So good luck and please be careful.'

Then, with a mass scraping of chairs, everyone stood and got ready to move out. Dane had time a quick conversation with Lamb and the detectives. The Support Group Sergeants inspected their teams who were all dressed in black coveralls, bulky body armour and heavy military style ballistic helmets with night vision goggles. Each officer carried either a Heckler & Koch MP5 carbine or a G36 rifle, depending on their role. A Glock pistol sat in a holster. Stun grenades, torches, and plastic ties to handcuff the prisoners dangled from raid vests, and flame-retardant masks covered their faces. Some carried Taser's, the usual bright yellow grips now painted black. With the inspection complete, weapons were loaded, and safety catches applied. The banter died out as everyone focused and moved into operational mode before boarding the vehicles.

Dane drove to the observation point with Alison. A technician had installed a powerful thermal image camera trained on the house, which streamed to one of two monitors on a table by the

## VENGEANCE DAY

window. The second showed live pictures beamed from Knocker's body camera. They took their seats facing the screens and put on headsets. At 0500hrs on Saturday morning, the order was given to move in. With no moonlight and heavy cloud, the bleak November night was black as pitch. A row of ghostly glowing figures appeared on the monitors, scuttling into position to take up firing positions and covering the building with their rifles. More entered the garden to cover the rear and sides. Dane could see the pin prick fluorescent green glow from their goggles on the monitor, like the eyes of a nocturnal animal caught in headlights. It reminded him of a wild-life film. The only thing missing was the hushed tones of a narrator describing how the hunters were surrounding their prey. Dane turned his attention to the live feed from Knocker as he arrived at the front door and waited.

'All unit's report when you are ready,' Alison said.

A series of clicks came over the airwaves that she ticked them off against her sheet. When they ended, Alison glanced at Dane, nodded, then spoke over the radio.

'All units stand by, stand by, stand by ...'

Everything was silent, except for the sounds of breathing over the open microphones. Alison listened on another channel for a few moments, then said. 'The power is off, strike, strike, strike and good luck.'

Dane watched on the monitor as Knocker slid the key into the lock and turned it. To everyone's obvious relief, the door opened an inch to reveal the glint of the security chain through the crack. A pair of bolt cutters appeared from behind Knocker and snipped it. He crossed the threshold, eyes, camera, and weapon sweeping left to right across the hallway. All clear. Three swift steps to reach the bottom of the stairs. Knocker advanced up them, placing his feet gently, testing for that creaking step. Dane held his breath. There had to be one. There always was.

At the top, Knocker stopped beside the first bedroom door, then turned as his number two tucked in behind him. An officer in the ground floor hallway confirmed that the downstairs was secure. Knocker chopped a quick hand signal and four more officers filed past him and along the landing. As the last couple reached their door, one of them stepped on the inevitable loose floorboard, which gave out a loud groan in protest at the pressure. Then it went noisy.

Knocker pushed his door open and lobbed a distraction grenade into the bedroom. Stunning explosions shattered the still night air, followed instantly by flashes of searing light which illuminated all the windows. Knocker's camera jerked as he darted in and to the left, his firearm sweeping the room. A figure rose from the far side of the double bed, holding a pistol which he fired twice. Knocker fired back, then advanced to check the man who had fallen beside the window. Dane saw a naked man with three neat bullet holes in the middle of his chest on the monitor. His eyes were wide in death and there was surprisingly little blood. Satisfied the terrorist was no longer a threat, Knocker returned to his number 2. After giving him first aid he reported, 'Shots fired. One target down, one friendly injured who requires casualty evacuation now.'

When he'd finished assisting his mate, Knocker walked along the hallway to check the other bedrooms. In each, a man lay handcuffed face down on the floor, with the officers covering them. Knocker returned to the original bedroom and reported again, his voice sounding tense.

'All secure. Subjects one and three are in custody, with no injuries. Send up the medics.'

Dane, followed by Alison, sprinted up the road, feeling sick to his stomach. This was all his responsibility. The operation and the tactics used had all been his idea. Now someone had died, and an officer was injured. He stopped, panting, at the gate and watched as the paramedics were escorted inside.

Dozens of neighbours in their night clothes stood silently in their gardens or peering out of upstairs windows. No one spoke, but their fear and anxiety about what was going on in their quiet, leafy street was obvious. Five minutes later, the medics reappeared, leading the casualty to the ambulance.

'How bad is he?' Dane said as they passed him.

## VENGEANCE DAY

'He can't be that seriously injured. He'd asked for my number before I'd taken his pulse,' the pretty blond paramedic replied.

Dane closed his eyes and sighed with relief before he poked his head inside the ambulance.

'Are you alright, Pete?'

'Yeah, no worries boss, bit sore, that's all, and this little nick is worth a fortune,' Pete responded with a wide grin that turned to a grimace as he moved his injured arm.

Two cars pulled into the driveway and the arrest teams jumped out. They all wore forensic suits with gloves and masks. A firearms officer met them and led them inside as Knocker appeared. Dane called him over.

Knocker shook his head, then lit a cigarette and leant against a police van, 'Why is there always a creaky floorboard?'

'We heard it,' Dane replied.

'That must have alerted my target.' Knocker paused for a puff before continuing. 'Christ, he was fast.' The big man's voice shook with emotion, 'I have lost count of how many of these operations I've been on and now I've killed a man.' Knocker sucked another lungful of smoke as Dane put a comforting hand on his shoulder.

'You've all done a fantastic job. No one else could have accomplished it any better.'

There was a flurry of activity at the front door as the arresting officers led the two surviving terrorists to the waiting cars. Both now wearing forensic suits with their hands and feet encased in nylon evidence bags.

Gordon, the team leader who secured the ground floor, came out and joined Dane and Knocker.

'The house is all clear. Your people can have it whenever you're ready, boss.'

'That's great. My guys will take your statements this evening,' Dane replied.

'You might like to come and have a squint at what we found in the garage.'

Dane pulled on a forensic suit and followed him. The van shone under the fluorescent lighting. He peered into the back and felt vindicated as he surveyed the terrorists' handiwork. The matt olive-green painted tube, with the sights fitted, was in position with the baseplate welded to the floor. An aluminium box was fixed next to the mortar with the tail fins of ten bombs poking out. A section of the roof was missing which was resting against the wall. Someone had screwed several clips to it, and Dane assumed they would fit it back in place until they got to their firing point. It looked a professional set up and they would have been able to drive into London, exciting no interest in the vehicle.

Dane wandered through the house with a growing sense of satisfaction that they'd disrupted this part of their planned attack. But where were the other three mortars? He glanced at his watch and was surprised to see it was only twenty past five. Dane could have sworn at least an hour had passed since Alison had given the go.

The personal carriers rolled down to collect the firearms team, who all piled in and left. Unarmed uniformed officers took their place, creating a cordon and closing the road for fifty yards each way. Most of the residents had gone back inside their homes.

Perkins arrived with the chief constable. Dane described what they had found and showed them the video of the operation.

'Knocker is shaky. He will need some support.'

'Leave that to us. You concentrate on the investigation,' Perkins said.

'Best I crack on then. How about the press?'

'We have released a statement confirming this was a counterterrorist operation. They'll all be here soon. Polly is on her way to manage all that' Perkins replied.

Dane was relieved he wouldn't have to deal with the reporters. Polly knew what she was doing and always oversaw the pack with polite firmness.

He spent an hour with Pauline Rose, the crime scene manager, assessing what needed to be done. Each room now contained forensic searchers looking for evidence and bagging up anything that looked interesting. Dr Hume arrived together with a biologist and a ballistic expert. All three took their time examining the

## VENGEANCE DAY

corpse. They counted the bullet holes in it and recorded its position and the blood staining before the body was removed.

Dane searched for the serial number on the mortar tube, but it had been ground off. They might be able to recover it in the lab. But he knew in his heart this must be one of the four stolen in Bahrain. It astonished him to discover how well armed the men were. There were eight full magazines for the AK 47s placed close to windows. There could have been a bloodbath if they hadn't used the tactics Dane had insisted on. The three terrorists occupied a bedroom each. There was little in any of them apart from clothing and toiletries. No suitcases and only a few books and comics in Subject One's room. A radio sat on the windowsill in the kitchen and there was a television in the lounge. But no iPad, laptop, or any other personal items. A metal dustbin on the patio contained the charred remains of papers and it was piping hot, suggesting there had been a recent fire. It would take until tomorrow to complete the full search, so Dane knew he would have to be patient. Detectives called at all the neighbours houses to inform the residents of the situation and reassure them.

The press arrived and demanded interviews and an explanation about the night's excitement. They weren't satisfied with the scant briefing they received from Polly. Reporters started calling at the neighbouring houses, trying to get information from the occupants.

By midday Pauline was dropping heavy hints that Dane was in the way. He drove over to the custody suite and found Dave Stone, who was co-ordinating the interviews with the suspects.

'How are you getting on?' Dane asked.

'We've completed the forensic examination of them both. So far, they've said nothing to anyone except to ask for the doctor and a solicitor. The Superintendent has signed the authority to hold them both incommunicado for twenty-four hours. The doc has seen Subject Two, and he's with the other guy now. Once that's wrapped up, we can get on with the initial interviews.'

Dane knew that terrorist organisations all trained their people on how to frustrate a police investigation. The two men they had in custody would know that if they declared an illness, the custody sergeant had to call a doctor for them. It was a classic delaying tactic, and although frustrating, it rarely did the suspects any good.

The medic joined them.

'There's nothing wrong with either of those young men. Apart from being the scariest people I have ever examined. They're both fit for you to detain and interview.'

'Thanks,' Stone replied, 'We'll make a start then.'

The two interviewing officers collected the first prisoner and escorted him to a video room and started the tapes. Dane sat in the monitoring cubicle and listened as they asked their questions. Subject One refused to utter a syllable in reply. Dane left them to it and drove to Chelmsford, where he rang Vicky.

'Looks like you've had a successful night,' she said.

'Not too bad. I'm worn out, but I'll get some sleep later. I won't be able to be with you all until tomorrow afternoon at the earliest.'

'Don't worry. We're having a great girly weekend. We visited your dad earlier. He's much better and is off the ventilator.'

'I wish I could be there with you all.'

'You just look after yourself and we'll see you when you get here.'

'I'll give you a ring in the morning.'

Dane walked over to meet Perkins for a conference call with Shaw where he briefed her on the outcome of the raid.

'We must assume there are still three mortars outstanding. I believe they're still going to attack the parade on Sunday.'

'I agree it's a strong possibility,' Shaw replied, 'But there are also developments on the other side I can't talk about on the phone. We are locking central London down from this evening. There will be increased patrols for up to three miles from Whitehall, but that's the best we can do with the available resources.'

'These weapons have a much longer range than that.'

'I know. But I think these arrests will deter the rest of them. We must concentrate all our resources on central London.'

## VENGEANCE DAY

Dane rubbed his eyes, then studied his watch. It took him a few seconds to calculate he had not slept for thirty-six hours.

'I want you to get your head down for a few hours before you keel over,' Perkins ordered.

'That's the next thing on my agenda.' Dane trudged back to his small office and pulled two chairs together, curled up on them, and was soon fast asleep.

SIMON DINSDALE

**Chapter 17**

Liam settled into the armchair to eat his Corn Flakes and watch the news. He'd managed a half decent night for a change. Mary and Patsy were still asleep upstairs, so he kept the sound down, barely listening as the anchors did their double act. As he shovelled a spoonful of cereal into his mouth, he glanced up and his jaw dropped with shock. A reporter was standing outside the house in Frinton. Liam lunged for the remote, sending the bowl bouncing across the floor, spilling milk, and scattering soggy bits of food.

It was the end of an outside report from the scene of a counterterrorist operation in Essex. The coverage returned to the studio, and Liam listened as a security expert babbled on about the current terrorist threat to the country. They didn't mention Frinton, and the straps across the screen were vague, only referring to two arrests and a death. All the other news channels ran the same story which they repeated every fifteen minutes.

Liam roused Mary and Patsy then remained rooted in front of the television, watching the coverage with growing fury. Once it was obvious no additional information was coming out, Liam turned it right down and closed his eyes.

'How did they find them?'

'Perhaps they slipped up,' Patsy replied.

'Who, Eddy? No, he's too canny to allow anyone to be so careless. Have you checked around this morning?'

'No, I've not,' Patsy replied.

'If they knew about this place, or the other three. We'd all be face down by now and they'd be bragging about it. They love to show off and tell the world how clever they are. But it's only Frinton.' Liam watched the silent footage as an icy calm descended over him.

Patsy drove Liam to Ware. They circled the safe house, looking for any sign of police activity. Once satisfied there were no surprises waiting for them, Patsy parked around the corner. As

## VENGEANCE DAY

Liam approached the front door a nervous Ruari opened it with obvious relief.

'We thought you'd all been lifted as well. I phoned but got no reply.'

'You shouldn't have done that,' Liam replied.

'It was getting tense in here. I needed to make sure you were alright.'

Liam noticed that Ruari's team were ready to meet the police should they come knocking. The other two were upstairs, armed and keeping watch. Woe betides any bloody cop who tried to get in here this morning.

'How did they discover them?' Ruari asked.

'I can't answer that. But Patsy and I have checked around here. I'm certain there're none of them out there. I'll make a couple of phone calls, then we'll be back, and we won't be leaving again.'

'The operation's still on then?'

'Too right it's on. We've come too far to stop now. There'll never be a better chance for us to succeed. So, yes, we go as planned.'

Patsy dropped Liam in Ware town centre, where he made two phone calls from different payphones. 'They're all fine,' Liam reported when he returned to the car, 'It looks like the guys in Frinton have been unlucky. But the cops can't know about us all, or what we're planning. There's nothing they can do to stop us.'

More information was released through the day by the police. That, and further reporting by the press, confirmed that one of their friends had died in Frinton. The news subdued them all. Liam had a long telephone conversation with Mary, then spent the afternoon dozing on the settee.

\*

Dane's eyes cracked open, blinking, and squinting in the light. With an effort, he rolled into a sitting position and rubbed his face. His head was pounding, and he pressed the heels of his hands into his eye sockets, trying to ease the pain. It didn't work. The headaches were becoming a regular occurrence. Mr Hurrell would not be happy to see the time Dane was putting in on this case. It wasn't the slow and steady return to work the surgeon advised. Three hours sleep was nowhere near enough, but it would have to do. Dane stood and stretched, then a sudden wave of nausea swept over him. His stomach flipped, and he dry retched for a couple of minutes.

The temperature outside was plummeting, and the heating wasn't on in the office. Dane shivered as he padded down the corridor to the changing rooms for a shower. At least the water was warmer than its usual tepid. He let it stream over him until he felt human again. Once dry and dressed, Dane found Paul Lamb, and they drove to a nearby pub for something to eat.

As they tucked into ham and eggs Lamb informed Dane that the first round of interviews with the suspects had finished with neither terrorist uttering a word. The search of the house was continuing with teams already designated to continue through the night. All the property found there was being taken to the incident room. The house-to-house enquiries round the house in Frinton had not produced any interesting information.

After the meal, Dane drove the few miles to the custody suite to meet Dave Stone. His officers had collected the terrorist's fingerprints and DNA which had all gone to the lab. Dane doubted that would identify either of them, although he was sure Subject One was Shanahan. It was even less likely the search of the house would reveal where the rest of the group were hiding. That would be too easy. The investigation team would have to find the hideouts the hard way, and Dane knew he was running out of time.

The interview teams were about to start the next round of interrogations. As they were waiting for the prisoners, Dane received a telephone call from Karen and left the room to take it. He returned in time to watch the first one being led into the room.

Subject One walked straight towards a chair.

'Other side please,' the officer, who was smaller and much skinnier than the terrorist, blocked his way, 'Over there.' The terrorist glared at him but took the seat. He crossed his legs and turned his body and head, looking over his left shoulder and up towards the ceiling.

## VENGEANCE DAY

The cameras could still see him, but he remained in that position throughout the twenty-minute interview, not responding to anything asked of him. It was the same with Subject Two. The officers gained nothing from this exercise except to give the detained men the opportunity to respond to their questions. Dane joined them as they debriefed the interviews and discussed the next phase.

'Boss, Subject One jumped out of his skin when he saw you.'

'When did that happen?' Dane replied.

'As we brought him up from the cells. You were on the phone. He looked up the corridor and stopped dead. I swear he turned white at the sight of you.'

'Why would he behave like that? Are you positive he was looking at me?'

'Oh yes. We were heading to the room. He didn't recover until he tried to take my chair. That was the first time he's done that. I assumed it was an attempt to dominate us.'

'Have you told him we know who he is yet?'

'No, that's coming up in the next interview. Up to now, we've been working to establish a rapport with him. But he won't even acknowledge our existence.'

'How long before you're going to take him out again?'

'In about an hour.'

'Don't start them just yet.' Dane found an empty office and called Karen.

'Is there anything in the background of Michael Shanahan that connects with me?'

'Nothing that I've seen. His family is clean. No known involvement with any paramilitary or political organisation. He wasn't alive when they signed the Good Friday agreement, never mind when you were over there. He's a classic clean skin.'

'Well, he recognised me.'

Dane sat back in the chair, wondering why this man should be so shocked to see him. There was only one way to find out.

The officers collected Subject One from his cell and led him to the door and waved him in.

'Hello Michael.'

Shanahan spun round to discover he was alone with Dane, who was leaning against the wall.

Dane took two steps and held his hand out. He did it quickly and before Shanahan could stop himself, he responded, shaking hands with the enemy. Realising what had happened, he jerked away as if a scorpion had stung him. But it was too late. They had made contact.

'I hope you don't mind me calling you Michael. Please. Grab a seat, whichever you want. It makes no difference to me. The cameras can see you wherever you sit.'

Shanahan sat, eyeing him warily, but said nothing.

'My name is Dane. I'm the officer in charge of the investigation that has led to your arrest. This isn't a social call. The caution still applies and everything you say is being recorded and will be used in evidence. Do you understand?'

No reply. Dane could almost hear his mind whirling, wondering what was going on. This wasn't what he'd been told to expect.

'I wondered if you'd like me to inform your mother that you're alright.'

There it was, the flicker of concern across his face, which was now not so deadpan. 'She worries about you and won't be getting her regular phone call this Thursday, will she?' A blink and genuine worry in the dark eyes that were trying so hard to remain impassive.

'I'll keep it simple. Just inform her you're in custody and in good health. Unlike your comrade, who's dead. Sorry about that. But he tried to kill my officers.'

Red spots of anger flared on his cheeks. A muscle ticked in the corner of his right eye.

'What do you say, Michael?' Dane stared at him without speaking and holding Shanahan's glare. The younger man broke eye contact first, glancing down at the floor but still saying nothing.

'We've got them all. And the four mortars. Thankfully, no one else had to die. It's sad when someone loses their life. On the

## VENGEANCE DAY

positive side we prevented you all from doing something I'm sure you would've regretted.'

Shanahan's face displayed despair. Then shock as what Dane had said sunk in.

'What made you think that slaughtering hundreds of innocent people at a Remembrance Parade would make you a hero? How did that go for the fools responsible for Enniskillen? They're regarded as the worst kind of scum, even on your own side. They couldn't wait to give them up to the authorities.' Dane paused for a beat, 'Just like you did to your friends.'

Shanahan glared at Dane.

'Yes. You broke security. How else do you think we were able to find you and your little band of merry men? And Mary.'

Another reaction, a double blink and his eyes darting about the room, fear perhaps. Sweat formed on his upper lip, and the blood drained from his face.

'I want a drink.'

Dane nodded and waved his hand. Seconds later, a plastic cup and a bottle of water were delivered. Shanahan slurped it down, dribbling some over his chin.

'What's your friend's name? The man who died?' Dane said.

No reply.

'We'll find out. It would be better to tell his family as quickly as possible. Much fairer that way.'

Still no response, but a single muscle quivered in the young man's cheek.

'Come on, Michael. All soldiers deserve to have their sacrifice recognised. Who is he?'

Shanahan twisted away, trying to break the contact.

'Perhaps your mother can help us with that. Does she know who you are hanging around with?'

'Leave my family out of this.'

'It's too late for that. You and your friends are all going to be inside for the rest of your lives. You realise that don't you? How will mum cope with that?'

Shanahan shook his head and stared at the floor.

## SIMON DINSDALE

'It's bad enough lying to her all this time. Telling her all about the fictional building site. Now she'll learn you've been planning mass murder. She wants you to go to university, doesn't she? There'll be lots of opportunity for studying degrees where you are going. I guess a bright fella like you could get a doctorate.'

'She doesn't...'

'It'll all come out at your trial, of course. It's unusual for us to disclose how we catch people like you. We rarely give up our methods but, in this case, I'm sure we'll make an exception. You couldn't go more than a week without a natter with your dear old mum. How safe is she going to be once that's out in the open?'

Shanahan looked up, his eyes blinking rapidly, concern etched on his face.

'Every Thursday. Seven in the evening. You're a fit young man and you like running. I can relate to that. Did you tell your mates what you were doing while you were out jogging?'

Shanahan's face was now a deathly pale, 'I didn't give them away. I never talked about what I was doing.'

'Nice cosy chats with your mum and next thing, bang, you're all in a cell. And your friend is dead. How's that going to go down with the boys?'

The tick on the cheek was out of control, 'No. That's all bullshit.'

'Is it? Think about it.'

'I don't believe you. If you had them, you wouldn't be allowed to keep me incommunicado. You've got nothing and I won't tell you anything.'

Dane held Shanahan's gaze until the young man broke again, looking down. Then he changed tack.

'Why did you break into my house?'

Shanahan's eyes flew wide with shock. His tongue flicked across dry lips. Dane realised he'd struck gold.

Soon after a journalist exposed him in the press during the Anderson investigation, Vicky came to stay with him for the weekend. While Dane was out, she disturbed an intruder. She was able to give an excellent description of that person, and it fitted Shanahan. As the interview progressed, the similarity had

# VENGEANCE DAY

occurred to him, and he threw the question in to catch him out and gauge his reaction. Dane pressed his advantage.

'Come on. Why were you in my home? You frightened my friend to death. She thought you were going to rape her.'

'I'd never do a thing like that,' Shanahan whispered, 'I'm not like that.'

'What were you after? Why were you targeting me?'

Shanahan shook his head and said nothing.

'It doesn't make much difference. You won't be bothering me again.'

'Don't you believe it, you smug bastard,' Shanahan snarled, then turned away, crossing his arms and legs, and looking up at the ceiling. His expression hardened, as resolve took over. Dane stopped the interview, and Shanahan was returned to the cells.

\*

Dane drove back to headquarters to find Perkins and they joined a Zoom call with Shaw, Karen, and Brown.

'Why tell him they were all in custody?' Shaw asked.

'To watch how he would react. He was shocked and deflated because he was expecting three more mortars to be firing tomorrow. His last comment confirms that. He said, *"if you had the others."* I'm certain they will still attack.'

'I doubt it,' Brown retorted, 'With the arrests, they must know they're blown. They'll abort to fight another day.'

'But what if they don't?'

'We can't cover the whole of London. We've already deployed two thousand extra officers,' Brown said.

'I understand this isn't easy and there are other considerations. But we can't just give them a free run,' Dane replied.

'What do you suggest?' Shaw said.

'How about aerial surveillance of all the major routes into the capital? Look for large vans with a section of the roof chopped out. That sort of modification should be easy to spot from the air.'

'That's an excellent idea and certainly viable. I'll talk to my colleagues about using their helicopters,' Shaw said.

## SIMON DINSDALE

'Why would this lot be breaking into your home?' Brown asked.

'These dissident groups don't play by the same rules as the IRA did. Perhaps they were preparing to target me.'

After the call, Dane walked to the operations room to search through the stuff recovered from the house. The cold, fresh air cleared his head. A deep sense of unease had settled over him since talking to Shanahan. The exchange convinced him that for whatever reason, these people were coming for him. He already had contingencies in place to defend himself. But the thought of them threatening his family scared him. How could he look after them all the time. Back in the office he rang Vicky.

'Listen, you must keep the button with you this weekend.'

'I'm already doing that.'

'I mean, in your pocket. Not in your handbag.'

'What's the matter? Has something happened?'

'Yes, there's been a development here. We've arrested the bloke you confronted in the house. He's one of the terrorists.'

Vicky was silent for a moment, 'Are you sure?'

'He admitted as much to me.'

'Right. What does that mean?'

'I couldn't get any more information out of him. I assume they were targeting me, and still intend to do that. My parent's home isn't a state secret, so you are all vulnerable and need to be alert, at least until I can get there tomorrow. That's why the button mustn't be far from your hand.'

'It won't be, I promise. Do you want to speak to your mum?'

'No, I've got to go. Keep all the doors and windows locked. Don't answer the door to any strangers. I'm being paranoid, but I'll feel a lot better knowing you're all inside and safe.'

'We'll be fine. See you tomorrow.'

# VENGEANCE DAY

## Chapter 18

Dane found Lamb and Hayley surrounded by twenty exhibit bags from the house. 'These are the contents from the first floor and include the three bedrooms. They will deliver more from the downstairs later tonight. Shall we make a start with this lot?' Dane said after reading the property list.

They dressed in forensic suits with gloves and started with the bag from the main bedroom. It contained two dark fleeces and a weatherproof topcoat belonging to the dead man. Lamb squeezed around the lining seams, and hems, then paused.

'Feel the collar,' he said, and passed it to Dane.

'Is this a hood?'

'No, I think something's hidden inside.'

Dane peered through a magnifying glass and smiled, 'The stitching has been unpicked. There's something in here.' After snipping with a pair of scissors, Dane pulled a wad of cash out, three hundred pounds in total.

'Escape money?' Hayley said.

'Did they find a mobile phone in this room?' Dane asked.

'Yes, the burner they used when they rented the cars. There have been no calls or text messages made with it.'

They then turned to the second room which yielded another seven hundred pounds hidden in two jackets, but nothing else. Shanahan had used the third bedroom. This contained clothes and books by a variety of authors, including Charles Dickens and Arthur Conan-Doyle. No laptop or other modern electronic devices. More cash came from the collar of a heavy winter coat. Hayley discovered a Yale key wrapped in a piece of white paper with a number written on it behind the maker's label.

'Must be a code. Come on then, first person to crack it gets the prize,' Dane said.

'Don't look at me,' Hayley replied, 'I can't even do the Sun crossword at the best of times. And my brain is like porridge right now.'

Dane glanced at his watch and was surprised to see it was half-past one in the morning.

## SIMON DINSDALE

'Let's stand down and come be here at ten.'

Dane pushed the chairs together and was soon asleep. A loud banging on the door woke him with a start at five thirty. He hauled himself up and rubbed his eyes clear of sleep. Two officers from the search team were outside with a plastic box. It was freezing, with a hoarfrost shimmering on the grass. Dane shivered when a sudden gust of icy air rushed through the foyer as they carried everything in.

'Morning fellers, what have you got for me?' Dane said.

'Not a lot, I'm afraid. Apart from the personal possessions in the bedrooms, there's not much from elsewhere. All the downstairs rooms are empty. There was nothing under the floorboards.'

Dane carried everything into his office and then went for a shower. The water never got beyond lukewarm, and his teeth chattered as he shaved. As he returned to the office, Karen rang him.

'You're up early,' Dane said.

'I haven't been to bed. When our friends in Belfast told Shanahan's mum he was in custody, and why, she collapsed. They rushed her to the hospital, so we'll get nothing from her today.'

'Oh well, I doubt she could have told us anything. What's wrong with her?'

'Just a fit of the vapours, I think. We might hear something from other directions later. An urgent request went out last night. I'll ring when I get a reply.'

'Okay, thanks for that. Where will you be sitting today?'

'At my desk in Thames House, at least there's a kettle here. Do you still think they'll try to carry out the attack?'

'I do and we won't be able to stop them.'

'You never know. They might wait to fight another day. Anyway, if I hear anything, I'll be in contact.'

'Fingers crossed. Thanks for the call.'

'Time for breakfast,' Dane muttered. He drove to the nearest McDonald's and ordered a couple of egg muffins and the biggest mug of tea they did to take out. The greasy food gave him an energy boost and he returned to the office to give his full

## VENGEANCE DAY

attention to the latest exhibits. It didn't take long to confirm the sacks of property contained nothing interesting. In the last bag was a dog-eared London A/Z map book. As Dane replaced it, he remembered seeing the remains of an identical book in the fire at the house. Why would they burn one and not the other? He checked the search log, which stated the intact A/Z was discovered underneath the settee in the front room. The only item recovered in that room. Perkins rang just after seven, and Dane briefed him on what had been found during the search and his plans for the day. Perkins told Dane he had business out of the county that day but would be on the phone. As they chatted Dane doodled, and his mind wandered to the piece of paper with the numbers. An idea popped into his head.

When Perkins rang off, Dane retrieved the paper and copied the number out on his notepad.

11227229191268222241219261587. He broke it down to seven, four figure map references. A check on the web placed them in the English Channel. Next, he tried six figure grids and got much the same results.

Dane attended a course on cryptology when he trained for his role in Ireland. It had been decreed that that all covert operators must be able to recognise and decode basic cryptograms. Maths was never Dane's favourite subject, so he struggled to understand the esoteric nature of the science. But some things stuck.

For instance, the letters ETA and O are the most used in English. The nonsensical phrase ETAOIN SHRDLU contained the twelve most frequently used letters in a typical English text. Dane wrote the alphabet out and then numbered each letter. From that, he decoded the number to read; KVGVISLFHEXLSZOHG. So, not an anagram. He thought back, trying to remember what the bearded geek from GCHQ had said about ciphers. Then a grin creased his face as he recalled the man had said in one particular lecture.

'Don't forget your common or garden IRA terrorist is dim. Once they've encrypted something, they must decrypt it. So, they invariably keep it simple.' Dane never forgot that nugget of wisdom. He stared at the line of figures and his alphabet. Five minutes later he had, PETERHOUSECORALST.

## SIMON DINSDALE

After connecting to a web address finder, Dane found a Coral Street in London, Liverpool, Leicester, Middlesbrough, and Saltburn-by-Sea, on the North Yorkshire coast. There was no Peter House listed at any of them.

This slip of paper must be a crib for Shanahan's own use, so as not to forget the address. Hence the simplicity. Once again, the young terrorist's slack approach to security was exposed.

The front doors opened, and Hayley appeared looking worn out. She was laden down with tea bags, coffee and milk.

'You're not supposed to be here until later?'

'I know, but I couldn't sleep. I wanted to have another look at the exhibits. There must be something to help us.'

'What do you think of this?' Dane said and pushed his pad across the desk.

Hayley read it and raised a single eyebrow.

'You are sometimes too clever for your own pants, boss. How did you work that out?'

'I applied a dose of logic to a dash of training dredged up from the depths of my past. Then I combined it with the mind of a terrorist. Shanahan took the alphabet and reversed the numbering. A became twenty-six and so on. It's the simplest substitution cypher there is. What we need to do now is research the address and locate a Peter House in it, quickly. The key we found must be for a safe house. Shanahan hid the paper with it. Did we find any more keys in the property?'

'Not that I recall. I'll double check.'

They searched all the bags again, but there were none.

'It must have been his job to hold it,' Hayley suggested.

'Probably. You crack on and find me a Peter House.'

While she did that, Dane made them both a mug of tea and pondered this discovery. The London Coral Street had to be their bolt hole. All the others are a long way from the capital. It would make sense for the terrorists to lie low after their attack. The police would lock the city down after an assault of this magnitude. Having a safe house nearby would enable them to be out of sight quickly. Once the dust settled, they'd be able to scatter, attracting no attention if they were careful. In fact, to get caught, someone must inform on them, or they make a

## VENGEANCE DAY

catastrophic error in their own security or wear a sign round their necks pointing out who they were. Before meeting Shanahan, Dane doubted that any of the above would have applied, but now, he was not so sure. They're not as good as we give them credit for, he thought.

Where is Coral Street, he wondered and glanced around for a map? He spotted the A/Z in the evidence bag on his desk and, putting a pair of gloves on, flipped to the index, which took him to page 146. That was a larger scale and showed that the street was behind Waterloo station, and less than a mile from Whitehall.

Dane called Hayley over and pointed out what he'd discovered.

'That must be the one. They can do the deed then escape through the underground and pop out at Waterloo.'

So now Dane knew the location of the safe house. But where are they going to shoot from. He visualised a mental map of London. Four mortars, no three, but where from? They could fire on Whitehall from Battersea or outside Heathrow and still hit their target. Those weapons were terrifyingly simple to use.

Just after nine, Lamb arrived. 'I've spoken to the interview team. They won't get much done today. Both prisoners have demanded a solicitor.'

'Who did they ask for?'

'That's the odd thing. They're both happy with the duty brief.'

Counter terrorist officers had for many years joked they would always know when a real bad guy was in their clutches by the lawyer who turned up to represent them. That Shanahan and his friend asked for a local advocate was an interesting development. This suggested they were outside the mainstream groups and without access to the usual legal firms who helped arrested terrorists.

Dane took Lamb through what he had discovered and picked up the map to point out where Coral Street was.

As he allowed the pages to flick through his fingers, something caught his eye, he riffled back until he found what he was looking for. Page 79, someone had drawn a small circle in ballpoint pen over an area of Rotherhithe in east London. On the next page at the far-left-hand margin was Waterloo station.

## SIMON DINSDALE

Whitehall was on page 77. The mark in Rotherhithe was exactly five thousand yards to the east of Whitehall.

'Look at this,' Dane said to Lamb.

'Anyone could have done that for many reasons,' Lamb replied after looking at the map.

'It's the right distance from what we think will be their target and well within range.'

'I suppose so. That's not a lot to go on.'

'I know. I can't find any similar marks anywhere else. You check if I've missed anything.'

The time was now 0955hrs, just over an hour before the Remembrance Parade was due to start. The old sweats would be mustering in and around Whitehall. Thousands would be on parade spanning seventy years of military campaigns. Hundreds of Northern Ireland veterans were marching this year as their service and sacrifice was being celebrated. The hairs on the back of Dane's head were prickling. This was something to do with the attack.

'I'm going to go and have a look.'

Lamb looked surprised, 'Do you want me to come with you?'

'No, this is nothing more than a hunch, and you have work to do here. But this doesn't feel right. This might be a coincidence that the mark is close to an address that could be a safe house. It's well within range of Whitehall. I won't be happy until I've settled this finally. You and Hayley research Coral Street, it's just behind Waterloo station,' Dane pointed to the map and Lamb realised what he was getting at.

'We'll sort that.'

Dane put his covert body armour on under his shirt and strapped his CS gas canister and ASP baton onto his belt. He was one of the few senior officers who bothered to carry their 'appointments', as the British police quaintly refer to the equipment. It was five past ten as Dane set off, heading for the A12 and London. Not much time to reach Rotherhithe before eleven. He rang Shaw's mobile.

'I'm glad you called because we've got an update for you. Alex Brown is on speaker,' Shaw said, 'Surrey police found a Citroen van abandoned at the Fleet services on the M3. An AA patrolman

## VENGEANCE DAY

glanced in the rear and saw a mortar. Local officers have attended and confirmed it. I've ordered patrols to search every service station round London for similar vehicles. They must have aborted and got out while they could.'

'Why dump it somewhere so public?' Dane replied and told them what he'd unearthed, 'I'm on my way to investigate the area marked in the map book. I'll be struggling to make it before eleven. Can you send a patrol to have a look?'

'We're tight for resources. I'll get a local unit to do that,' Brown said.

'Did you say Fleet services?'

'Yes.'

'Do we know when the van was dumped?'

'Not yet. The patrolman is still being spoken too. When we receive an update, I'll call.'

'The reason I ask is that Fleet is on the railway line that runs into Waterloo.'

'That's right, why?'

'Coral Street is behind Waterloo station.'

'I see what you're getting at,' Brown said, 'You go to Rotherhithe. We'll find out what the AA man has to say.'

'Thanks,' Dane replied, then put his foot down.

Dane reached the bottom of the A12 when Brown rang him.

'The guy from the AA saw three people. Two men and a woman, just after seven this morning. Their van wouldn't start, and they asked him to help. One of them said they were on an urgent job and needed to be in London before the roads closed. That's why he thought it was strange when they disappeared.'

'That hardly sounds like a planned abort, does it?'

'No, it doesn't. We've just heard that a patrol has driven around the area in Rotherhithe. It was all clear. There were no large vans anywhere.'

'Okay. I should be there in the next fifteen minutes.'

Dane switched the blue lights and siren on, which made the Sunday morning traffic move out of his way. He had a clear run onto the south bank of the river and followed the loop in the Thames through Deptford to the junction of Brunel Road and Canon Beck Road. Sweat trickled down between his shoulder blades, caused by driving fifty miles flat out. Two hundred yards in front of Dane a white Mercedes Sprinter van was parked on Rotherhithe Road

It was nine minutes to eleven. Dane rang Shaw and told her what he was watching.

'I can't see the roof, but the engine is running. Someone is sitting in the cab. This does not look good.'

'Stay where you are. I'll send an armed unit to join you.' Dane waited, nervously checking his watch every thirty seconds. Seven minutes passed with no patrol, and his concern was rising. There'd been no movement in or around the van, although the engine was still running. Dane was about to drive down the road himself when a marked police vehicle pulled alongside him, and the passenger wound his window down.

'Morning, are you Mr Dane?'

'Yes,' he pointed, 'That's the one we're interested in.'

'You hang on here. We'll sort them out.'

'Be careful. If they are who I think they are, they're armed and bloody dangerous.'

'No worries,' the officer said, and they drove away.

To Dane's surprise the patrol car stopped and parked about fifty yards short. His surprise grew to concern when the two officers climbed out of the car and walked nonchalantly down the middle of the road.

Dane groaned, 'For God's sake, what are you doing?'

\*

Liam volunteered to stay up and keep watch. He didn't want to suffer those images again. They would leave him once he fulfilled the pledge made all those years ago, and there would be plenty of time to sleep afterwards. So, he spent the night waiting for the new dawn and contemplating what was to come. Liam had been planning this for as long as he could remember and even delayed his plans, so they could carry out the attack on this day. This was the anniversary of Martin's murder. Twenty-five years to the day since those two killers had blown his brother's brains out. Liam was determined that no one would forget the Rafferty brothers.

## VENGEANCE DAY

At five, Liam received two text messages confirming the other teams were on the move. He woke the others, and they were all ready to go by eight. Spirits were high when they set off towards destiny. Carol drove with Ewan beside her. Liam and Ruari were in the back. Patsy was following in the car and would pick Liam up when they had finished. Liam was going to fire the salvo and the first shot was going to leave the barrel exactly ten seconds before the hour.

As they approached their firing position, Liam saw it was clear and smiled. They couldn't fail. Carol had proved to be the best driver in practice, and as Ewan set the compass bearing, she drove into position. Liam checked his watch. Ten minutes to go. A little early, but that didn't matter. So long as they were ready at the right time. No one said anything as they waited. Liam helped Ruari unclip and removed the section of roof. Then Ruari withdrew the first bomb, checked the fuse, and handed it to Liam before preparing the second. As the last seconds ticked away, Liam's thoughts were of Martin, recalling the fun they'd shared and the love he still had for him. Even after twenty-five years, almost to the minute. This act would release him from the guilt and nightmares. It would serve as the requiem the Church never afforded Martin and would avenge the boy murdered by the state. Ruari watched his friend and mentor as a look of ecstasy settled onto his face.

'Fifteen seconds,' he muttered.

Liam counted to five, then kissed the bomb and whispered, 'Rest in peace, Martin.' Tears were streaming down his cheeks as he placed it into the tube and let go.

# SIMON DINSDALE

## Chapter 19

The sight of the two police officers walking towards the parked van without an apparent care in the world horrified Dane. They were both carrying a Heckler and Koch MP5 machine pistol on slings across their chests and appeared to be chatting to each other. When they were about thirty yards away, a stunning bang came from the van and they both flinched. Dane almost jumped out of his skin and realised he'd seen a muzzle flash above its roof.

The powerful forces generated by the mortar drove the rear end of the van down on its suspension, which rebounded, bouncing the vehicle a foot in the air. As it settled on its wheels, the passenger door opened and a man leaned out, raising an AK47 assault rifle into his shoulder. The distinctive chatter of the weapon firing followed. Dane watched in disbelief as a stream of bullets tore into the two officers. They both staggered under the relentless impact before collapsing face down beside each other. The door slammed shut as the van manoeuvred.

It took a moment for the enormity of what he had just witnessed to hit him. Then a blazing fury coursed through his gut.

'You murdering bastards,' Dane snarled. He pulled out of the parking spot and drove past the bodies towards his target.

\*

The violent reaction shocked Liam, and he smacked his head on the roof when they bounced. What Jake hadn't explained was the physics of the weapon firing, and how that would drive the base plate downwards. He didn't mention that a mortar crew would usually fire a couple of rounds first to bed it in. Jake told them they could fire from a vehicle, which was true. But hadn't emphasised that the military only used heavily armoured vehicles as platforms. If Liam had asked about using a civilian commercial van, Jake would have laughed and said it couldn't work.

# VENGEANCE DAY

Liam swore in frustration, then heard the gunfire, 'What's going on?'

'A couple of cops!' Ewan shouted, excitement making his voice shrill, 'I took them out.'

'Well done. Line us up again.'

Carol reversed, then, with a deft touch of the steering wheel, drove back towards their firing point. As she applied the brakes, there was a sudden crashing impact, throwing her and Ewan sideways across the cab. Liam and Ruari had just regained their balance when they were both knocked off their feet again. The weld holding the mortar failed, and it bounced up, sending the baseplate crashing onto Rauri's leg, shattering his femur.

\*

Dane slowed at the T junction. He intended to ram the van but had to keep his speed steady at about fourteen or fifteen miles an hour. Any faster, and the air bag would deploy. He aimed and sped up, hitting the van's rear nearside wheel full on. There was a crunch of tearing metal as the car came to an abrupt stop, hurling him forward into his seat belt. He selected first gear and increased the revs until it slowly started forward pushing the van sideways. As they gained momentum the van keeled over onto two wheels. The houses lining the south side of the street backed onto the river, and there was a staircase between two of them leading to the towpath. Dane kept the accelerator hard down until the rear end of the van dropped into the stairwell, leaving the cab in the air with its front wheels slowly spinning.

With a loud grating from the gearbox, Dane engaged reverse. The engine roared, and the wheels spun. 'It's jammed,' he thought. With the screech of tearing metal, the car came free and leapt backwards leaving the front bumper jammed under the van. He gathered speed before turning to swing sideways and skidding to a halt alongside the fallen officers with the vehicle covering them. Dane rolled out of the driver's door beside the men who hadn't stood a chance. He flinched as bullets slammed into the car and whistled past him. The sharp cracks of the high velocity rounds breaking the sound barrier made his ears ring. People were peering out of their doors, but quickly ducked back as bullets struck the front of their houses. Dane lay face down, hugging the tarmac, and peered underneath the vehicle. A pair of legs and a steam of ejected brass cartridge cases bouncing on the road were next to the van.

The two officers had collapsed on top of their carbines, and Dane couldn't free either of them. He grabbed a Glock pistol from the holster on one man's leg, aimed under his vehicle, and fired four shots. With a grunt of satisfaction, he saw the shooter crash to the ground having been hit in the ankle. The rifle bounced away from him. Out of the corner of his eye, Dane spotted another pair of feet walking along the footpath towards him. He rolled onto his back as a woman appeared. Her arms were extended straight out in front of her body, and she was holding a gun. Without warning, she fired into the dead men, advanced a step, then saw Dane. Before she could adjust, he shot her five times. Each round drove her backwards until her legs gave way, and she toppled face down on the pavement.

Dane grabbed two more magazines from the officer's gun belt, reloaded and chanced a look over the bonnet. A blue saloon car screeched to a halt beside the van as a man was climbing out holding another AK47.

Their eyes met, and Dane hesitated. Here was the short dark-haired man who had been plaguing his fragmented memory. The person who had killed Anderson and shot him. Everything from the day he'd nearly died came flooding back. Searching the apartment with Hayley, the telephone call to Perkins, spotting Anderson and chasing him through the streets. The smelly staircase into the basement of the car park. Searing pain then the cold concrete floor digging into his back. Anderson standing over him callously admitting there had been no need to kill the boy that day in Derry. Providing the answer he had risked so much to get. The man now standing opposite him appearing. His sneering voice, with the Northern Irish accent rang in Dane's ears. *'Every time I see you, you're flat on your back with someone pointing a gun at you. You really should get a grip of yourself.'* The sound of the shots. Anderson falling and then his own pain. All caused by the man in front of him. Then another image. One seared into

## VENGEANCE DAY

Dane's memory so many years ago. A young boy, quivering with shock on the doorstep of his home. Filthy face steaked with tears. The brother of the boy killed by Anderson. This was Liam Rafferty.

A roar of rage snapped Dane back to the present as Rafferty raised the rifle to his shoulder.

'Oh shit…' Dane muttered then dropped to the floor. The world around him started to disintegrate. Bullets sprayed glass and chunks of bodywork over him as he crawled to the front wheel and cowered behind it. The engine block should give him some protection. Then he recalled firing an AK47 on the ranges at a car. The bullets had gone through the engine like a knife through butter. Dane tried to make himself as small as possible, tensing his body and holding his breath, anticipating the crushing blow of a bullet. Flying debris stung the top of his head, and his hands. Something plucked at the back of his shirt. The noise was deafening and seemed never ending.

'Dear God, protect me,' he whispered.

Silence fell and Dane rolled sideways. He chanced a peek through the shattered windows. The man Dane had shot shouted something to Rafferty, who glared at Dane with a look of pure hatred. He nodded to his comrade and lobbed his weapon, which landed with a clatter on the road. With a final glance towards Dane, Rafferty jumped into the car, which then roared away.

Dane stood and took aim over the roof of the car.

'Armed police freeze,' he bellowed.

The terrorist grabbed the rifle and fired a burst before he could get a tight enough grip. The muzzle rode high, spraying bullets into the sky. Dane pulled the trigger, twice in quick succession. Both rounds hit the target killing the man instantly.

Dane checked the woman to confirm she was dead, then kicked her gun away. He moved forward cautiously to the other body then heard groaning coming from the back of the van. He checked the cab before jumping in the back. Another terrorist lay writhing and moaning in pain, clawing at his misshapen leg. Dane searched him and made sure he wasn't losing blood before climbing back out.

## SIMON DINSDALE

The residents were now flooding outside, inspecting the damage to their homes, and staring at the bodies. Dane took a deep breath and returned to his car.

'Has someone called the police?' A chorus of voices confirmed they had, 'Go inside, please. This is a crime scene.'

'Your heads bleeding,' a woman said.

Dane tentatively ran his fingertips through his hair. A small cascaded of window glass fell out and he felt a sting then the stickiness of blood. The backs of both his hands were peppered with small cuts and grazes.

'Here, let me have a look,' the lady said and pulled Dane's head towards her. 'It's just a nick.' She turned him round. 'There's blood on your back,' she pulled is shirt up, 'You've got a cut here. It's not deep but it will need a dressing.'

'Thank you,' Dane said, then looked around the street. Most of the nearby houses bore evidence of bullet strikes. Windows were smashed, and alarms were screeching. Parked cars were damaged or sitting on flat tyres.

Dane leaned on the bonnet of his car, breathing hard, patting his pockets for his mobile phone. He found it and dialled Shaw's number, checking his watch as he did so. It was three minutes past eleven.

'Shaw.'

'It's Dane.'

'What's happening?'

'I have four dead and one injured.' His voice was strained, and it took a second to get his emotions under control, 'Two terrorists have escaped in a blue saloon. They fired the mortar before I could stop them...'

'The bomb landed short on the Embankment and caused dozens of casualties,' Shaw replied.

'Has it all stopped?'

'Yes, everyone has been cleared from the area. We're getting reports of projectiles landing in the Thames near Vauxhall and an explosion in Kensington. But they missed the parade, thank God.'

'I'm going to need some assistance here.'

## VENGEANCE DAY

'We've dispatched units and they're on the way to you. Are you hurt?'

'I'm alright,' he replied, and rang off to contact Perkins.

Dane explained the events of his morning and that he recognised one of the terrorists.

'I've remembered it all. His name is Liam Rafferty. He's the brother of the boy Anderson killed in Ireland. Get some armed protection outside my mother's house quick. Rafferty knows about Vicky and they're all together there.'

'Don't worry. I'll organise that.'

A convoy of marked police vehicles came into view and disgorged uniformed officers.

'I'd better go.'

The cops fanned out to take control of the scene and set up a cordon. Dane found an inspector and after identifying himself briefed him on what had happened. An ambulance arrived and a medic cleaned and treated Dane's cuts and bruises then dressed the wound on his back with steri strips. His hands wouldn't stop shaking, and he felt dizzy and exhausted. A car arrived and took him to the Special Operations room in central London where Shaw and Brown were waiting.

The large room was a mass of people. All rushing about, or talking on phones, or tapping on their computers. It looked like chaos, but Dane knew there was an order to it as they coordinated the huge police response to the atrocity. Shaw pulled him aside.

'A second van blew up in Kensington after they fired five rounds. They all landed in the river. We think three terrorists died in it. A civilian couple were passing in their car when it exploded. They were both killed, and another two pedestrians hurt. Six died and eighty were injured in Westminster. Many of them are critical. That includes dozens of our people.'

Dane stumbled into a small anteroom where someone handed him a mug of tea. He took a few minutes to sip that and settle himself. When he was sure he wouldn't lose it, he called his mother.

## SIMON DINSDALE

'I suppose you are in the middle of all this, aren't you?' she said.

'I'm afraid so. Sorry.'

'Well, this is a to-do, I must say. What's the matter with these people? Are you coming home?'

'I should be there later. Can I talk to Vicky?'

'I won't ask if you're alright,' Vicky said, her voice strained.

'I've got to be here for a while.'

'Don't worry about us. We are all fine here. Shocked at what's happened, but we're staying busy.'

'Has anyone arrived there yet?'

'No, should there be?'

'I asked Perkins to send some people, just in case.'

'In case of what?'

'I saw the man who shot me. He was one of the terrorists and recognised me before he escaped. I have asked for a guard to be posted outside the house until I can get there. Tell the others it's a precaution to frighten the press off. I'll find out where they are. Text me when they arrive, please.'

'Okay, take care. See you later.'

Dane rang Perkins, 'There's no one at my parent's place yet. Where are they?'

'I've left instructions for an armed unit to be deployed. Leave it with me and I will chase them.'

Shaw called him over, as he approached her a still picture appeared on the eighty-inch plasma TV on the wall. It was him, with a pistol standing over the woman he'd shot. Shaw noticed where he was looking.

'I'm sorry, but you're famous again. They have footage from Rotherhithe and they're identifying you.'

'Great. That's all I need. I had enough of this the last time.'

'Don't worry. You are an important witness. They will have to leave you alone.'

'What about the address on Coral Street?'

'DI Lamb has done a cracking job and identified a block of flats there called Peter House. A surveillance team is surrounding it as we speak. We're trying to identify the occupants.'

# VENGEANCE DAY

Dane rang Vicky back to warn her about the press.

'You forgot to mention you'd been in a gunfight,' Vicky said. 'We are all proud of you. But I should warn you that your mum is going to give you a clout for getting into danger again.'

Dane managed a weak laugh. 'Don't answer the phone to them...'

'Too late. They have already been on. We're only answering calls that we can identify.'

'I'll be home as soon as I can get away from here.'

'I know, we'll see you later.'

'Have the officers arrived?'

'They're outside.' Dane sighed with the relief of knowing that his family was safe and being protected.

Karen bustled into the room. 'The source has come up with the probable identity of the leader of this gang.' She cast a glance at Dane, and he knew what was coming next.

'Who is he?' Shaw asked.

'Liam Rafferty,' Dane interjected.

Karen looked startled. 'Yes, it is.'

'I recognised him in Rotherhithe this morning. He's the man who shot me and Anderson. I can remember it all.'

'Oh no. I'm sorry we didn't hear this before. I suspect our source has been economical with what he's been passing on.' Karen said and took Dane's hand, 'You're sure it was him?'

'Yep. I should thank him for restoring my memory. The doctor told me it could return unexpectedly. I doubt they had something like this in mind though.'

'Is there any information about where they might go?' Shaw asked.

'No, we have nothing about possible safe houses.'

'So, our best bet is Coral Street. Let's run with that and see where it takes us.'

'What about the suicide attacks?' Dane said.

'They didn't happen,' Brown said, his face flushed with anger, 'We've been following a dozen young Muslim men who, we were told, were planning to attack the ceremony. Everything they have done in the last few weeks seemed to confirm that. They all left their homes this morning carrying heavy rucksacks and met at the Brent Cross shopping centre. Four more men arrived in a minibus. That was loaded with tents and other camping equipment. At ten forty-five, they joined the M4 heading west. They're all going on holiday.'

For the next few hours, Dane sat in the operations room as Shaw and her officers planned the approach to Peter House. Brown continued to monitor the movements of the Muslim men who, by that time, were well on their way to the Brecon Beacons in mid-Wales. A young woman who looked familiar arrived and Brown took her into a side office. Their terse conversation ended with him shouting at her. She stalked out with a face like thunder. An hour later she returned, accompanied by David Fawn from MI6. Dane now realised the woman was his assistant, Laura. The two joined Brown and had a heated exchange. As they left, Fawn spotted Dane and made a point of walking over to shake his hand.

'I'm pleased to see you escaped unscathed following your little adventure this morning. Well done. You appear to have averted a bloody catastrophe.'

'I was lucky. I assume Mr Brown has been acting on intelligence from your desk?'

There was a sharp intake of breath from Laura.

'You realise I can't answer that,' Fawn replied.

'Tell me what you think about this for a hypothesis. Once upon a time. Iranian agents steal four mortars and forty bombs and hand them over to Irish dissidents. They want to conduct a spectacular attack and these toys are just the ticket. Someone discovers the theft sooner than expected. To cover for that, those pesky Iranians feed intelligence suggesting they gave them to Hezbollah. More follows, warning of a suicide bombing on today's parade and identifying the likely bombers as probably Islamic extremists. They know we must respond to such information and concentrate our resources on monitoring them. They lead everyone a merry dance, deflecting any interest in the Irish. We don't need to take them seriously, do we? They're not a

## VENGEANCE DAY

genuine threat nowadays, are they? These are the musings of a lowly police officer, you understand.'

Fawn studied his face, 'Mr Dane, it has been good to see you again. As to your interesting hypothesis. I couldn't possibly comment. Well done today and good luck for the future.'

Brown saw the exchange and as the MI6 spooks left, he walked over. 'What's your connection with those two idiots?'

'We met during my investigation into the murder of George Blaine in Bahrain. I assume they're the origin of your intelligence about the suicide attack?'

Brown nodded, 'Their information came from the Americans who insisted it as grade A. And it was on the face of it. It corroborated other information we had developed. That led us to the men we have been following. They were all behaving as if they were in the planning stage of something. It all fitted, until today. It was all a setup to give the Irish dissidents a free run. But you seem to have got everything right. How did you manage that?'

Dane stared at the Scotsman and shook his head, 'I'm not some semi-literate hayseed. We know how to investigate crimes in the sticks. What is your problem?'

His tone stung Brown. 'I take what I do seriously, and I suppose I've become used to the idea that only I can do it.' he hesitated for a second, 'But I owe you an apology. I didn't think we needed you, nor did I trust you. I also apologise for what I got Samson to do. That was wrong. Carol White has put me straight as well. She told me things that made me want to weep. But what they did was my fault, and I accept full responsibility. I'm going to retire. So, you won't have to worry about me for much longer.' He turned and walked away without waiting for a reply.

Shaw came over and sat beside Dane.

'The bomb disposal guys think a misfire caused the Kensington explosion. They've examined the mortar and say the loader probably didn't realise it hadn't gone off and dumped the next one on top and everything blew up. They tell me it's not unusual.'

## SIMON DINSDALE

The investigation into Peter House soon revealed that the same families had occupied four of the six flats in the building for years. The others were sublet. The owners had let flat two on the ground floor about a year before and number six much more recently. Surveillance officers had blocked all the entrances, and anyone approaching was being stopped and asked to identify themselves. Through that exercise, the police moved the residents of flats one, four and five out. Intelligence gleaned from them established that the tenants in number three were a disabled couple who rarely left their home. The family in flat two were Nigerian immigrants.

Plain-clothes police knocked on their doors and led them to safety. The net slowly tightened around flat six. Technicians entered number four and placed a listening device on the ceiling. It didn't take long to establish that there were at least three people in there, two men and a woman. At six o'clock that evening, an armed team using a hydraulic jack and a heavy battering ram, known as a 'Ramit', smashed the door in. The lead officer called for the occupants to show themselves. At first there was no response, then a voice answered, and a standoff ensued. Negotiators started persuading them to come out with their hands up.

Dane watched the footage of the Remembrance Parade. Just before eleven the King and senior royals filed out into Whitehall and took up their positions.

Seconds before Big Ben struck the hour, the crump of the explosion reverberated across the silent streets and hundreds of startled pigeons flew into the air. The camera stayed on the King, who did not move a muscle. Dane spotted the Kings personal protection officer at the top of the picture. The blast startled him, then he ran towards his principal, elbowing his way through the dignitaries, followed by more bodyguards. They gathered up the royals and whisked them into the Foreign Office building. There was then a general rush as the politicians and other bigwigs scuttled out of sight.

There were no more explosions. The screen switched to Horse Guards Avenue. Camera crews were there filming scenes of

## VENGEANCE DAY

panic and carnage. The mortar bomb had detonated five feet above ground level between the statue of Charles Gordon and the junction of Victoria Embankment and Horse Guards Avenue. A deadly cloud of shrapnel had spread out in every direction, peppering the front of the Ministry of Defence building and shattering dozens of windows. Hundreds of people, who were standing nearby on the Embankment, all hoping to glimpse the parade were cut down as the razor-sharp pieces of metal scythed into them. There was blood everywhere, and confused and injured people were milling around in shock. Several torn and bloodied bodies wearing fluorescent jackets, lay on the ground. Dane knew they were police and community support officers, who had all been there to protect the public. The news channels were praising the royal family and everyone else for their fortitude. The picture cut to Rotherhithe with a correspondent talking outside the cordon. The coverage was interspersed with pictures of Dane, and his bullet riddled vehicle. It looked like a colander with every window smashed, the tyres flat and reminded him of Bonnie and Clyde's car after the ambush.

At least they were only showing stills. The video footage was, as the news anchors gleefully informed the public, too graphic to show. Although there had been no official confirmation it was Dane at Rotherhithe, all the channels were running with his name and background. The networks rolled out their favourite talking heads to speculate about what had happened and outguess each other about the number of dead and wounded.

Dane's mobile rang, and he saw it was John Lord.

'Hi, it's not a good time to talk right now'.

'Christian, where are you?'

'I'm still at work. Why?'

'Vicky's alarm has activated.'

## SIMON DINSDALE

### Chapter 20

Patsy floored the accelerator, and they sped away from the scene. He glanced nervously at Liam, who was screaming obscenities as he punched and kicked the dashboard.

'For the love of God, calm down. What happened?'

Liam was quiet for a moment. The muscles in his cheek working as the anger boiled through him.

'He was there and ruined everything.'

'Who?'

'Dane. It all went wrong. When I fired the first bomb, the whole van bounced into the air. Carol was trying to move the bloody thing back into position when he rammed it.' Liam turned the radio on and listened as the news reported a single explosion in Westminster.

'Just the one,' Liam whispered, 'What happened to the others?'

Patsy said nothing, his eyes darting to the mirrors, half expecting to see blue lights bearing down on them at any second.

'We've got to ditch this. He saw us in it.'

'Hang on. Let me think. Head north of the river, we'll dump it in the East End.'

They drove through the Blackwall Tunnel and turned towards the city. The media then reported a vehicle exploding in Kensington, which they linked to the attack in Whitehall.

'Could they have escaped?' Patsy said.

'If they did, they'll head for the safe house. But I want to know where the rest of them were. How come they didn't fire? They had better not have lost their nerves.'

Liam's voice was strained with the emotion of his failure. All that work and preparation made the bitter ache of disappointment course through his veins like acid. He rang Mary.

'Where are you?' he listened and nodded, 'We'll catch a train to Ipswich. Pick us up there. We're still on for later.'

Patsy parked the car behind the London Hospital. They took the underground to Liverpool Street station where they caught the next train. As it pulled in at Ipswich, Liam was off before it

# VENGEANCE DAY

had stopped and sprinted out to find Mary. As they drove away, she couldn't conceal her concern.

'What happened?'

'I'll explain while you take us to the hotel.'

Mary had rented three adjoining rooms in a travel lodge on the outskirts of the town, and they got in with no one seeing them. Liam switched the television on and spent the next hour glued to the coverage. Whenever Dane was mentioned, he became almost demented with rage, kicking the furniture, and throwing things across the room. Mary watched, concerned that the noise would attract a complaint.

'Liam, keep it down. We don't need to draw attention to ourselves.'

He looked at her and grinned mirthlessly, 'Makes me feel better.'

'Are we doing it?' she asked.

'Of course, we are, why wouldn't we?'

'What are we doing now?' Patsy said.

'I'm going to kill him. Mary has set it all up and we can't fail this time,' Liam stated, and explained the plan.

Patsy sat back and pursed his lips, 'I'll follow you anywhere, you know that, but are you sure?' Liam glared at him, his eyes like flint as his friend continued. 'I mean, you've just seen him. And he saw you. He must realise you'll be coming and where he's vulnerable. They'll have taken precautions to protect them, won't they?'

'Dane will do anything to save those closest to him. That's what I'm counting on. Mary can have a look at the house and if it's clear, we'll arrest them. Once they're secure. I'll call him on and execute him. Are you with me?'

'I am always with you. I don't want you getting caught for something as dumb as this.'

Liam leapt out of his chair and grabbed Patsy by the throat, forcing him against the wall.

'Revenge for my brother is all that matters,' he bellowed, spraying flecks of spittle. It took all Mary's strength to pull him off.

'That's not what he meant. He's concerned they might catch you when we could hang back a while and make sure the coast is clear. You should listen and think on.'

Liam was panting with anger as he stalked around the room, his eyes flaring.

'I've got to do this. If I don't take him tonight…' Liam fought to bring his emotions under control, and took a deep, shuddering breath. 'I may never have another chance and I can't wait any longer. I need to do this now, do you see?'

'Yes, Liam, I do. But you can't go into this in a blind rage. We must plan it properly.'

'Mary's done all that. It's fool proof, we can't miss this time.'

'Well then. If you're sure, then I'm with you,' Patsy replied.

Mary slipped out and returned soon after five.

'There's a police car parked outside. But there are only two officers, and they're not armed.'

Liam grinned in triumph, 'They won't know what hit them. This is how we'll do it.'

\*

The news from Lord surprised and concerned Dane.

'When did that happen?'

'About three minutes ago. We've checked the signal. She's at your mothers.'

Dane thought for a second, 'Have you seen what's been going on?'

'Yes, you can't miss it. We were all here and stopped to watch the fireworks. I'm still at the office and was here when the activation happened.'

'I saw the man who shot me. He was in Rotherhithe, and we recognised each other.' Dane hesitated for a moment, not wanting to accept what he was hearing. 'There should be an armed guard at my mother's house. Have you monitored her phone yet?'

'No, I needed to speak to you first. It might be a false alarm.'

'How many times has she set it off accidentally?'

'Never,' Lord replied, 'That's why I called you. Something's wrong.'

## VENGEANCE DAY

Dane looked around him. Dozens of police and support officers were working in the operations room, and there was a buzz of excitement about the place. Shaw and Brown were next to each other watching the live feed from Coral Street. Dane's handset vibrated, showing another call coming in. The caller ID told him it was from Vicky's number.

'John, this call is from her. Monitor and record this please and stay on the line.'

Dane accepted the incoming call, 'Hello.'

'I'm sorry if you were expecting the delightful Vicky. I'm afraid she can't come to the phone right now.'

Dane's stomach lurched, and he had to fight the urge to vomit. He recognised the voice with its harsh Irish accent, which confirmed all his fears. If this madman had Vicky, he had Robyn and his mother as well. A thrill of fear ran through his body like an electrical shock. His throat was dry, and he had to compose himself before he could reply.

'Who is this?'

'I'm your worst nightmare and there'll be blood on these walls if you don't do as you're told. Do you understand me?'

'Yes, I do.'

'Good, so listen carefully. You've got an hour to come alone to the front door of your mother's house.'

'I will follow your instructions to the letter. But you must know where I am. I'll never be able to get there in an hour.'

'That's your problem, not mine. People die in sixty minutes.'

'How do I know they're not already dead?'

'You don't.'

'Be reasonable. I can't fly there. I need transport and I've got to make the right arrangements.'

The line was silent for a few seconds.

'You have two hours. That's it. A minute over and they all die. Your mum's a nice old lady. She'll be first. And she will suffer.'

'You've made your point. Take them to a place of your choosing and we can exchange me for them. I'll be there.'

'No. You come here. Oh, and before you think about getting your friends to help you, remember this. I know how you people operate. If I get a feeling in my water that you're not alone. If the wind is blowing from the wrong direction, or I hear something I don't like. I'll kill them all. If I receive a call from anyone but you, they die. If you try a negotiator, they die. You have one small opportunity to save them. Don't be a hero and waste that chance. This is between you and me. If anyone else is nearby, or in sight, they die. Do I make myself clear?'

'Yes, you do. I'm on my way. Let me speak to them, please.'

'No.' The line went dead.

Dane stared at the phone and switched to Lord, 'Did you get all that?'

'We did, and everything from inside the house is now being recorded via Vicky's handset.'

'Good. Can you keep doing that until we have resolved this?'

'No problem. So long as we're intercepting these communications with your authority, it's lawful.'

'I must go there. You heard him if he gets a sniff of anyone else about.' Dane paused, and his voice caught.

'I have several operators here who're more than willing to help,' Lord offered.

'Thanks. But I have to do this myself.'

'Are you telling your boss?'

'No. That's the last thing I want to do. These people are skilled in countering our tactics, and I know they've been practicing recently. Do you have someone who could pick me up?'

'We can arrange that.'

'What is happening there now?'

'Give me five minutes to organise things and I'll call you back.'

'John, what's going on? Tell me,' Dane demanded, his voice shaking.

'There's been a disturbance. Shouts, and screams, but no shots. Hang on,' Lord paused. 'It's all calmed down now.'

Dane took a moment to clear his head and take in what had happened. A wave of fear threatened to swamp him, then a bubbling anger before he settled into an icy calm. He didn't have the luxury of getting help or wimping out. If he talked to Shaw or

## VENGEANCE DAY

Perkins, they were duty bound to play it by the book. That would mean the death of his loved ones. He was also under no illusion that Rafferty would let anyone go free. They would all die unless he got his game face on and dealt with the problem.

'I'm leaving here now. Can you send someone to meet me outside Westminster tube station?'

'On the way. It's a motorbike and he'll have a helmet for you.'

'I had better come to your place first and I'll need some kit.' He recited a list of items.

Dane watched Shaw and joined her when she moved away from Brown.

'I'm doing nothing here. Do you mind if I duck out? I should be in darkest Essex for my mother's eightieth birthday party.'

'Of course. You should've gone ages ago.' She studied his face, and her concern was obvious, 'Are you alright? You look like you've seen a ghost.'

'I'm just feeling a bit shaky. It's a reaction to what's happened I suppose. I've arranged for a friend to collect me. How do I get out of here without the press seeing me?'

'That's easy,' she replied, and picked up the phone on her desk.

A powerful Ducati motor bike purred round the corner onto Bridge Street opposite the houses of Parliament and pulled up beside Dane. The rider passed him a crash helmet, and he hopped on the pillion seat and only just had time to take hold before the machine took off.

\*

Liam dropped the mobile on the table and glared down at Vicky where she lay on the kitchen floor. Her left eye was swelling shut, and a deep purple bruise was forming around it. A nosebleed was slowing to a trickle and bloodied her face. Her hands were tied behind her back. She winced in pain as she tried to ease her position.

'Please loosen the ropes on my Granma. They're too tight. You're hurting her,' Robyn pleaded from the sitting room.

Liam ignored her as Patsy appeared and said, 'All clear upstairs,' He opened the cellar door, disappearing for a minute,

'There's space for them all down there and this is the only access.'

'Good, put them all in there. Except Vicky. She stays up here with us.'

Mary pulled Mrs Dane by the hair, hauling her to her feet and causing her to gasp in pain. Patsy did the same with the first police officer who barged him aside, striding towards Mary.

'You vicious cow. There's no need to treat her that way. She can't hurt you.'

Patsy grabbed him, 'Keep your mouth shut.'

The officer spun round and head-butted Patsy, knocking him back a pace as blood spurted from his nose. Liam stepped forward, swinging the butt of the AK 47 and clubbed the young cop over his right ear. He collapsed like a rag doll. With a snarl of anger, Patsy weighed in, kicking him repeatedly in the head.

'Stop that,' Mrs Dane shouted, 'Stop him,' she appealed to Liam.

'I told you all. Any resistance, and you die,' he turned to Patsy and Mary, 'Get them out of my sight.'

Mrs Dane tried to shrug Mary off, 'I don't require your help, thank you, young lady,' she declared, shuffling down the wooden steps into the cellar. Robyn followed, her face pale as she glanced down at Vicky who tried a weak smile of encouragement.

'Do as they say. Your dad will be here soon.'

The second officer was staring at her colleague lying motionless, blood seeping from his ear.

'He needs a doctor. Please help him,' she whispered. Liam punched her in the face, splitting the skin over her right eyebrow.

'Get down there,' he snarled, and pushed her through the door before tipping the unconscious officer after her. There was a series of sickening thumps as the body tumbled down the stairs. Patsy followed and was back a minute later, grinning.

'They won't cause us any bother.'

'Good, secure the perimeter.'

Patsy swung a heavy rucksack over his shoulder and, with Mary, went out into the garden.

## VENGEANCE DAY

Liam prowled round the ground floor. He settled in the sitting room and watched the television. He glanced over to Vicky, 'Quite the hero, your boy, eh?'

When she didn't reply, he stood menacingly over her.

'I suppose you're responsible for the attacks this morning?' she said.

'Yes. I am. And we would've succeeded. But for bad luck.'

'You failed. Because of Christian.'

Liam kicked her hard in the body, 'No. it was just bad luck. That happens sometimes. But you people have to be lucky all the time, so the odds are in my favour.'

It took a while before Vicky could speak again. 'Do you think you'll get away with this?' she gasped, 'How many innocents did you kill this morning? How did that madness further your cause?'

'We achieved our aim. We killed enough for you all to be afraid.'

'Enough! What sort of creature are you? All you did was murder innocent people who have never caused you any harm. They will hunt you down like the animals you all are. You'll need more than luck to escape them.'

'Perhaps. I'm sure your precious Christian has told them all about me. You will find it won't be easy to beat us.'

'He didn't kill your brother.'

Liam head snapped round. 'So, you know. Did he tell you how they murdered him while he lay defenceless on the ground?'

'But it was Anderson who fired that shot. And you've paid him back.'

'He was the reason it all happened,' Liam muttered in a flat tone, 'If he hadn't been there, my brother would still be alive.'

'He won't lie down and let you kill him. Do you suppose the three of you are enough to take him?' Vicky declared, her voice rising, 'He's a better man than you. All you're good for is killing and terrorising helpless people. You and your lunatic friends are the worst sort of cowards. You disgust me.'

'I'm not interested in what you think. He'll pay for his meddling, and you'll watch little Vicky. You will all have a few minutes to appreciate what it's like to lose someone you love. But you won't have too long because I'll be merciful and put you all out of your misery.'

He turned back to the news coverage and ignored her. Half an hour later, the other two returned and Patsy dropped the now empty rucksack on the floor.

'We've covered every approach. I doubt anyone'll get close without us knowing. I'll stand at the gate.' He pulled the police officer's fluorescent coat and his cap on, picked up an assault rifle, and walked outside. Mary locked up behind him and checked all the other doors and windows on the ground floor.

\*

Dane jumped off the bike and jogged up the stairs to Lord's office.

'I've got a couple of vehicles with some operators on route to your mum's.' Lord held his hand up as Dane protested, 'They'll not go close to the house. One is our technical support vehicle, which we will need to talk to each other. They can also intercept their communications. The other is a plain van that might be useful to extract the hostages. The people in them all live up that way and have volunteered to do this. They will be on station soon.'

'Thanks, but make sure they keep their distance. I've not told my bosses and when it all comes out, I'm going to have a lot of explaining to do. The fewer I involve in this escapade, the less grief I'll bring to others.'

'Don't worry about that. We are picking up conversation from the mobile. The opposition comprises two men and a woman who sounds a complete nightmare. They've herded your mother, Robyn, and the police officers into the cellar. Vicky's being held in the kitchen.'

Dane's mind had been working, and he already had a plan to infiltrate the house. This information was useful, and he couldn't help the smile that creased his lips. He's playing into my hands, he thought.

'Have you got the kit I asked for?'

## VENGEANCE DAY

'Follow me.' Lord led the way to the storeroom where a man in his late sixties was waiting, 'This is Ted, and these are all his toys.' On a six-foot table was a pile of clothing and other bits of assorted equipment. The scene reminded Dane of his first day in the Army when he walked through a similar room being issued with his kit.

Ted measured him and as Dane stripped off, found the right size lightweight thermal long johns and a T-shirt. Over that Dane pulled on black flame-retardant overalls. They were thick, warm, and zipped up to his throat. Then heavy ballistic body armour, over which went a nylon waistcoat, known as a raid vest, with pockets arranged on the chest and two across the small of his back. The ensemble was complete with combat boots, a full-face balaclava, and gloves.

'This is a fibre optic camera and viewer. Try not to break it, it cost me a bloody fortune,' Lord said.

It was lightweight with a colour screen about the size of a smart phone. Lord pulled out a telescopic arm, no thicker than a shoelace and switched the device on.

'It's simple to operate,' Lord explained. As he slid the tip of his finger across the screen, the arm wriggled like a worm. 'It will extend out to a foot and is small enough to slip through just about any crack.'

Ted held out NVE-7 level 3-night vision goggles with rubber eye pieces that shielded the eyes and a single monocular lens.

'These are the best around. They operate in all light conditions from zero to bright sunlight and not lose any effectiveness. It's charged, and the batteries will last for hours. Do you want to use a helmet?'

'No, it might restrict my movements. Can I wear them over the balaclava?'

'No problem,' Ted replied and produced another pair with a harness that looked like the type on an American electric chair. They fitted the goggles and adjusted the straps. Dane switched them on, and everything turned a pale green. Adjusting the focus, he played with the controls and held his hands out. It was almost as good as using his eyeball. His depth of vision was unaffected.

'These are brilliant,' he declared, taking them off, 'Much better than the stuff I've used before and they're well balanced.'

'The best money can buy. They come with a nifty million candle power infrared spotlight. It'll illuminate your path for a hundred and fifty meters, and it is invisible to the naked eye.'

'Unless there is someone at the other end with a detector.'

'Yes, there is that caveat. If you prefer to be picky,' Lord said. 'Take it anyway, it's only half a kilo.'

Dane pushed a mobile phone earpiece into his left ear and a radio one in the other. Now he could use both devices with the switches clipped on the vest. He filled his pockets with nylon zip locks for restraints, a roll of duct tape, small wooden wedges, screwdrivers, plyers, and a Stanley knife. With his lock picks, a conventional torch, and asp baton stowed, he was ready to go.

Lord eyed the weapon, 'Is that all you are taking?'

'It's all I need.'

They tested the communications equipment and packed everything into a rucksack. Dane climbed onto the waiting motorcycle.

'Good luck. I'll be monitoring from here. If there are any updates, we'll contact you via the radio,' Lord said.

'Thanks,' Dane replied. They shook hands and he checked his watch. Forty minutes had elapsed since the telephone call from Rafferty. Another hour and twenty to get in position and save the three women he loved more than life itself. Dane tapped the rider on the shoulder, and they rode out of the yard towards Essex.

leaving Lord's office, he hopped off the motorbike and tapped the rider on the shoulder.

'Thanks for the ride.'

'Good luck, boss.' The bike drove off at a much more sedate and legal pace.

Dane was alone and looked around to fix his bearings. To his right was the gate to Temple Farm, owned by old friends who worked the surrounding land. He was on a country road that went to the next village. The lay-by with the terrorist's possible getaway car was a mile away. Dane settled down beside a wall to inspect his backpack and equipment and ensure nothing would rattle. He slipped the goggles over his head and tightened the straps. When they were comfortable and secure, he switched them on and sat for a minute until his eyes had adjusted to the artificial light.

'Radio check,' he murmured, and Lord responded.

'Loud and clear. The sentry is still outside. The woman has just given him a hot mug of something. They have drawn all the curtains. We are certain there are no cameras operating.'

'Roger. Has the guard walked around at all?'

'He has done that twice. He stayed on the lawn and circled the property. We have eyes on him and will warn you next time he moves.'

'Received. I'm moving now.'

He jogged along the road until the glow of the security lights in his parent's garden came into view in the distance. In between were four hundred yards of cultivated fields sown with spring crops. The ground was bare, with no cover at all. At the headland of each field were deep ditches, like the one he found his father in. This would be his route home. He slid down through the hedge into a ditch. There was a trickle of water running at the bottom. Not enough to hold him up.

Dane checked his watch. He had half an hour left. The weather was dull and overcast, with heavy clouds threatening rain. With the night vision gear, he had a clear view for about thirty yards. As keen as he was to get home, he couldn't afford to rush. If the terrorists had laid traps in the garden, then they might have considered the approach routes across the field. He picked his way carefully along the ditch. It took him six minutes to reach a point fifty yards from the fence surrounding his parents' garden.

He settled down to listen. Something rustled nearby and slowly turning his head saw a fox fifteen feet away. It was motionless, nose twitching as it stared in his direction, with one leg off the ground. It suddenly ran off and galloped across the field before stopping for another nervous glance back. Dane moved, his eyes constantly scanning the ground in front of him for obstacles.

At the fence, he paused again, checking the surroundings and his route into the stream bed. There was a gap of about two feet for him to crawl under. He plucked a long stem of grass and held it between thumb and forefinger, the full length of it pointing towards the ground. He gently extended his arm. Nothing impeded the grass. He lowered himself down and crawled forward, an arm's length. He shivered as the cold water soaked through his clothing. On the third repetition, the grass hit an obstruction. By this time, Dane was halfway under the fence, and he could see the garden on his left. The stream ran to the road a hundred and fifteen feet away and where he expected to find the lookout. Dane reached to where the grass had hit the obstacle. A length of thin wire stretched across his path, with one end tied to a tree. At the other end, it was connected to an oblong object, about eight by six inches, hidden in the undergrowth. He crabbed sideways and peered at it through the goggles and made out the words "Front towards the Enemy" embossed on it.

Dane recognised it immediately and swore under his breath. Where the hell did they get these from? He thought. It was a US Army M18 Claymore mine. A lethal anti-personnel device, packed with C4 explosive and seven hundred steel balls. These would spray out like a giant shotgun blast when the mine detonated. Dane carefully did a fingertip search of the ground around the base of the mine. When soldiers laid them, they would place the safety pin at the base of the weapon. A standard operating procedure so everyone knew where to find it if they needed to disarm it. It did not surprise him when he couldn't find

## VENGEANCE DAY

it. The terrorists were probably going to abandon this one, so had taken it with them. If they had one, there would be others.

Dane untied the trip wire from the tree and was about to proceed when he had a thought. He gingerly lifted the live mine from its hiding place and wriggled back out into the ditch to consider his options for a moment. His strategy was high risk. The chances of success were low, even with the element of surprise. Rafferty and his gang must have an escape plan, and Dane guessed their route out would be through the rear gate to their car. If they were able to do that, it would mean Dane and his family would probably be dead. He saw no reason to make life easy for the terrorists, so he decided to set his own trap. Dane relaid the mine, taking care to aim it along the outside of the fence. He positioned the tripwire so that anyone coming out that way would hit it and detonate the claymore. After camouflaging and rearming it, he resumed his approach.

Once through the fence, he shuffled sideways a few feet to get out of the stream bed. The sentry was beyond his view, but he had a good idea where the man would be. Dane spotted another trip wire attached to the back gate, which disappeared into the flower beds. That wouldn't concern him. He switched the infrared spotlight on to study his route. It was as effective as Lord had boasted, and in the ghostly light he saw his quarry, standing where he expected to find him. Halfway between them was another booby trap, which he noted, then moved. He checked with the grass, if there were no obstructions, he raised his body up on elbows and toes, then gently levered himself forward to advance an arm's length at a time. It was taking much too long, and Dane was acutely aware he was falling behind schedule. The night vision goggles were causing a small but irritating problem. They only weighed a couple of pounds, but he found it difficult to keep his head up while flat on his belly. He was still well short of the gate when the radio crackled to life.

'Stand by. The sentry is moving.'

Dane had already spotted the terrorist pick up his rifle. He watched as the man trudged down the lawn, his eyes sweeping the area. Dane lay still but knew he would be invisible, the lights illuminating the garden would have ruined the man's night vision. As he disappeared round the building, Dane stood and scuttled through the undergrowth and carefully backed into the shrubbery behind where the guard had been standing. He reappeared a minutes later and sauntered along the front of the house. When he reached his place, he propped the weapon against the gatepost and pulled a hand-held radio from his pocket. He was so close Dane could smell the sweat from him.

'I've checked the perimeter. It's all clear.'

There was a crackle, and a voice replied, 'Okay. Stay put. No more communication until he arrives.'

Lord spoke, 'No movement from inside that we can detect. You are two minutes past your deadline. Next phase moving.'

Dane tensed as headlights appeared up the road. The lights grew stronger as they came straight towards the gate, dazzling the guard. As he reached for his rifle, Dane stepped forward and looped his right arm around the terrorist's throat. The crook of his elbow closed over the man's Adam's apple. Dane braced it with his left forearm behind the neck. Then half turned, and leant sideways, lifting him, and squeezed. It was a classic choke hold, depriving the brain of blood and oxygen. The terrorist's fingers scrabbled at Dane's arm, desperately trying to prise it away. Within seconds, his body went limp. Dane lowered him to the floor, secured his hands and feet with zip ties then gagged him with a strip of duct tape. As his eyes flickered open, Dane whispered in his ear, 'If you move or try to escape. My friends will kill you. Do you understand?'

The stunned sentry stared at the figure bending over him in astonishment and nodded.

'One down and secured,' Dane muttered.

'Roger,' Lord replied, 'You are now four minutes late. No movement noted at any of the windows.'

It took seconds to reach the side door to the garage, which was locked. He shone the lamp through the window. His mother's car was parked in its usual place. Another trip wire was tied to the inside of the door handle. Dane pulled his lock picks out and got to work. A minute later, the door cracked open, and

## VENGEANCE DAY

he slipped his fingers through the gap and snipped the wire. He crept inside and stood still. The army trained him to search rooms in complete darkness, using only touch and his other senses. Unlike cryptology, Dane had been good at this and rarely left any sign of his presence. He didn't need to be so careful tonight and swept the infrared beam around. Another claymore was at the end of the wire he had just cut, but there was nothing else. The integral kitchen door was shut, so he gently pushed a wedge into the frame, jamming it closed.

The front wheel of his mother's car was sitting far enough onto the cellar's hatch to block it. He considered the possibility that the terrorists had done this deliberately but discounted it. This was where his mother had parked, and Dane would have to move it.

The car doors were locked, and he wouldn't be able to bounce it out of the way. That would make too much noise. Dane searched his father's tool bench and found a claw hammer and two old dust sheets, which he spread over the passenger side window. After a practice swing, he took a deep breath and hit the glass. A dull thump reverberated round the garage, which sounded very loud to Dane. The window remained intact, and he paused. He couldn't hear any movement from inside, so tried again.

It took three blows before the toughened glass shattered and fell into the car with a whoosh. Dane leant through and released the handbrake. As he heaved the car back a couple of feet, the dressing on his back tore, and he felt blood trickling from the wound. After reapplying the brake, he cut an oblong section out of the carpet, exposing the hatch beneath, and placed his ear on it.

There were no sounds below him, so he opened it and pointed the torch down. His mother was sitting below him with her eyes shut and head resting on Robyn's shoulder. The sudden movement above caught his daughter's attention. She looked up, fear etched on her face. They both had their hands tied behind their backs. A woman police officer was opposite them, and another figure lay motionless beside her. Dane dropped next to Robyn, who cringed at his touch.

'It's dad,' he whispered into her ear.

She tried to speak, but he stopped her, 'Let's get you all out.'

He crept to the bottom of the stairs and switched the camera on. The screen flickered to life, and he slid the fibre optic under the door. Vicky came into focus, lying on the kitchen floor, and Dane felt his stomach flip as he stared at her. He could now see if anyone approached or intended to come into the cellar or the garage. Dane propped the screen so he could keep an eye on it and returned to Robyn.

'When I cut you free, it will hurt like hell. You must keep quiet, okay?' She nodded, and he sliced through the nylon rope. Robyn moaned gently as the blood rushed into her hands.

'Good girl,' he mumbled and turned to his mother. Her eyes were wide open, her head tilted, and a quizzical expression on her face. There was a dark bruise along her jawline.

Dane touched her shoulder, 'Hi mum. Happy birthday.'

'You're late,' she whispered.

'Sorry about that,' he replied, and cut her bonds. She gasped and shuddered in pain as he rubbed her wrists. Her arms were black with the bruising caused by the ropes. Dane had difficulty controlling his emotions. He left Robyn to care for his mother and moved to the woman officer. His anger grew at the sight of her blood-stained face and the deep laceration over her eye, 'It's Superintendent Dane, remember me? We met when my father disappeared. You're Becky James.'

She stared straight ahead, her eyes like saucers, 'Oh, thank God,' she whispered as he picked the lock on her handcuffs.

'I need your help. Are you up to it?'

'Yes,' she replied, and crouched down beside her partner, 'He needs a doctor.'

Dane checked for a pulse but couldn't find one. He removed the cuffs and rolled the body into the recovery position.

'We can't move him. He's too badly injured. Once the medics arrive, they'll help him.'

'Okay,' she whispered.

## VENGEANCE DAY

'I will lift you up into the garage. Then I want you to lead these two out. There are some people waiting. When you reach them, contact the control room. Tell them what's happened and that I'm inside. They must send an armed response and ambulances. Have you got that?'

Becky nodded. After whispering instructions, Dane boosted them all up through the hatch and led them outside.

'Party of three to come out,' he muttered over the radio.

'No movement visible. Safe to proceed.'

Dane turned to Becky, 'Stick to the wall. Go through the gate and turn right. There's a van parked up there waiting to help you.'

Robyn was staring at her father, 'What about Vicky?'

'She's next. I need you to take your grandmother to safety. Three moving now,' he muttered into the radio.

'Roger,' Lord replied.

'Go and don't stop.'

Robyn and Becky carried his mother between them. As they passed out of sight, relief flooded over him. He returned to the cellar and checked the officer again. His skin was already cold.

Dane crept up the steps, testing each one before putting all his weight on it. As he did so Lord reported in his ear, 'Package collected and safe. The cavalry is being called.'

Dane stood next to the main fuse box with its red master switch. He grasped the latch and watched the viewer. Vicky hadn't moved, and Mary was now standing over her. She appeared to be talking to someone. As he watched, Mary suddenly walked out of sight, and he paused.

\*

Liam stared at his watch. Dane was nearly twenty-five minutes late. He rubbed his face and turned to look at Mary, 'What do you think?'

'Perhaps he couldn't get transport. Or someone delayed him.'

'I don't like it. There's something wrong, I can feel it.' He picked up the radio and weighed it in his hand. Then he put it to his mouth and pressed the switch. 'Any movement out there?'

There was no reply. Liam waited a beat and tried again.

'The battery might be dead,' Mary said. She walked to the front window and cautiously pulled the edge of the curtain aside to peer out.

'Is he there?'

'I can't see him. He should be by the gate.'

'Maybe he's checking round the back.'

Mary ran to the conservatory and carefully looked round the closed blinds, 'He's not out here.' She chanced another look and re-joined Liam, 'He won't suddenly decide to go walkabout will he. Not when Dane is due.'

Liam looked through the curtains again. 'You're right. They're out there. I told Dane. I warned him what would happen if…' His face was pale and devoid of expression, his eyes like flint, 'Get her.' He nodded towards Vicky and drew his pistol. 'Let's see how they enjoy watching her head explode, shall we? If they still want to play, we've got the rest of them to barter with.'

*

Lord spoke, 'They're calling the sentry. There is movement at the window. Someone is looking out.'

Dane watched Mary hurry through the kitchen and out into the conservatory and return moments later.

'They've twigged something is wrong. You need to move now,' Lord said.

Mary reappeared, pistol in her hand, and grabbed Vicky by the hair, hauling her to her feet. Taking a deep breath, Dane flicked the power switch, plunging the house into darkness. He pulled the door open and moved straight to Mary.

She still held Vicky, but was looking around, startled. A man's voice exclaimed from the sitting room. As Mary turned her pistol towards Vicky, Dane lashed down with his baton. The centrifugal force of the swing forced the twenty inches of steel to extend from the handle. It all clicked into place as it struck her wrist. Dane drove the blow down like a sword strike.

The dull thump of a shot made Dane's ears ring as Mary yelped and dropped her gun. Vicky collapsed to the floor as Dane grabbed a handful of Mary's sweatshirt. Rafferty was eight feet away, one hand out, groping in the darkness and holding a weapon. Dane yanked Mary forward, propelling her into Rafferty. Their heads collided with a sharp crack like billiard balls striking, and they both fell in a tangle.

He stepped over them and snapped handcuffs onto Mary, then threw her aside. Rafferty was struggling upright, searching for the pistol he'd dropped. Dane kicked him in the face, knocking him flat on his back. He flipped Rafferty over, then drove his knee into his back, pinning him down before securing him with a zip tie. Dane frisked them both, threw their weapons out of reach, then looked round for Vicky. She was lying six feet away, motionless. He knelt by her side and cradled her head.

'It's me Vicky.'

'Christian...'

The rush of relief he felt when she spoke to him was indescribable, 'Hang on.' He turned the power back on, then pulled the goggles off and knelt beside her. She blinked her one good eye in the sudden light. As he cut the ropes, she gave a gasp of pain, which became low moans as the circulation returned to her hands.

Dane called Lord, 'All secure, no casualties.'

'Received. Police and ambulance are on route. Well done.'

'Can someone retrieve the sentry?'

'Roger.'

'Your mum, and Robyn...' Vicky said.

'They're safe.'

'But they were in the... Ah, the trapdoor.'

He nodded, 'I got them out with Becky.'

'What about her partner?'

Dane shook his head. He checked her for injuries, then helped her to sit up and saw the damage to her face. 'Who did this to you?'

She glanced quickly at Rafferty. Dane gathered her into his arms and carried her to the sitting room and laid her on the settee.

There was a knock on the door. Dane opened it to find Patsy being supported between two of Lord's men.

'Thanks guys. I'll take him from here. You had better make yourselves scarce.'

## SIMON DINSDALE

They both grinned, 'Good job, boss.'

Dane half dragged Patsy into the kitchen and threw him down beside the others. They all glared at him, raw hatred twisting their features.

'You're all under arrest for murder and kidnapping. The first of many other charges, I'm sure, but that should do for now,' he said, and cautioned them.

'This isn't over,' Liam snarled.

'After what you creatures have done today, they will throw the keys away. But if there is a next time, I won't be so gentle.'

Dane filled a bowl with hot water and found a clean cloth before sitting beside Vicky. He gently dabbed the cut over her eye and wiped the blood from her face. 'How're you feeling?'

'My chest hurts,' she peered at him, 'And I am seeing two of you.'

'Help will be here soon.'

She took in his sodden, mud smeared clothes and equipment. Then glanced towards the front door, looking confused.

'Where's everyone else?'

'What do you mean?' Dane replied.

'The back up... Oh God you didn't do this alone, did you?'

'Not quite. I had some help.'

'Who from?'

'John Lord and his men.'

She gaped at him, then she closed her one good eye and shook her head. 'You haven't told anyone, have you?'

Dane shrugged his shoulders, 'I couldn't. He gave me very explicit instructions. And made it abundantly clear what he would do if I didn't follow them.'

'We all heard him give them to you.'

'Then you know why I had to do as he wanted.'

She grasped his hand. 'I'm glad you did.

'How did they get in?'

'They forced John to ring the doorbell by threatening to shoot Becky,' She glared over at the three terrorists, 'It's my fault. I opened the door. The leader barged in and hit me with his rifle butt. I only just had time to push the panic button.'

## VENGEANCE DAY

Dane held her by the shoulders. 'It is not your fault. If you hadn't, they would have broken in. And things might have been much worse.'

'After the telephone call, they put the others in the cellar. That evil woman punched your mother. For nothing.' Vicky shook her head in disgust. 'Those two men are bad enough. But her…'

'They won't be hurting anyone else for a long time.'

'I hope so. John was so brave. He fought them. They beat him while his hands were tied behind his back.'

'We will make sure no one forgets him.'

They were silent for a few moments before Vicky said, 'It will be an interesting conversation with Perkins when he finds out what you've been up to.'

'I'll worry about that later. Right now, my priorities are you, Robyn, and mum.'

The distant sound of sirens grew until several vehicles pulled up outside and flickering blue lights illuminated the room. Dane helped Vicky up and they opened the front door. A uniform inspector with a young woman constable were walking towards them. Dane heard a cry and looked up to see Robyn running towards him.

'Dad, it's grandma. She's collapsed. Come quick.'

Dane grabbed the inspector, 'There are three people inside. All secured and under arrest. They are responsible for the attacks in London this morning and the kidnap of my family. Guard them until relieved. You must not talk to or go anywhere near them. They are extremely dangerous. Do not take any chances.'

'Leave it with me, sir. I can handle this,' the inspector replied, and, with the constable in tow, marched inside.

Dane and Vicky followed Robyn to an ambulance. A paramedic was kneeling astride his mother's body on the stretcher. Her straight arms pounding up and down as she delivered chest massage.

'She's suffered a cardiac arrest. Call it in. We must run now,' she shouted.'

Dane gestured to Robyn and Vicky, 'Go with them. I'll follow as soon as I've sorted this lot out. Where are you taking her?' he called to the medic.

'Colchester. Get in if you're coming because we're leaving.'

The doors slammed shut, and they roared away, blue lights flashing and siren wailing. Dane returned to the gate, where a chief inspector with four officers and another ambulance had arrived. As he briefed the paramedics, there were muffled shouts and the sound of smashing glass. Seconds later, the constable ran out of the house.

'They've escaped,' she screamed.

Some of the cops started to move forward.

'Wait,' Dane bellowed. 'Stand still. They have booby trapped the place. Stay where you are. No one is to go off the path.'

A sudden bright flash illuminated the sky. A tremendous explosion from behind the house followed it. Everyone automatically ducked, and a thick pall of acrid smoke rolled over the garden and enveloped them.

# VENGEANCE DAY

## Chapter 22

Dane jogged up the path to the door, where he paused and peered inside. He crept along the passage and into the kitchen. The inspector was lying on his back with his arms splayed out beside him. Blood seeping from a serious head injury. Dane could feel a faint pulse and shouted through the door, 'Bring the paramedics up here.' Two female medics came in moments later and took over from him. A quick check confirmed there was no sign of the terrorists. Dane looked through the conservatory door and saw the back fence was in tatters.

The chief inspector was waiting outside the front door, 'Do you know the officers in here?' Dane asked.

'Yes, Ian Patterson and PC John Olds.'

'I'm afraid Olds is dead, and Patterson is seriously injured.'

'Oh no. Are you sure?' When Dane confirmed that the man looked stricken, and for a moment clearly didn't know what to do next.

'We must preserve the property as a crime scene. Post a guard on the road at the far side of the fields,' Dane prompted.

'Yes, of course. Sorry you must think I'm an idiot,' the chief inspector replied.

'No, I don't. But you've lost friends. I know what that's like. Make sure that everyone stays off the farmland until the area has been cleared and made safe. Under no circumstances is anyone to move off this front path. There are more explosive charges in the garden.'

'Who were these people?'

'The terrorists who perpetrated the attack in London this morning.'

'What were they doing here?'

'I upset them.' The chief inspector looked bewildered by that answer. 'It's a personal thing between me and the man who was leading them.

The medics confirmed the death of Constable Olds and after treating Inspector Patterson they lifted him into the ambulance.

## SIMON DINSDALE

More police were arriving, and they soon had the scene under control.

Before he left, Dane changed his clothes then cautiously picked his way across the lawn to the fence line. There was a strong smell of gunpowder in the air, but it was still and silent. He played the torch beam over the field and into the ditch. A shattered torso lay twenty yards away, beyond that a naked leg shone in the torchlight next to a human head. More hunks of flesh and shattered bone were scattered around. There was no movement. The three of them had run into the Claymore he'd moved and set up to foil their escape. They had stood no chance and must have died instantly.

Dane didn't feel an ounce of guilt or remorse, 'I told you I wouldn't be so gentle,' he muttered.

He begged a lift to the hospital and halfway there, Perkins rang him.

'I've received calls about a terrorist incident at your parents' home. What on earth is going on?'

Dane had been expecting this conversation and took a moment to compose himself and keep his anger in check, 'Before I answer that. Why there were only two, unarmed, officers posted outside the house?'

'What do you mean? That's not what I ordered.'

'Well, something went wrong. Rafferty and his gang seized them, together with my family. They murdered one of the officers. And the last time I saw my mother, or Vicky, they were in an ambulance.'

'Oh God. I gave explicit instructions to deploy an armed response team. I will sort that out. But what happened there?'

'Rafferty told me to go to my parents' home, alone. He made it clear that if anyone else became involved, he'd kill them all. And I believed him.'

'What did you do?'

'I did as I was instructed. When I got there, I released the hostages. Then subdued and arrested Rafferty and friends. My mother collapsed so I had to leave them being guarded by two officers. Somehow, they got free and nearly killed one of them.'

## VENGEANCE DAY

'What a mess,' Perkins groaned. 'Where are you?'
'Halfway to Colchester hospital.'
'Okay. I'll find you there later. Are you alright?'
'I've escaped unscathed. Which is more than can be said for everyone else in there,' Dane snapped, and without waiting for a reply, broke the connection. He spent the rest of the journey in silence, staring out of the window.

Dane found Vicky in the treatment area of accident and emergency, being examined by a doctor.

When he finished, he took Dane aside, 'She has a concussion and a couple of broken ribs. We'll keep her in overnight as a precaution.'

Dane stared at Vicky's battered face and fought to keep back the tears, 'I'm so sorry.'

'What for? This isn't your fault. You couldn't have done any more to save us all. How is your mum?'

'I don't know,' He turned to the nurse, 'Where did they take her?'

'She's in the cardiac unit.'

'You had better go to her. I'll be okay.'

He sprinted through the long corridors, following the signs hanging from the ceiling. At the ward reception desk, a formidable-looking sister demanded to know who he was. Once he'd identified himself, her demeanour changed, and she showed him into a room where Robyn was sitting on the edge of a chair. She jumped up and threw her arms around him.

'Grama's not doing too well. They're operating on her.' They hugged each other before he held Robyn at arm's length and looked at her.

'Did they hurt you?'

'My wrists are sore but apart from that I'm not injured. They were so mean to Vicky and Gran. What about John and Becky?'

'I'm afraid John is dead. I've not seen her.'

'They took her into casualty when we arrived,' Robyn slumped against his chest and sobbed, 'He was so brave and tried to protect us. The leader smashed him over the head with the gun. It was terrible, dad. Why do that to someone who couldn't hurt them?'

'I can't answer that. I don't understand it either.'

'I hope they burn in hell.' she declared.

They both fell silent again as they waited for what seemed an eternity until a doctor arrived and sat down with them.

'Your mother has suffered a massive heart attack. Almost certainly caused by an embolism which formed when she was tied up. We've managed to stabilise her. But I must be frank with you. Her prognosis is poor.'

'May we see her?'

'Of course. The nurse will show you the way.'

They sat at her bedside. Dane watched her chest rise and fall to the rhythm of the ventilator. She looked peaceful and in no pain but was in an induced coma. Her arms and face bore the marks of her mistreatment. As the long night wore on, Dane recalled all the wonderful memories he had of his parents and their lovely home. The hours spent with his father in the cellar. Fresh cakes and bread in the kitchen baked by his mother. But the images of the two officers kept intruding and clouding the happiness. How could it ever be the same again? As dawn broke, Robyn had fallen asleep and his right arm was numb from the pressure of her head, but he wouldn't disturb her.

At seven, there was a racket in the corridor and the sound of furniture being dragged along the floor. Dane found two armed police officers setting up a table and chairs.

'Morning boss. Sorry to disturb you. We have been sent to mount a guard. There are also teams with Ms Needham and your father.'

'Why now?'

'The press is all over the place asking questions. And it's not been confirmed that all the terrorists died. So, there's still a threat and we're here to watch out for you.'

Dane left Robyn at his mother's bedside and went to check on Vicky. She was sitting up in bed but was pale and winced in pain when she moved to kiss him.

## VENGEANCE DAY

'I have got a banging headache, and I hurt all over. How's your mum?'

'She's fighting, but they don't think she'll pull through,' he replied, then his resolve slipped as tears stung his eyes. She grabbed his hand and squeezed.

Dane explained why an armed guard had appeared and after promising to come back later left her to visit Becky James. The young constable's bruised and swollen face was a testament to her ordeal. She had learned of the death of her friend and was being comforted by her husband. Dane spent half an hour with them, thanking Becky for what she had done for his family. He returned to Robyn who was whispering to her grandmother and stroking her hand. He left her to it and went to sit in the waiting room where he was joined by Perkins.

'First, I must apologise for what's happened. As you know I was out of the county when you called me yesterday. I issued clear orders about what should be done. The person who received those instructions ignored them. The chief has suspended him pending a full investigation.'

'Who is it?'

'Grant.'

Dane closed his eyes, 'What did he do?'

'He thought you were overreacting. He decided it would be a waste of money calling out the firearms team. So, he instructed the local division to do what they did.'

'Well, he'll have to live with the consequences. Do we know how they escaped?'

'The young officer has been interviewed. She told us the woman, Mary, complained that you had broken her arm and demanded they remove the handcuffs. At first Inspector Patterson ignored her. But she persisted and threatened retribution should she suffer further injury and her civil rights be infringed. It appears Patterson was frightened of getting a complaint. So, released her, intending to handcuff her hands to the front. The instant she was free, she pushed him away, snatched an iron skillet off the stove and bashed him over the head. Mary then turned on the constable. She had the good sense to run for it.'

'Thank heavens she did. How is Patterson?'

'Not good. He suffered serious head injuries and has been taken to London for specialist care. The bomb disposal teams have located two more claymores in the garden and are working their way across the fields. The forensic team won't get access until later this afternoon. You can't return to your parents' home for the time being.'

'Once I know what's happening with my mother, we'll stay at my place.'

'Good. As of today, you are on indefinite leave. After what you've been through in the past twenty-four hours, you need time to sort yourself out. This is not a suspension. Nor are you being punished.' Dane protested, but Perkins stopped him.

'Listen. I think I understand why you did what you did. But the story has leaked to the press. That, coupled with your exploits in London, has excited them. So, you're on leave and recovering from your ordeal with your family. It must be better for you to stay out of the public eye.'

'It smacks of me being hidden away.'

'The best thing for you is to look after your loved ones. We will keep you informed of any progress in the investigation.'

'What about the flat in Coral Street?'

'Three people surrendered early this morning. The search team found weapons and explosives in the flat.'

'Have we identified them yet?'

'No, they all clammed up. You were right all along. There are the six from Frinton and Coral Street, the crew you tackled in Rotherhithe and those who died in their van in Kensington. It looks like the last three blundered into their own booby trap and set it off. I suppose they forgot about it in their rush to escape.'

'That's their bad luck,' Dane replied.

'Why did you do it?'

'Let me turn that round. What would you have done if I came to you and told you what was happening?'

## VENGEANCE DAY

'We'd have mobilised the troops and surrounded the place. They would never have escaped.'

'But that wouldn't have saved my family. The minute a negotiator made contact, or they spotted someone other than me, Rafferty would have slaughtered them all. They did it all to lure me there so he could kill me. Once he'd succeeded Rafferty was going to murder everyone else.'

'You can't be certain of that.'

'I can. I have a recording of our conversation to prove it. To paraphrase him. If he thought anyone was outside or if the wind were blowing in the wrong direction, they would all die. I had to do it myself. And it worked. They were all in custody with no casualties and they would be in the cell now, but for the misguided actions of that poor inspector.'

'I'll convey that explanation to the boss. You understand you'll have to explain your actions many times over in the coming weeks. Don't you?'

'I'm prepared for that. I have no regrets about what I did. If I'd come to you, you would've done your duty to the best of your ability. But I would have lost them all.'

There was a sudden commotion outside the room. People were running, then he heard Robyn shouting, 'Dad. Where are you…' She was standing outside the ward as doctors and nurses rushed past, pushing the crash trolley.

They held each other and watched as the medics surrounded the bed, all working to save his mother.

After twenty nerve wracking minutes, a young doctor stood back and glanced round at them, 'She's survived that scare and is hanging in there.'

\*

At home in Kent, Angus Boyd received a phone call from a well-placed source. As he listened, a grin spread across his face. Since the decision to clear Dane over the Isle of Dogs shooting, the media had dropped him. This snippet could give him the boost he needed to restore his fortunes.

'So, you are saying he took independent action which led to the deaths?'

'That's right. I have spoken to people who saw him at the house. He was dressed up like a bloody Ninja. Dane broke into the house without informing anyone what he was doing. He's got a mate in the security business who helped him out.'

'Who is that?'

'I don't know yet. I'm working on it.'

'You do that. Is there anything more?'

'No. When I get something, you'll be the first person I call.'

'Make sure I am. I'd better not read about this anywhere else. There'll be an envelope for you tomorrow.'

Within hours, Boyd had an article online and another ready for the following morning. A news channel promised a TV interview the day after, depending on how the story developed.

\*

Dane and Robyn remained beside his mother's bed. She looked serene but remained close to death. Robyn sobbed as he held her in his arms, then wiped her nose, 'I don't want to lose her. I've only just got to know her.'

'You're not going to. She won't give up, I promise you.' He checked his watch. 'I'm going to see Vicky.'

'Give her my love,' Robyn said and picked up her grandmother's hand.

Vicky's parents were visiting when he arrived. Her father was a distinguished looking man in his late sixties. Mrs Needham was about the same age, slim and impeccably dressed. Dane had met them once, and he got on well with Mr Needham. His wife was not keen on him. She regarded Dane with a haughty look, which slid when he told them what had happened to his mother. It was obvious she blamed Dane for Vicky's injuries and barely spoke to him before they left.

'Sorry. There's no need for her to behave like that,' Vicky said.

'It's alright. She's worried about you and after this little lot, I don't blame her. Ever since you met me, I've been a magnet for trouble. Are you sure we should carry on?'

'Of course, I am. None of this is your fault and if you go all guilty on me, I'll gave you a slap. You didn't kill that poor officer or put any of us in danger. Rafferty and his friends did.'

## VENGEANCE DAY

A doctor arrived to examine her and was happy she could be discharged. Vicky gathered her things together and they visited Dane's father. The old man was slowly recovering but still heavily sedated. The staff promised to ring Dane if there was any change in his condition. They returned to his mother's ward to collect Robyn. There was nothing more they could do at the hospital. They returned to Dane's house to find a team of officers waiting outside.

'We've searched, and it's all clear and safe,' the sergeant in charge said.

Sixteen hours later, Dane woke with a dull thumping headache and stumbled to the bathroom to spend ten minutes doubled over the bowel dry retching. He knew it was stress related. But it was getting worse every day and taking longer to bring his stomach under control.

Perkins arrived after lunch. He had a stack of newspapers under his arm.

'Have you seen the media?'

'No, what are they writing this time?'

'That reporter Boyd has written a piece accusing you of charging in like a reckless idiot. And by taking the law into your own hands, you caused the deaths at the house. We're receiving calls requesting a comment and we are reaching the point where we must respond.'

'I hope you're not expecting me to be involved.'

'No, I wasn't suggesting that. But I will issue a statement later today to quell the wilder accusations that are being bandied about.'

'They can write what they like. I've done nothing wrong.'

'The other thing to tell you is that the forensic experts have only found the remains of two people.'

'Are they sure?'

'Doctor Hume is certain he only has one man and a woman.'

Dane sighed and glanced over at Robyn and Vicky who had heard the exchange.

## Chapter 23

On Wednesday morning, Dane spent an hour with his father and tried to explain what had happened. The old man was slowly being weaned off the sedatives but was still very weak and confused, so soon fell asleep. His mother remained unconscious and dependent on the life-support machine, but he stayed for a while, whispering to her. He drove home feeling more miserable than he could ever recall. Perkins called round that evening, with news from the investigation.

'The vehicle seen close to your parents' house has turned up in the crew car park at Harwich port. The security guards spoke to the driver who left it there and he fit's Rafferty's description. He showed a seafarer's card registered to a luxury yacht. The records show that vessel sailed late on Sunday evening.'

'Who owns it, and where did it go?' Dane replied.

'It belongs to an American financier and was in Harwich for repairs. The Border Force has located it sailing west off the coast of Cornwall.'

'Is it out of our reach?'

'No, it isn't. There are a team of people on their way to intercept it. Let's keep our fingers crossed, and hope Rafferty is on there. How are Vicky and Robyn?'

'They are both on the mend. Has there been anything else in the press?'

'No, but Boyd is becoming a nuisance. It looks like he's got a well-placed source is supplying him with information that can only have come from within the investigation. He fills in the gaps with wild conjecture about you.'

'That's nothing new. I'm beyond caring about what he writes.'

'It makes no difference to the truth. There is a consensus forming that what you did was unorthodox but justified. You'll hear that officially next week. None of this should have happened, though. I am so sorry.'

'It's not your fault. What's done is done, so let's move on.'

## VENGEANCE DAY

Once Perkins had left, Dane contacted Lord, 'Have they visited you yet?'

'Yes. We've supplied the recordings and transcripts of the telephone conversation with Rafferty and the radio chatter. Are they causing you any bother?'

'Not really. My bosses seem to understand why I did what I did. I hope your involvement doesn't cause you a problem?'

'Not a chance. I showed them all the written authorities to monitor your phones. I think we've surprised a few people with what we are capable of. That can only be good for business.'

'You had better send me your bill.'

'I can't charge you for that. It was my patriotic duty to help you.'

'My lot and the Independent Office of Police Conduct are aware I employed your company to watch our back. That will also come out during the trial of the surviving terrorists. I'd be happier if I can prove I paid for your services. Then no one can say I've been getting a freebie, or it's a corrupt relationship. On top of all that. The press is creeping around and someone close to the investigation is talking out of turn. It won't be long before your involvement is splashed over the papers.'

'Well, if you insist. I'll send you an invoice. It might make your eyes water, though. We're not cheap.'

'I didn't think you were. That's why I hired you. Would you thank all the operators who helped me, please.'

'I've already done that. They wanted me to congratulate you to.'

*

Pete Higgins was at the helm of Water Horse and, for the umpteenth time in the last hour, checked the radar. The blip was still there. They were a hundred and fifty miles southwest of Plymouth. Billy was with him on the darkened bridge. Higgins had received a frantic telephone call the previous Sunday and, as a result, set sail in a hurry. Their passage through the Channel passed without incident, and as the Cornish coast slipped over the horizon, he had finally relaxed. Then, this vessel appeared and rapidly closed behind them. It was too big to be a fishing trawler and far too small to be a cruise ship. They were holding position a mile astern invisible in the darkness. Higgins peered through binoculars but couldn't even see their navigation lights. They had to be Navy, he thought, but why sit there like that? Earlier he had changed course to a more southerly heading, and the mysterious craft had matched him.

'They're closing,' Billy said.

'Guess we'll find out who they are soon.'

Five minutes later, the marine VHF radio crackled to life, and a voice came over the airwaves.

'His Majesties War Ship to Water Horse, come in on channel sixteen over.'

Higgins took a deep breath, 'Water Horse to His Majesties War Ship. Good evening, over.'

'His Majesties War Ship to Water Horse switch to Channel ten, out.' The curt instruction left him in no doubt that something was wrong. He changed the frequency as instructed and hailed them.

Powerful searchlights illuminated Water Horse's starboard quarter. Higgins and Billy instinctively turned to look out of the window. As they did so the door opened behind them. Higgins was grabbed and pushed face down on the deck. As he tried to struggle a foot between his shoulder blades pinned him down.

'We are a Royal Navy boarding party. Don't move. This vessel and crew are under arrest.'

Strong hands handcuffed Higgins, then lifted him into a sitting position. He was astonished to see five men all dressed in black with body armour and machine pistols strapped across their chests. One took over the helm, switched off the autopilot, and adjusted the yacht's speed and course with an easy familiarity. Two more commandos trussed Billy up and dumped him next to Higgins.

'Bridge is secure,' a masked figure said, then faced them, 'Who's the Master?'

'I am,' Higgins replied.

'How many more are there on board and where are they?'

'One should be in the galley and another in his cabin.'

'Names please.'

## VENGEANCE DAY

'I'm Peter Higgins. This is Billy Ellis, my first mate. Down below will be Neil Luckett and the other guy. He joined us in Harwich, I can't remember his name.'

'It's Jimmy Pierce.' Billy said.

'How come you don't know the names of your crew?'

'I told you, he only signed on the other day. I've not had much to do with him. I'd forgotten. Which is hardly surprising when I'm jumped on like this. This is a US registered boat, and we are American citizens. What is going on?'

Ignoring him, the leader started issuing instructions to other unseen members of his team. As he did so Water Horse came about.

'Where are we heading?' Higgins asked the helmsman, who didn't answer him. Their guards hauled them to their feet and frogmarched them down to the main salon. Neil was sitting in the corner looking bewildered, next to him were more commandos watching a tall black man who was dressed in boxer's shorts, his long dreadlocks falling over his shoulder.

'Is this your complete crew, Captain?'

'Yes, that's Neal, and this is Jimmy.'

'Is there anyone else on board?'

'No, we're sailing to the Caribbean to pick up the owner. Now what the hell is this is all about?'

'You are all under arrest and being taken to Plymouth.'

'On what charges? We are Americans. You can't just climb on my vessel and do this.'

'On suspicion of being involved in acts of terrorism,' the Commando said.

A thrill of fear passed through Higgins. He'd kept his nose out of his boss's business and sailed the yacht. But he knew what Rafferty and his friends were. They had all watched the news at the weekend and guessed who was responsible for the attack in London. If the Brits could prove what they had been doing, and Higgins suspected they would, then they were all in deep trouble.

*

By the end of the week, Vicky had recovered enough to accompany Dane and Robyn to visit his parents. His father was getting stronger by the day but hadn't been told about his wife yet. The doctors were concerned the news could cause him to relapse. It was impossible to hold a coherent conversation with him. Dane's mother was awake, and although she was off the ventilator, found it hard to speak. They spent some time with her before the nurse chivvied them out so she could get some rest. As they walked together towards their car, a reporter followed by a cameraman confronted them.

'Mr Dane. Can you tell us how your parents are doing?'
'They are recovering, thank you.'

He kept walking, forcing her to jog alongside him in her high heels, 'How does it feel to be the hero of the hour?'

'That's not how I see myself.'

'But you are. Many more people would have lost their lives but for your intervention.'

'I did my job, and I was lucky. Now if you'll excuse me.' He brushed past the journalists and walked quickly back to their car.

'How did they know we were here? Why can't they just leave us alone?' Dane complained as they drove away.

'They're camped outside waiting on the off chance. I know they are a pain, but you would appear rude if you ignored them. It's better to give them a moment of your time,' Vicky replied.

Dane had turned his phone off while they were in the hospital. When he switched it back on later that evening, a dozen text message alerts pinged. He glanced down the list and his eye caught a number he didn't recognise. He opened it and read.

*I only have to be lucky once this is not over.*

\*\*\*

In Tehran, Zand entered the office and stood at attention in front of the enormous desk. The General ignored him for five minutes as he dealt with the papers in front of him. He placed the last signed sheet aside, then fixed the man in front of him with a cold, hard gaze. Zand was reminded of a hawk glaring at its prey before the final deadly swoop. He had served the General for years and had an unblemished record, but knew his life now hung in the balance. He had failed. Or rather, those incompetent fools in London had and exposed him to this danger.

## VENGEANCE DAY

'What happened?'

'I made enquiries, Baradar General. It would appear the Irish freedom fighters were slack in their security. The police captured one team a day before the attack date. The rest bravely pressed on but were only able to fire one round before the police attacked and arrested them.' Zand paused.

'And what has become of him? This mighty freedom fighter?'

'He later attempted to murder the police officer responsible for disrupting his operation. Sadly, he failed in that enterprise as well. His current location is unknown. This setback will not diminish his desire to damage the British. I suspect he will be even more determined in the future.'

'He must do that without our help. You persuaded me to entertain these fools and their stupid enterprise, and they repay us with their incompetence. To make matters worse, we compromised valuable assets in Britain to cover for their pathetic attack. Our network there, developed at enormous cost, is now useless.' The General pressed a button on the desk. The door behind him opened and two guards walked in and stood on either side of Zand.

'This operation was ill conceived and has caused me personal inconvenience and embarrassment. You failed, and I can't accept that. I expected better from you.

The young revolutionary guardsmen seized Zand by the elbows and frogmarched him from the room. His legs buckled as they dragged him down the stairs and out into the former private garden of the US Ambassador to Iran. They forced him to his knees and, before he had time to offer a prayer, shot him in the back of the head. A week later, a report of the execution reached CIA headquarters in Langley, Virginia. The analysts assessed the information, then filed it without passing it to the wise men.

## Chapter 24

Liam huddled on the settee in the front room of the house he had shared with Mary and Patsy. He had spent the last few days watching the news channels, desperate for news about the fate of his comrades. The police had found the safe houses in the West Country. The letting agents recognised the descriptions of the people circulated in the media. Since then, less and less information was being released and the media were moving on to the next story.

Liam was left to stare out of the windows, waiting for the cops. There wasn't much chance of them finding this place. Mary rented the house more than a year before wearing a wig and speaking in her best English accent. None of the others knew about it. But in case the police got lucky all the doors were booby trapped and he didn't move without the AK47 in his arms and a pistol on his hip. If they came for him, they would pay a heavy price for his head. Sleep remained a problem, whenever he dropped off, the nightmares plague him.

The house was full of reminders of Mary and Patsy which depressed him even more. The only people he had ever allowed close enough to become friends were gone. Annihilated in an instant. That scene played out in his mind's eye. Mary had got them free. It took her seconds to dupe that stupid cop into undoing her handcuffs, and she struck like a cobra. They reached the fence where he removed the trip wire from the gate. He told them to go on while he re-set the booby trap. As he crouched down, the explosion blew him off his feet. Patsy and Mary had laid all those mines. So how did they run into one of them? It didn't make sense. He'd looked for them in the vain hope they might have survived but soon saw there was no chance.

Liam evaded the police and after staggering across the fields, escaped to Harwich. The memory of the empty wharf still made his blood boil. Higgins answered his call and told him his boss had ordered him to sail and not turn back. There had been no point raging at Higgins or contacting O'Halloran. It would make no difference and Liam knew he'd been abandoned. There would

## VENGEANCE DAY

be time to seek retribution for this treachery later. Besides, he had unfinished business to attend to here. And he was not about to give up.

Once back in the safety of the house Liam carefully analysed every move he'd made over the previous year. Every meeting and telephone call. Anything to do with the planning of the mission was taken to pieces in his head.

Liam knew their security had been tight. Apart from Mary and himself, no one knew the final targets until the day before the attack. Yet everything had fallen apart at the last moment. How could that have happened? There was only one logical conclusion. Someone had betrayed him. There was no other rational explanation for Dane having been at the firing point in Rotherhithe. Or arresting Eddy's crew in Frinton. But Liam had no idea how that had happened.

He watched the footage of Dane leaving the hospital and snarled defiance at the screen.

'I'll give you luck,' he snarled, then sent the text. He did it in anger and knew as soon as he pressed the send button, it was a serious mistake. But it brought him to his senses. He'd been hiding like an animal for a week. Wallowing in his own self-pity and filth. Liam looked down at himself in disgust.

'Pull yourself together and finish this,' he muttered.

He showered and changed into fresh clothes and packed a bag. Once ready, he set the last two Claymores before switching the phone on and placing it on the table. He drove away with a sense of purpose, invigorated by his determination to complete this final mission.

\*

Dane stared at the text for a moment and noticed he also had three missed calls from Perkins so rang him.

'I'm glad you called I've been trying to reach you.'

'I turned the phone off.' He told Perkins about the text message.

'I'll have someone investigate it. Can you tell the chaps outside so they're aware?'

'Yes, I will. But we're not moving out. Robyn is going home soon. I don't want to disrupt her anymore.'

## SIMON DINSDALE

'It's probably best if you all remain inside. We'll also put a discrete presence in to cover your parents.'

'Thanks. What happened with the yacht?'

'The SBS boarded it overnight and took it to Plymouth. Rafferty wasn't on board and the crew is staying silent. So, the chances are, he's still in the country, and thinking about another pop at you.'

Dane pondered that for a moment, 'We're not planning any trips out apart from a last visit to my parents before Robyn fly's home. If we go anywhere, I'll let you know.'

'Good. I will start the ball rolling about the message.'

For the first time in many years, Dane wasn't interested in the progress of an investigation. He intended to focus on his family for once. Perkins rang him the following morning to inform him they had located the house from where the text was sent. It was empty and wired with explosives. The bomb squad estimated it would take them three days to make the building safe. There would be no chance of any information from that source in the short term.

*

Liam took care and only drove past Dane's home once. He learned enough to realise it wouldn't be easy with police officers standing in the street. In the early hours of the following morning, he crept along the fence line on the property behind Dane's.

The security lights illuminated everything, and he saw more guards in the rear garden. It was not possible to directly observe the house. They had discovered that from the surveillance Mary and the others conducted when they first identified Dane. So, he broke into the residence opposite and tied the couple who lived there up and dumped them in their bedroom. He settled down in their front room with a clear view of the front of Dane's home.

The next morning, Liam watched as Dane and the two women were collected from the house and driven away. An hour later he dialled 999 and reported a suspicious man with a gun at an address four hundred yards away. He waited impatiently then smiled with satisfaction as the four cops stationed at the front jumped into their vehicle and sped off.

# VENGEANCE DAY

*

The welts around Robyn's wrists had faded, but Vicky's injuries were more obvious. The swelling around her eye had gone down, but a yellow bruise encircled it. She used a foundation to hide the damage and covered it all with a large round pair of dark glasses. It was the day Robyn was due to fly home to Canada. They had discussed the possibility of her staying until her grandparents were released from hospital but as that could be weeks she knew she had to go home. A driver arrived to take them to headquarters to collect a hire car. Then they drove to the hospital to say goodbye to Robyn's grandparents.

Mr and Mrs Dane remained in their respective wards. Mrs Dane was well enough to manage a prolonged hug with her granddaughter. They then visited Dane's father who now knew his wife lay in another ward, but not the full circumstances of how she got there. The news had distressed the old man, and he had relapsed over the last few days. When they arrived at the ward, they found he had been sedated again. It was upsetting for Robyn who was unable to say a proper farewell to her grandfather.

Dane drove to Heathrow airport at a sedate pace. He intended to savour every minute he had with Robyn before she had to check in for her flight. The atmosphere was subdued as they hugged each other before he and Vicky waved Robyn through the security gate. Dane was bereft and Vicky self-consciously wiped tears away, smudging her carefully applied makeup. They returned to Essex in silence.

On the way Vicky suggested a diversion to Lakeside shopping centre. Their mood lifted as they toured the shops in the massive mall. Dane smiled for the first time in days at the simple pleasure of watching Vicky enjoying herself as she indulged in an afternoon's retail therapy. His eyes never stopped scanning the crowds though.

The police guards greeted them when they arrived home and chatted as they unloaded the car. Dane carried the shopping bags upstairs and laid them on their bed, before using the bathroom. He washed his hands and turned to find a towel and froze. Two muddy footprints were around the plughole in the bath. Someone wearing shoes had stood behind the shower curtain in the small puddle of water left by their showers that morning. He checked the three bedrooms finding no other sign of an intruder.

As he came down the stairs, he could hear Vicky clattering about in the kitchen, 'Is that tea ready?'

'It's in the pot,' she replied, as he walked down the drive to speak to the guards.

'Has there been any excitement here today?'

'No boss. We came on duty at six and it has been quiet. There was a report of an armed man up the road this morning. A couple of the lads here went to help but it turned out to be a hoax,' the officer replied.

'Was the house left unattended?'

'No, and they searched everywhere on their return. Just to be on the safe side, is anything wrong?'

'No, just checking. Are you all right for a hot drink?'

'We're fine, thank you.'

As he walked back though the door Dane called out, but Vicky didn't reply. He walked down the hall towards the kitchen and saw her holding a mug of tea. Vicky was staring at something out of his sight. There was a look of abject terror on her face that made him freeze for the second time in as many minutes.

A familiar voice said, 'Come in, why don't you. We are just getting reacquainted, aren't we Vicky?'

Dane moved forward to find Rafferty standing about six feet away, aiming a pistol at them.

'You thought I'd disappear with my tail between my legs, didn't you? It doesn't matter how many guns you surround yourself with, you'll never be free from me. But you needn't worry anymore because you're both going to die.'

As the gun tracked towards Dane, there was a shout from outside, and the kitchen window disintegrated. Rafferty hesitated for a moment and Vicky threw the mug at his face. The scalding tea caused him to flinch and yelp in pain. Dane leapt across and grabbed his arm, deflecting the pistol up as Rafferty fired. The heat from the muzzle flash seared Dane's hair, the concussion making his ears ring. Dane used his other hand to smother the

## VENGEANCE DAY

pistol's top slide, forcing it back a fraction of an inch. When Rafferty tried to pull the trigger again, it misfired.

Vicky remained rooted to the spot for a second, before running off.

Rafferty clawed at Dane's eyes as they revolved around the kitchen, struggling in a deadly embrace bumping into the table and sending chairs crashing over. Dane brought his knee up, aiming for Rafferty's groin, only catching him on the thigh. He head-butted Rafferty twice on the nose, half stunning himself. Rafferty staggered and Dane felt him weaken, so hooked his foot behind Rafferty's leg, tripping him, and they both crashed to the floor. Dane landed on top, gripping the pistol, and punched him hard in the throat. Rafferty heaved his body and jerked his hand free. The pistol's slide clicked back into place. Dane grabbed Rafferty's wrist, and they wrestled for control of the gun as slowly, inexorably; the muzzle turned in to their bodies. A muffled shot rang out, and they both lay still. There was a scream as Vicky returned, followed by two officers who ran to stand over them.

'Roll off, boss.'

Dane rolled sideways onto his back, his chest heaving. Blood ran from a cut over his eye, but he was holding the pistol.

Rafferty lay on his back panting from the exertion. A bloodstain was creeping along his shirt, low on the side of his body.

'I'm alright,' Dane grunted.

One cop stood over Rafferty, while the second frisked him and handcuffed his hands to his front.

Dane unloaded the weapon and placed it beside the sink. He turned to Vicky who dabbed his brow with a tea towel, mopping up the blood.

'He's got a wound to his side. It looks like a through and through. He'll live, worse luck,' one officer said.

Vicky stared down at the terrorist who glared defiantly back, 'Will we ever be free of him?'

'I hope so,' Dane replied. They waited in silence until the ambulance arrived. The two officers went to let the paramedics in.

'Christian,' Vicky said, with urgency.

He heard a grunt and turned as Rafferty hauled himself to his feet, 'Stay where you are. There's nothing you can do now. It's finished.'

Rafferty looked around then spying a knife block snatched up a carving knife. He steadied himself and came forward.

Dane pulled Vicky behind him, and they both backed away. Rafferty continued to advance towards them.

'Come on. Do you really think you can take me now. Drop the knife,' Dane said.

Rafferty ignored him and came on. As they passed the sink unit Dane picked up the unloaded pistol. He slapped the magazine in and thumbed the lock, releasing the slide and loading it.

'Stay there or I'll fire,' Dane shouted, as Vicky's back hit the wall. There was nowhere else for them to go.

Rafferty held the knife in both hands, 'I'm going to kill you, you bastard,' he growled, and prepared to launch himself.

Dane fired two shots in a blur of sound. The bullets struck the centre of Rafferty's chest, knocking him back a pace. His legs quivered then buckled and he collapsed.

'Get out of here,' Dane instructed Vicky and she darted out of the door. Dane stood over Rafferty who stared at the ceiling. He coughed and blood flecked his lips.

A smile spread across his face. 'Martin,' he said, and died.

The armed officers charged into the room and stared in horror at the body on the floor.

A paramedic was brought in who examined Rafferty. 'He's dead. Let's have a look at you. That looks like a nasty cut,' she said to Dane.

Dane sat patiently while she dressed his injury but refused to go to hospital. The house was sealed as a crime scene and an officer drove them to Chelmsford, where Perkins was waiting. Dane recounted what had happened.

'God. What a nightmare. I doubt he would have ever given up. He was obviously demented,' Perkins replied.

'He blamed me for his brother's death. He saw it happen which can't have been easy.'

## VENGEANCE DAY

'How on earth did he get in? And where did he hide? He just appeared in front of me when you went outside,' Vicky said.

'We will soon establish that. I'm afraid you can't stay at your home for a while,' Perkins said.

'We'll be at Vicky's. I hope this is all finished because I'm running out of places to live.'

The following morning the daughter of the neighbours Liam had tied up found them traumatised but alive. In the days that followed, the investigation established that the hoax call had come from the mobile phone found on Liam's body. He also had a key to Dane's front door in his pocket. It was assumed to be a copy Shanahan had made when he burgled Dane's home.

The front of the house had been left unattended for no more than a minute when the officers responded to the hoax call. It had been enough for Liam to get in and evade the subsequent search. Dane made a point of absolving all the guards of any blame. If they had discovered him, someone would have died, and no one wanted that.

\*

In London, Angus Boyd's source kept him fully appraised of what had happened and suggested Dane had been alone in the house with Liam Rafferty. This gave Boyd a new and even better angle to pursue, and he exploited it to the full. He wrote a piece questioning the official version of events and floated the theory that Rafferty had been executed. This piqued the interest of the rest of the media. To Boyd's delight he became a regular contributor to news programs.

\*

Three days after Rafferty's death Karen Teller rang Dane and after asking after his family said, 'My boss has asked me to pass you a message.'

'Who from?'

'It originates from an unnamed source via what we euphemistically call back channels. It reads, "The nationalist community is horrified by the recent events in London and the attacks on Detective Superintendent Dane and his family. Those responsible were not acting on behalf of, or in the interest of, the nationalist community in Northern Ireland. The actions of those renegades are regrettable and to be roundly condemned by all right-minded people. It is hoped that all those injured have a speedy recovery to full health. There is no threat to Mr Dane personally from anyone in the republican movement".'

'That's nice of them. It's a shame they hadn't been so forthcoming sooner,' Dane replied.

'I agree, but at least we're talking to them. Rafferty's actions and the revelations about the weapons he stole have embarrassed them. After all this I think the threat from the dissident factions will reduce. I doubt their leaders will sanction any attacks for a while.'

'Let's hope so. So long as they leave us alone, that'll do for me. Am I expected to reply to them?'

'No. This is not for public consumption. You won't hear from them again.'

'I can live with that. Thanks for telling me. Will I see you at the next reunion?'

'Oh yes. The drinks are on me.'

\*

In the northeastern desert of Syria, Husam fitted the last of the suicide belts to the four young men who were the next group of martyrs. They all listened carefully as he explained how they were to approach their designated targets and detonate the bombs. Husam shook hands with each one then left them to their devotions. He walked outside for a breath of air and stood in the courtyard of the large property. High walls surrounded the central mud brick house. Husam's fighters had commandeered it the week before and the previous occupiers, a family of eight, were all buried next to the back wall. Husam took a deep breath then cocked his head to one side and listened. Something was wrong, but he couldn't put his finger on what it was. He turned to his bodyguard.

'Have you heard anything?'

'Nothing. It is silent.'

'Yes, too quiet,' Husam muttered then realised it was the dogs. There were three other compounds nearby all with dogs chained up outside the gates. The sounds of them snarling and barking at something could be heard in the distance. The two great rangy brutes outside this property usually joined in, but tonight they were silent.

Before Husam could react, the big double wooden gates set in the perimeter wall erupted in an orange flash bringing the entire frame crashing down in a cloud of dust. The guard recovered first but ran into a burst of automatic fire from two Kurdish Special Forces soldiers as they appeared through the smoke.

Husam swung his AK47 to his shoulder and fired. Sergeant Billy Smart of 'A' Squadron SAS saw his friends fall and instinctively knew they were dead. He'd trained them, they were true patriots with a fierce passion for their country and he liked them. Billy identified the man who'd killed them and engaged him. The terrorist was dead before his body hit the floor. It took mere minutes for the joint team of Kurds and SAS to secure the compound after eliminating the remaining ISIS insurgents. They gathered a DNA swab from each corpse then fingerprinted and photographed them before leaving the bodies where they fell.

Two nights later Major Nick Blaine reviewed the after-action contact report submitted by Billy Smart. As he looked through the sheaf of photographs something clicked in his memory. Nick studied the third picture for nearly a minute. Tears stung his eyes, 'God bless you dad, rest in peace.' Making a note in the margin he closed the file.

A couple of days before he was due to return to work, Dane received a call from a withheld number.

'Christian? it's Nick Blaine here.'

'Hello, how are you?'

'I'm fine. Listen, I don't have much time. Remember the foreign chap you wanted to talk to about that business in Bahrain?'

'Yes.'

'He's dead.'

The information stunned Dane, 'Was that you…'

Nick's voice echoed then sounded tinny as the signal wavered. Dane guessed he must be calling on a satellite phone.

'No, it wasn't me. But I know who did and we have the means to confirm it. I have sent the relevant material home for the attention of a man called Fawn. I believe you met him.'

'Yes, I have.'

'He has promised to get the DNA checked against the profile you discovered. When he receives the results, he'll inform the coroner.'

'How did you find him?'

'He got in the way of one of our operations and paid the price. Would you mind telling my mother, please?'

'Don't you want to do that?'

'No. I would rather she didn't know of my involvement. Tell her you have received the information through channels.'

'Okay, I'll visit her tomorrow.'

'Thanks, I must go. I hope you and your family are all on the mend?'

'We're all doing fine.'

'Great. I will ring when I'm back and take you for a beer.'

'That is a date.'

\*\*\*

Dane's mother grew stronger, and the doctors predicted she would be home by Christmas. His father was also improving and after his relapse was now spending time out of bed. Dane called in to visit him, but to his surprise, found the room empty. The bedding had been stripped and all his personal possessions were gone. A pulse of fear lurched through his gut as he checked his phone. The hospital had promised they would contact him if there was any change in his father's condition, but he'd received no messages. Dane bumped into a cleaner in the corridor, but she knew nothing. With his concerns growing he went to the nurse's station which was empty. Dane looked along the ward in both directions and spotted a young nurse and ran up to her.

'I'm sorry to bother you. Do you know what's happened to my father? He was in room fourteen?'

'I have only just come on duty. Come with me and we can check.'

Dane followed the young woman, and his frustration grew when she was unable to log into the ward computer system.

'I'm sorry, it's playing up' She looked around, 'They are doing the handover. Sister will be back in a moment. She will know what's going on. I'm sure there's nothing to worry about.'

## VENGEANCE DAY

Dane waited for fifteen minutes, his frustration and imagination going into overdrive. The staff would clear a room after the patient is discharged. His father was nowhere near that stage in his recovery. The only other reason was the unthinkable.

'Please God, not now. Not after everything else we've been through,' he muttered. He was about to go in search of the sister when he saw her walking towards him.

'Good afternoon, Mr Dane.'

'Where is my father?'

She was startled by his demeanour and Dane saw the comprehension flare in her eyes. She held her hands up, 'Please tell me someone has informed you?'

'No, I've heard nothing.'

'I'm so sorry. We moved him this morning to be with your mother. I was assured you had been told. I can only apologise.'

'Never mind,' Dane replied, 'That's a relief. I'll go and see them. Thank you for everything you have done for him.'

As Dane's heart rate slowed, he jogged to his mother's room. His father was sitting in a wheelchair beside the bed, holding her hand as she slept.

'Hi dad. How are you today?'

'I am feeling a lot better. Thank you.'

'That's good to hear. Is mum okay?'

'We were having a chat. I think I wore her out with my questions because she's dropped off.'

'There's colour in her cheeks.'

Peter Dane nodded, 'She's on the road to recovery, God willing. She told me how you found me in the ditch and carried me home.'

'Well, I couldn't leave you there.'

'I am glad you didn't. I'm sorry to have caused so much trouble. I know what happened that day I wandered off and what you did in London,' he squeezed his son's hand, 'I am immensely proud of you. We've been at odds for so long and I know I'm the cause of that.'

'No, dad. I have a lot to answer for as well. I should have done more to try and mend our differences.'

'Let's agree that we're both to blame. Can we be a family again? And put the past behind us?'

'There is nothing I want more,' Dane replied.

The door opened to admit a man wearing a clerical dog collar. Peter Dane smiled a welcome.

'This is the hospital Chaplin. I have asked him to lead your mother and I in prayers. To give thanks for our deliverance and recovery.

'Perhaps I could join you?' Dane replied.